Shinta Fuji

Illustrated by
Susumu Kuroi

APPARENTLY, DISILLUSIONED ADVENTURERS WILL SAVE THE WORLD

4

The Idol Appreciation Concert

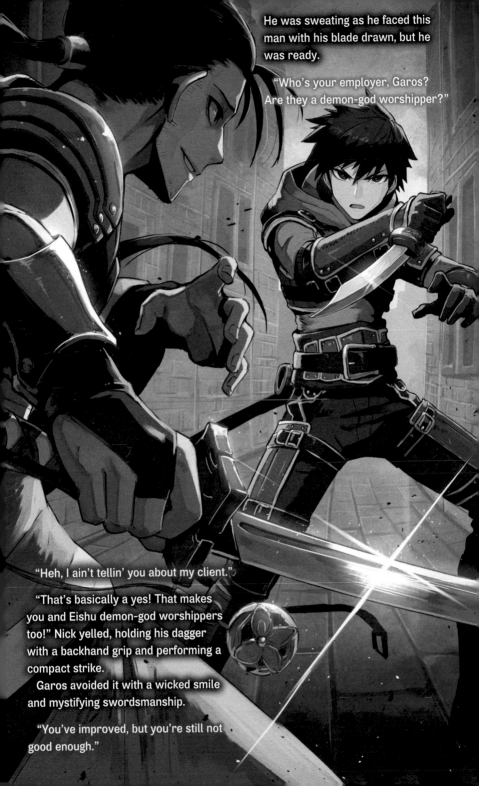

He was sweating as he faced this man with his blade drawn, but he was ready.

"Who's your employer, Garos? Are they a demon-god worshipper?"

"Heh, I ain't tellin' you about my client."

"That's basically a yes! That makes you and Eishu demon-god worshippers too!" Nick yelled, holding his dagger with a backhand grip and performing a compact strike.
Garos avoided it with a wicked smile and mystifying swordsmanship.

"You've improved, but you're still not good enough."

APPARENTLY, DISILLUSIONED ADVENTURERS WILL SAVE THE WORLD

The Idol Appreciation Concert

4

Shinta Fuji

Illustration by **Susumu Kuroi**

YEN ON
New York

APPARENTLY, DISILLUSIONED ADVENTURERS WILL SAVE THE WORLD

The Idol Appreciation Concert ④

Shinta Fuji

Translation by *Luke Hutton*

Cover art by **Susumu Kuroi**

This book is a work of fiction. Names, characters, places, and incidents are the product of the author's imagination or are used fictitiously. Any resemblance to actual events, locales, or persons, living or dead, is coincidental.

NINGENFUSHIN NO BOKENSHATACHI GA SEKAI WO SUKUYODESU Vol. 4 ~GINYUSHIJIN DAIKANSHASAI HEN~
© Fuji Shinta 2022
First published in Japan in 2022 by KADOKAWA CORPORATION, Tokyo
English translation rights arranged with KADOKAWA CORPORATION, Tokyo, through TUTTLE-MORI AGENCY, INC., Tokyo.

English translation © 2024 by Yen Press, LLC

Yen On
150 West 30th Street, 19th Floor
New York, NY 10001

Visit us at yenpress.com
facebook.com/yenpress
twitter.com/yenpress
yenpress.tumblr.com
instagram.com/yenpress

First Yen On Edition: April 2024
Edited by Yen On Editorial: Anna Powers
Designed by Yen Press Design: Andy Swist

Yen On is an imprint of Yen Press, LLC.
The Yen On name and logo are trademarks of Yen Press, LLC.

The publisher is not responsible for websites (or their content) that are not owned by the publisher.

Library of Congress Cataloging-in-Publication Data
Names: Fuji, Shinta, author. | Kuroi, Susumu, illustrator. | Hutton, Luke, translator.
Title: Apparently, disillusioned adventurers will save the world / Shinta Fuji ; illustration by Susumu Kuroi ; translation by Luke Hutton.
Other titles: Ningen fushin no bōkensha-tachi ga sekai o sukuu yō desu. English
Description: First Yen On edition. | New York, NY : Yen On, 2022- |
Identifiers: LCCN 2022020938 | ISBN 9781975349981 (v. 1 ; trade paperback) | ISBN 9781975351861 (v. 2 ; trade paperback) | ISBN 9781975351885 (v. 3 ; trade paperback) | ISBN 9781975376895 (v. 4 ; trade paperback)
Subjects: CYAC: Fantasy. | Adventure and adventurers—Fiction. | Politics, Practical—Fiction. | LCGFT: Action and adventure fiction. | Fantasy fiction. |Light novels.
Classification: LCC PZ7.1.F8 Ap 2022 | DDC [Fic]—dc23
LC record available at https://lccn.loc.gov/2022020938

ISBNs: 978-1-9753-7689-5 (paperback)
978-1-9753-7690-1 (ebook)

10 9 8 7 6 5 4 3 2 1

LSC-C

Printed in the United States of America

Contents

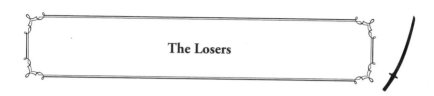

The Losers

We lost.

Did you think we won just because you survived?

Don't be a fool. I took too much damage to maintain my artificial personality. You're at the end of your rope, too.

They broke my core with their fists. There are no excuses. Admit defeat.

I've never lost to such rabble in my entire life. Not when I was alive, and not after I died and became a spirit.

...What? You want to know what kind of person I was? It's not like you to ask such a question. It's unsettling.

Well, I was no one special. I was the type who pretended to be a hero while only looking out for himself... I suppose you would call that an adventurer in this era.

Adventurers are different, you say? Really? I don't see it.

Anyway, I joined the clan and took up my sword to vie for supremacy and hunt monsters. Unfortunately, the clan's leader decided I was dangerous. He set a trap for me on a monster-hunting trip, and I was killed by fellow clan members.

Our current employer saved me, though my physical body was lost. I became a spirit known as White Mask, got my revenge... and you know the rest.

Did I feel indebted to him after that, you ask? Heavens no. I would not be surprised if our employer had me dancing in the palm of his hand the entire time. Well, maybe not. I'm not sure he's capable of such meticulous manipulation. He can be quite an unserious person. I can think of numerous occasions when he's made sure to let enemies live.

I did not use the forbidden weapon out of any sense of duty, either. I felt guilty about turning it on such a useful pawn, but it goes against my nature to leave loose ends on a job.

...I think I have about an hour before I disappear completely. I don't feel much of anything.

You want to know if I have regrets? Since when were you the type to ask such deep questions? We've known each other for years, but I could count the number of real conversations between us on one hand.

To answer your question, no. I'm not like you.

You're the one trapped by regrets.

Do what you must to atone for your crimes before you die. I doubt you'll have long to live after losing the holy armor.

What? I'm only speaking the truth. Or did you want me to lie?

Find your resolve and get your life back. It's not too late, even if you don't have long before you meet your miserable end.

Farewell, partner.

The Survivors

In this world, there was a fish called an oil-eater. It was a fat, misshapen creature that resembled an anglerfish and was about the size of a bucket used to draw water from a well.

Oil-eaters were totally unique creatures. They were often mistakenly believed to be monsters, but they did not live in labyrinths, which meant they were animals. According to biologists, they couldn't technically be classified as fish, and it was hard to call them amphibians, too. They were a hotly debated species in the field of biological classification.

Oil-eaters reached adulthood three years after hatching. It was then that they reached a crossroads; depending on the environment they grew up in, they could become saltwater fish, freshwater fish, or grow legs like a frog and live on land. They could even adapt to extreme environments such as the desert or the deep sea, though at the cost of a shorter life.

But that metamorphosis was only the second of the oil-eaters' defining traits. The fishes' most unique habit was that they, well, ate oil. Not edible ones like rapeseed oil or beef tallow, but oil-based products such as cushioning, packaging materials, and other relics created by the ancient civilization.

Oil-eaters ate these items and excreted them, along with

digested leaves and micro-organisms from aquatic plants. The oil created by refining their feces was very useful. It was a cheap source for indoor heating, and it was easy to preserve and transport. It also didn't produce mana while being used, meaning it didn't interfere with intricate spells or magic items.

"Magic Search."

A wick doused in black oil burned brightly within a crude lamp, illuminating the room. The oil released a grilled-fish scent that could not be totally removed in the refinement process.

"...Okay. There's no sign of searching spells or magic items in our vicinity," a petite blond girl said to the others in the room. Though her words were meant to reassure, there was no emotion in her face.

Although she was beautiful and well-dressed, her ever-present stern countenance made her difficult to approach. Her eyes tended to be especially stern when she cast magic. She was aware of that habit but did nothing to fix it; in her opinion, no one had any right to judge her when she was hard at work. Tiana was that kind of mage.

"That is a relief. Shall we open the safe?" asked a young man with chestnut hair, who was sitting next to Tiana. He pulled out a key decorated with an ornament. The lamp cast a bewitching light on the key, but it couldn't rival the captivating, tranquil beauty of the man himself.

He wore priestly clothing but lacked the medal that all priests were supposed to wear around their necks. That meant he had been excommunicated. That fact may have been off-putting to some, but it only made him more attractive to the many women he had seduced into a one-night stand. Zem projected an alluring aura, like a magic lamp on a moonless night.

"Wait, Zem," said a red-haired girl sitting next to Zem. She guarded the locked safe with her scaled hands. These people may have been her companions, but she wouldn't let them touch it until she was ready.

"What's wrong?" Zem asked.

"He's not done with the ledger," the girl said, flicking her tail to point next to her.

That tail was only one trait that set her apart from ordinary humans; she was much taller than the average woman, her arms were covered in scales, and two marvelous horns grew from her head. Karan was a dragonian, a humanoid race with dragon-like traits. Her figure appeared soft and feminine at first glance, but a close look at her physique showed her untiring training. She had a more stoic personality than either Tiana or Zem.

"Gimme a sec, Karan. I'm almost done with last month's ledger," the young man said. He was writing something in a binder while Karan was pointing at him.

"Hurry up," Karan complained.

"I'd been putting this off 'cause of all the work we've had to do with the Steppingman mess. I don't wanna delay this any further."

"But no one else keeps a ledger. I heard most people just rush to a tax consultant at the beginning of the year."

"Yeah, and those people end up flipping over their bed looking for lost receipts, then finishing their paperwork only to realize there are omissions in their bookkeeping. Then they turn in their return at the last second, which pisses off the tax collector. It's better this way," the young man argued as his quill pen flew across the page.

He had a slender build, but no one would mistake him for being weak. He was a fighter, one even sharper than Karan, and that was apparent in the way he carried himself. His handwriting was surprisingly neat for how quickly he was writing, each straight line and curve drawn exactly right. If handwriting was a reflection of the person, you could say Nick's demonstrated his honesty and playful heart.

"...Done!" Nick said. He wrote the following in his binder.

Cashbook.
Year 439 of the King's Calendar.
Party: Survivors.

* * *

Nick used this binder to record all the money that entered and left the Survivors' funds. The records were proof of their great success as a party. The first page showed modest rewards for fighting monsters in beginner labyrinths such as Gooey Waterworks and Goblin Forest, but the amounts of money they earned only grew from there. Two early entries stood out.

> *Idle Moon, 13th day. Labyrinth of Bonds. Reward for exploration and for excavating the Sword of Bonds: 500,000 dina.*
>
> *Gloomy Moon, 25th day. Reward for arresting the Iron Tiger Troop: 300,000 dina.*

But those were dwarfed by the entry Nick had just added.

"Rainy Moon, twenty-ninth day. Reward for subjugating the Steppingman: one million dina. Reward for helping to rescue the abducted children: two million dina... That is quite the haul," a small boy said after grabbing the ledger. He had silver hair and an androgynous appearance. His face resembled Nick's, but cuter and friendlier.

"We deserve it, too! Help us out here, Bond. I want to see if the money matches his records," Tiana urged.

The boy shrugged. "Dear me, you all are so untrusting. Let's see... Yes, exactly three hundred," he said after making a circle with his fingers and glancing at the gold coins on the table. That was all the time he needed to count them.

"No silver or copper coins slipped in by mistake?"

"My visual processors tell me they are all gold coins. I also picked them up and confirmed their weight. Everything's perfect!"

The boy—whose name was Bond—had used a special ability called Search to inspect the coins, which was not magic that normal people could use. The ability heightened his audiovisual senses so he could pick up volumes and audio frequencies that humans couldn't detect; he could also see distant objects as if they were close to him.

But that was only a secondary ability of his. It was also not immediately clear whether "he" was even the right way to refer to him—he was both cutely feminine and coolly masculine. In truth, he didn't have a gender, and he wasn't even human.

"Can you all refrain from using me only as a tool for your convenience? You should use my primary function more often," Bond complained.

"You've got a point, actually. We wouldn't have survived that last fight without you," Nick agreed.

"Oh? Have you finally seen the light, Nick? I am the holy sword called the Sword of Bonds, not a smart meter or a security item. Don't you forget that," Bond announced proudly.

Bond was the final member of the Survivors. He was currently using a body he created based on his wielder Nick's, but his true form was a holy sword created with the advanced technology of the ancient civilization.

"Speaking of things we can't forget, let's divvy up the reward," Nick said. The other Survivors' faces lit up.

The party had just received their reward for the biggest job of their careers—defeating the Steppingman, a mysterious kidnapper who was abducting children in Teran, the Labyrinth City.

"Hmm-hmm-hmm… I didn't know how I was going to afford special spectator seating for the Dragon God Cup!" Tiana cheered.

"A northern-style barbecue restaurant opened recently. They're serving a limited amount of luxurious duck-winged deer meat that's normally only eaten by royal families, and people are bidding over the reserved seating… I can't pass up this chance," Karan said.

"I booked a hotel in a harbor town for a weeklong vacation with a hostess. Please refrain from taking on any jobs during that time," Zem requested.

"I have plans as well. I want to buy the new issue of *Sixth*

Shining—it's about a person with supernatural abilities who fights evil spirits," Bond added.

They all seemed ecstatic as they thought about what they wanted to do with their time off—except for Nick.

Each member of the Survivors had a slightly embarrassing hobby. Tiana was a gambler who was especially obsessed with dragon racing. Karan was a gourmet who enjoyed sampling food from stalls opened in public parks, although lately she had started enjoying luxurious restaurants with a dress code. Zem's hobby was the most problematic of all—he was a womanizer who frequented the red-light district and inspired many rumors in the business districts of Labyrinth City.

Nick also had such a hobby, but unlike the others, he kept his cool.

"I wanna buy a ticket to the Jewelry Production One Hundredth Anniversary Concert. Actually, I'm gonna go do that right after this... But first we have some expenses to cover, starting with three hundred thousand dina for Anemone Alehouse as an apology and to pay for our meals," he said, transferring thirty of the gold coins into a pouch.

Anemone Alehouse was a bar whose assistant manager allowed the Survivors to use it as a base. They would strategize and sleep there as they hunted for their bounty. The other Survivors watched the gold go with resigned disappointment.

"Next is the money to repair our weapons and equipment. We'll need two hundred thousand dina total for the five of us."

The others were again disappointed but understanding as Nick placed those gold coins into a different bag.

"Lastly... We broke the roof of a nearby building during our fight. We'll need one hundred thousand dina for the repair costs."

"Huh? What are you talking about?!" Tiana asked accusingly.

"I can't blame you for reacting that way," Nick said, remaining calm. "It caught me off guard when I heard about it, too. You know how the factory exploded after that fight? Some fragments of broken washing tubs went flying and fell through the roof of another factory. The president of that place was pissed."

The other Survivors looked like they'd been punched in the gut. "But that damage occurred in the course of an Adventurers Guild job! Shouldn't *they* be compensating us?!" Tiana implored.

"They would've if we'd caught White Mask. He got away, so they can't compensate us." Nick sighed, sounding exhausted. The feeling spread to the others.

"So much for special seating...," Tiana muttered.

"There goes my barbecue...," Karan lamented.

"My romantic adventure at the harbor town remains a dream...," Zem said wistfully.

Karan and Zem regretfully watched the gold coins go into the bag. Only half of their reward remained.

"Hey, that's not so bad. There is still plenty left. Are we splitting this five ways?" Bond asked, attempting to soothe the group.

"No, six ways," Nick corrected. The rest looked at him with confusion, but then comprehension dawned on their faces. "She gave us a lotta help. It sucks, but she deserves her share. Is there anything else we need to discuss?"

The others responded that there wasn't. Nick smiled and stood.

"All right, guys! The Survivors are on holiday, starting now! Go and make the best of it!"

""""You got it!"""" the others responded.

And so, having had their fill of adventures for now, the Survivors split up for a much-needed rest.

Work days started late at the publishing company called Mysterious Teran. That was a necessity, as night was the best time for its reporters to pursue the suspicious rumors on which they based their articles. They could interview adventurers who were off the clock and nightlife workers who were on the clock; they could even witness article-worthy cases directly. The reporters typically finished working around midnight and woke up the next day, when most people were finishing lunch.

As such, it was nearly evening when Nick and Bond met with their acquaintance to offer her share of the reward to her.

"Are you sure about this? I was kinda undercover, so I'm not sure I should accept this money," she said, giggling to herself as she inspected the bag full of gold coins.

Nick and Bond were in a reception room on the third floor of Mysterious Teran with a bespectacled girl who wore an old coat despite being indoors. Her name was Olivia. The building was just as empty as the last time they'd visited; it seemed Olivia was the only one sitting around with no work to do.

"We'll gladly keep it if you don't want it. I don't envy life as a volunteer. You have my nonfinancial support," Nick responded sarcastically.

"On second thought, I'll take it. Thank you very much. I'll be writing a receipt." Olivia snatched up the bag with impossible speed just as Nick tried to put it away.

"Then you should've just taken it instead of beating around the bush," Nick complained. He didn't like that he wasn't able to follow her movements with his eyes. It wasn't just Olivia's speed that was impressive; she was able to read his body's movement to tell that he was going to lower his arm before he began to do it. That was a special skill that could only be obtained with serious training; as a practitioner of martial arts, Nick was well aware of that. "Anyway...you smell terrible."

"Hey! Rude! It's not my fault! I went through the underground tunnels earlier in pursuit of a case!" Olivia fumed, before taking a sniff of her coat and grimacing.

"The underground tunnels?" Nick said. "There's nothing down there but sewage."

There was a whole subterranean network beneath Labyrinth

City. They mainly existed as maintenance passageways for the sewers and as escape routes for aristocrats. Many people saw the tunnels as mysterious in some way, but they were completely ordinary. The Order of the Sun Knights and the Organization for Labyrinth City Development cooperated to make a detailed map of the tunnels, and they were regularly patrolled. Security was actually tighter underground than above it.

"I've been wondering about them lately, though. I want to figure out how White Mask got around the city, so I'm checking places that I initially excluded," Olivia said.

"Oh, you were actually doing serious work," Nick responded.

"Well, I was looking for material at the same time. Sneaking around underground to avoid detection was a thrilling experience."

"I would tell you to take better care of yourself at work, but you're not human, so I guess it doesn't really matter."

"Hey, I find that phrasing offensive."

What Nick said was true—Olivia wasn't human.

"Yeah! Intelligent magic items have rights! They should be respected in the workplace!" Bond proclaimed.

"Why are you getting angry?" Nick asked.

"Because we're the same. Sort of."

Olivia's true identity was the Sword of Might, a holy sword developed by the ancient civilization, just like Bond. Nick had a hard time seeing her as such a legendary being, but she had saved the Survivors with her incredible fighting ability when they were in grave danger against White Mask.

"That 'sort of' was uncalled for. Is that any way to speak to me after I helped you?" Olivia whined.

"I say that only because you may no longer be a holy sword... You've mutated, haven't you?" Bond asked.

Olivia smiled. "So you figured that out."

"Your name is proof enough. It has nothing to do with your

origin. Your name would have to be something like 'Valerie' for *valor* or 'Powpow' for *power* to prevent mutation."

"'Powpow'? Really? That doesn't suit my elegant image."

"Huh? Why're we talking about her name?" Nick interjected.

"Remember when Tiana said you shouldn't change the name of an advanced magic item too drastically?" Bond asked.

Nick thought for a moment and nodded. "Yeah, I do. She said if you name a holy sword 'Mop' it'll gain cleaning properties."

"Your name is different from your production name, which means that you must have mutated. What happened to you?" Bond inquired.

Olivia laughed awkwardly and scratched her cheek. "It's kind of a long story... I guess it boils down to falling in love and going to war."

"Man, sounds like you could write a book," Nick said, eliciting a laugh from Olivia. "Does it really matter if you've mutated, though? It's not like you turned into a mop."

"Well, I don't like to admit it, but there are some issues," Olivia replied. "For starters, advanced magic items like us have design specifications sealed deep within our core. As long as we have that, we can regenerate from any injury, even something as drastic as a smashed head or a severed blade. You wouldn't be wrong to call us immortal. Unfortunately, we lose our design specifications when we mutate."

"Really...?" Nick said.

"That is only an aftereffect of the mutation, not the mutation itself," Bond interrupted, clearing his throat. "Losing your immortality is trivial compared with the risk of your mission being distorted. Worst case, a holy sword could turn on the human civilization that created it. Then it's no better than a monster."

"Like when the Sword of Evolution became the Sword of Ruin?" Nick asked.

"No. He didn't abandon his mission, he simply twisted it to find logic that allowed him to attack mankind. I imagine Olivia has mutated much more significantly," Bond answered.

"So the Sword of Evolution went astray? What a shame...," Olivia said.

"You sound like you just found out a friend's child dropped out of school...," Nick interjected.

"Where is the Sword of Evolution now?" Olivia asked.

"Sealed in an undisclosed location. We gave him some books and other things to entertain himself with. Stuff like adventure novels and audiovisual data from idol concerts," Nick responded.

"I have major questions about those choices, but I'd rather not get involved. The less people know where he is, the better. He's not as dangerous as the Sword of Distortion anyway."

"The Sword of Distortion?" Nick echoed.

The distaste on Bond's face suggested that he knew the name. "Surely she's not still active."

"The Teran Distortion Agency, which housed her main body, was totally destroyed. Their headquarters has been a vacant lot for centuries, and now a concert hall is being built there. I think it's going to be called Starmine Hall," Olivia responded.

"Oh, I know that place. Jewelry Production is going to perform the Hundredth Anniversary Concert there," Nick said.

"You're really obsessed with idols, Nick," Olivia commented, and Nick snapped at her.

"Shut up."

Bond looked conflicted. "I—I see... She was something of a headache, but I do miss her," he said.

"Care to tell me who you're talking about? Their name sounds pretty messed up," Nick asked, confused.

"Oh, have you never heard of her? I thought the name *Teran Distortion Agency* was remembered in history," Olivia said.

"I'm not from around here," Nick explained.

"Fair enough. Allow me to elucidate. Ahem! Once upon a time in a land not so far away—"

"Cut the theatrics, please."

Despite Nick's interruption, Olivia continued speaking. "The Teran Distortion Agency was an organization founded to warp and purify the calls of the demon god, and to chant a city-class ritual spell called 'Distort' to weaken the demon god. The Sword of Destruction was the name of the holy sword who cast the spell. She also went by the name of Hizumi."

Olivia's voice was uncharacteristically serious when she said that name. It was obvious she had mixed feelings about this holy sword. Nick thought her organization sounded completely beneficial to society, however.

"Her name is kinda terrifying, but it sounds like she did good," Nick said.

"Her actions certainly did help everyone in the end. She contributed greatly to the sealing of the demon god," Bond interjected.

"Her achievements are undeniable, but her methods were more than a little problematic," Olivia added.

Nick gulped upon seeing their bitter expressions. "In what way?"

"Hizumi petitioned the king to gather young people with ample mana and send them to Teran. She then locked them all in isolated cells where they could hear nothing but the evil voice of the demon god and her own soothing voice," Olivia answered.

Nick pictured one of those cells and began to sweat. "Hold on. Why'd she lock them up like they were criminals? And whaddaya mean by 'the demon god's voice'?"

"The demon god speaks telepathically. The sound sends humans into a state of panic, strengthens monsters, and spreads miasma. They do this through a technique called Mantra," Olivia explained.

"Huh…"

"The demon god's Mantra has terrible power. It's capable of turning an entire small village into a labyrinth. Barriers were erected to ward off Mantras during the war, but Hizumi intentionally opened a hole in the barrier to let the voices in and strike fear into the hearts of the young people she trapped," Olivia continued.

"...And then the Sword of Distortion healed them. She gave them both the carrot and the stick," Nick said.

"That's exactly right," Olivia said quietly. "The young people came to hate the demon god from the bottoms of their hearts and devoutly worship Hizumi."

"Hizumi's worshippers became one with her power and gained the ability to invert and distort the demon god's thoughts, which they could use to attack not just monsters but the labyrinths themselves. This turned the war in humanity's favor. This only evened the odds between the demon god and humanity, but without her, humanity would certainly have lost," Bond explained.

"So she was pivotal to humanity's victory, but she went too far with her methods... Hold on," Nick said, realizing that there was something off about the story.

"Hmm? What is it?" Bond asked.

"Didn't you say that holy swords have a code of ethics that prevents them from gambling and getting into trouble?" Nick asked.

"Hizumi was very good at avoiding its activation. She would guide people to make certain decisions instead of her and craft budgets so that things would work out exactly as she wanted," Bond answered.

"She never harmed anyone directly, but that didn't make her any less problematic," Olivia added.

They both nodded knowingly.

Nick could tell their feelings toward the Sword of Distortion were complicated. He chose to keep quiet and listen.

"She was a good leader, but she had a difficult personality and a very particular taste in people," Olivia said.

"She was no leader. She just liked to boss everyone around. She indulged in every luxury and used her position to make her collection of beautiful boys and girls serve and polish her," Bond argued.

"I remember she had bodyguards to protect her sword body."

"Yes, she did. But she immediately fired anyone who displeased her. She would command them to go back to the country even as they cried and begged to stay by her side!"

"I saw her do that a few times, too!"

"Sounds like she was pretty abusive. Was she mutated?" Nick asked.

Neither of them answered.

"Don't leave me hanging."

"…That was just her nature. It is possible for a holy sword to have a twisted personality before any mutation occurs," Bond answered.

"Huh. What about you, Olivia?" Nick asked.

"Whuh? Me?"

"I'm asking how much you've mutated. That's where this whole conversation started, remember?"

Olivia laughed awkwardly and shrugged. "Don't worry about me. I haven't changed too much. I've simply changed my interpretation of my mission."

Nick looked at Olivia dubiously. "What exactly is your mission? You said you were a training tool, or something like that."

"That's right. I was made to train people who stood up to face the threat of the demon god. I'm the Sword of Might, a Spirit-Class Anti-Demon Combat Training Program. Though I call myself Olivia now," she said.

"Oh yeah, you mentioned that."

"But I eventually decided that my apprentices don't need to fight the demon god. I now simply hope that I can increase the number of able fighters in the event that humanity faces a crisis."

"Wha…? It sounds like you have almost totally abandoned your mission!" Bond was aghast.

Olivia shrugged her shoulders indifferently. "Does it really matter? The idea that a human could defeat the demon god with a little exercise was stupid in the first place. I'm sure we could come up with plenty of more plans that are more appropriate and humane."

"Don't treat Stepping like it's a simple exercise plan... I see your point, though. It's not like it's a weapon that's gonna turn the tides of a war," Nick said.

"So you decided that humans are not physically capable of defeating the demon god... I suppose you cannot be blamed for that," Bond relented.

"Oh, no, I can say with confidence that a human *could* physically defeat the demon god," Olivia responded, eliciting surprised reactions from Nick and Bond. "It would be possible if I found a person with innate talent, taught them everything I know, and helped them overcome the boundary between life and death. I once had ambitions of creating such a perfect warrior, but..."

Olivia sighed painfully.

"Anyone that superhuman would have no need for me. They'd figure out how to grow strong on their own and decide for themselves if they wanted to fight the demon god. An apprentice like that would make me lose confidence as a trainer," she continued.

"You think it wouldn't be rewarding for you," Nick observed.

"I prefer raising young apprentices who need me. I like helping them discover talents they didn't know they had and gradually opening up new possibilities for them. Eventually they learn enough to become a teacher themselves and pass on their knowledge. Such are the ups and downs in the life of a trainer," Olivia said, breaking into her usual broad smile. "I hope Hizumi can find something to make her happy, too."

"Yes, me too," Bond agreed earnestly.

"Do you feel more at home as a magazine reporter than as a trainer, though?" Nick asked.

"There are a lot of complications that come with running a dojo. I prefer having less responsibility," Olivia responded.

"I don't think there's anything wrong with that. The demon god is sealed, right? Or dead? You should enjoy your life the way you want."

"Huh? What are you saying?" Olivia asked, looking at Nick with surprise.

Nick stared back, thrown off by her reaction. "I was just trying to be nice..."

"No, not that. They're not dead, you know?"

"Who's not dead?"

"The demon god. Not only are they alive, their reawakening at the hands of their worshippers could be approaching."

Nick's jaw dropped. Olivia and Bond rolled their eyes at him.

"Hey, don't do that. How do you expect me to react?!" Nick complained.

"Who do you think we just fought, Nick? White Mask is a demon-god worshipper. There's no way his kind would operate so openly if humanity had destroyed the demon god entirely," Olivia said.

"Exactly. You must not act like the demon god threat does not exist. If we truly were at peace, I would have no need to pass down my knowledge of heroes and holy sword wielders," Bond added.

Nick rubbed his temples. "Tell me you're joking... We're done for if another guy like White Mask comes for us."

"Don't worry about that," said Olivia. I think they'll be out of action for a while."

"How could I possibly not worry? White Mask's armor was destroyed, but he got away," Nick argued.

"I'm sure whoever was inside the armor was greatly weakened. The demon-god worshippers also won't be able to use White Mask's weapons and spells without that holy armor," Olivia said.

"Huh? Why not?" Nick asked.

Bond answered that question. "Holy armor was developed so people could explore legendary labyrinths such as the Great Red Spot and the Monster Belt. These locations can have temperatures in the thousands of degrees or at absolute zero due to no air at all. Survival in such locations is impossible without impenetrable defense and special abilities."

"Special abilities? I get how holy armor would help people endure those harsh environments, but gear can't give someone abilities they don't already have," Nick said.

Bond shook his head. "Actually, holy armor awards the abilities of its past wearers to whoever equips it. For example, equipping a set of holy armor that was once worn by a dragonian, a mage, a light warrior, and a priest would enable you to use all their abilities."

"Seriously?!"

"The holy armor practically transcribes the souls of its past wearers, giving whoever equips it access to their knowledge and memories. It can use that information to perform advanced calculations and determine what its past wearers would do or say if they were present. It is as if the holy armor itself houses their entire personalities."

"That's amazing," Nick said with a shudder.

"Destroying holy armor means burying the mighty abilities within it for good. That's a huge blow to the demon-god worshippers," Olivia said.

"That's correct. Defeating someone who misuses holy armor is a great accomplishment," Bond added.

"You've got that right!" Olivia agreed.

The two holy swords laughed innocently, but that did nothing to dispel Nick's discomfort.

"...You said holy armor has personality. Does that mean the White Mask we fought and spoke to could have had nothing to do with whoever was inside the armor? Could everything they said have come from the false personality?" he asked.

"Yes. It's very likely that the wearer used the holy armor partially to keep their identity hidden," Olivia responded.

"So they got away without leaving a single clue about who they are. If they were smart enough to take that precaution, I'm sure they're already thinking of their next plan," Nick said.

"Hmm, you have a point. We'll have to prepare ourselves for

that threat," she said, and something seemed to shift in the room. Nick sensed danger and instinctively grabbed the dagger at his hip. Olivia whipped her left arm at him like a snake, and he drew the dagger to swing it and ward her off.

"Not bad. There aren't many people with the reflexes to react to me at this distance."

Olivia caught the blade in her fingers. With almost magnetic force, she had stopped not only his blade but his entire wrist and arm. Before Nick knew it, he was outside, a fierce pain ravaging his back, his lungs empty, his brain foggy. It was then that he realized Olivia had thrown him backward through the window and that he was falling to the ground.

"Light Body!"

Nick used a spell to lessen his weight, then twisted to kick the gutters and streetlights to slow himself as he fell. By the time he landed, there was almost no impact. He climbed to his feet and glared up at the third floor, but he saw only the broken window he'd crashed through. Olivia wasn't there.

"What took you so long?"

Olivia was already standing right next to Nick. She gently put a hand to his chest.

"Gah?!" Nick yelled as a violent shock ran through his body, sending him flying backward. He crashed into a building across the street from Mysterious Teran and glared daggers at Olivia. She returned his look with a satisfied smile.

"Once you can do what I just did, you'll be able to fight White Mask in hand-to-hand combat. Don't neglect your training," she said.

"Damn you...!" Nick cursed.

"Anyway, I'm going on an extended trip! Let's find the identity of the man—or woman—inside White Mask's armor!" Olivia declared before jumping up a wall step-by-step. She accelerated and quickly left Nick's sight.

* * *

After much pestering from Bond, Nick brought the holy sword to a secondhand bookshop on the way home.

"Man, that was embarrassing," Nick muttered.

"Olivia is a holy sword. There is no shame in her getting the best of you... Oooh, there's a special issue of *Lemuria Monthly*. I'll give it a read," Bond said excitedly.

"You can look at any page once and store it in your memory. Why not just read it here and put it back?"

"That would be stealing, you fool. I buy all the magazines I read."

Bond was a bibliomaniac and had built up quite the collection of books since joining the party. He read anything from newspapers and dry scholarly papers to fun works like novels and old comic novellas. Nick had thought his occult phase was coming to an end, but Bond flipped through the pages with a furious speed he had never seen.

"I thought you were getting tired of that stuff," Nick said.

"I've just been curious about something. Why do you think she's publishing magazines like these?" Bond asked.

"'Cause she enjoys it?"

"I believe that is part of it, but I find it strange that she chose to work at an occult publishing company despite all the knowledge she possesses. She is her own news source. There is no way she bases all her articles on groundless rumors. She wrote a special feature on White Mask, after all."

"You're saying her articles are actually credible?"

"That is what I want to ascertain."

"Why would she go out of her way to publish her stories in a dubious magazine that just screams 'every word of this is a lie'? The only people who will take it seriously are occult fanatics and us... Ah." Comprehension dawned on Nick's face. "She does it to avoid drawing too much attention to her writing."

"She slips some truth into all the false information. There is likely some way of determining which articles are true."

"That would catapult the value of this magazine for anyone who realized that."

"What should we do, Nick? I want to investigate, but withdrawing from all of this might be a good idea, too," Bond asked, looking up from the magazine to meet Nick's eyes.

"No... We've already fought a demon-god worshipper. Trying to back out at this point might actually put us in more danger," Nick replied.

A chill ran down his spine as he said that. It was becoming clear just how much darkness lurked in Labyrinth City, unbeknownst to its citizens. He had always had a vague notion that the city contained such dangerous presences, but he never imagined he would find himself fighting one himself.

"Nick, hold out your hand," Bond requested.

"Why?" Nick asked, doing as he was told.

"Blargh."

Bond spit up a beautiful jewel into Nick's hand.

"What the hell?! That's disgusting! I don't want your half-eaten candy!" Nick shouted.

"It's not candy! This is a knowledge orb. The data from all the magazines I've read is stored on it. Fill it with mana, and you can read them, too."

"That sounds useful. Just warn me next time you're about to hack one up and spit it at me."

"I am not too skilled at this type of investigation. Study it when you have time."

"I doubt I'm much better than you... Well, I do know someone who's good at literary study. I'll ask them."

A voice echoed in Nick's head after he said that.

"Nick! Help me!"

"Karan?!"

It was his teammate.

"Karan reached out to us using Telepathy... She sounded quite desperate," Bond said.

"I've never heard her sound so helpless...," Nick said.

Bond gulped, and a deep sense of worry quickly overtook Nick's mind.

"Let's go!" he said.

Nick and Bond ran toward Karan. Fortunately, she wasn't far; she was outside a café near the Mysterious Teran office.

"Hey, Nick! Please help me!" Karan pleaded.

"I'm coming, I'm coming!" Nick called back.

Karan looked exhausted, and the reason was apparent. She was holding and trying to comfort a toddler who would not stop crying.

"Ah... Karan. When did you become a mom?" Nick asked.

"He's not my child!" she shouted angrily, and the toddler started screaming. "Oh, s-sorry! There, there... Everything's okay!" Karan said, trying to soothe the little boy, but he showed no signs of calming down.

"Bond. Are you installed with any babysitting experience?" Nick asked.

"I am not," Bond responded.

"Yeah, that was a long shot," Nick said.

"Don't just stand there. Help me already...," Karan whined.

She sounded so exhausted, Nick actually began to worry for her. "Sorry. Here, hand him to me so you can rest," he said.

"Okay."

"Man, this kid's got some serious lungs on him... Whose is he? He looks dragonian..."

Karan opened her mouth to explain, but she was interrupted when the café door rattled open.

"Karan, I didn't know where you'd gone! Don't scare me like that! And Ares, stop crying!" a beautiful blue-haired woman complained as soon as she walked outside.

"You went to the bathroom! What was I supposed to do?!" Karan retorted.

"He's so shy. I swear, the waterworks are never far with this one," the woman said with a shrug before she took the boy from Karan and cradled him. She seemed like his mother. "...Hmm? Who are you two?"

The woman studied Nick and Bond. Nick wanted to ask the same question about her.

Karan answered them both. "This is Nick, my party leader, and Bond, another member of my party. Nick, this is my older sister... Well, I call her that, but she's actually my cousin."

The café was called Knocker Donuts. It was located on the western side of Labyrinth City and primarily served coffee and donuts. Its namesake was a legendary fairy called a "knocker" that would show miners where good ore veins were. There were no mines nearby, however; instead, the area was a lively scene for the performing arts, with many parks where plays and outdoor concerts could be held, which resulted in an abundance of customers, performers, and staff. People came to Knocker Donuts to relax with a dark-roast coffee and mine for inspiration.

"So you're the leader of the Survivors. I've heard so much about you all. I'm Daffodil, Karan's cousin. This is my son, Ares," Daffodil said after sitting across from Nick at the table. She looked at him appraisingly.

Nick observed her closely as well. She had horns like Karan. She resembled her cousin, with the most obvious differences being her scales and hair. They were both a shiny blue, and her long hair was slightly wavy and tied in a braid.

"Daffy lived with me in my home village. I hadn't seen her since she left the village, though. I thought she was dead," Karan said.

"Why would you think that?!" Daffodil exclaimed.

"You left ten years ago with your head in the clouds because you wanted to become a professional dancer."

"I *did* become a professional dancer! I work as a trainer now, too! And you're not one to talk about having your head in the clouds!"

"At least I act like a dragonian!"

Karan looked at Daffodil with accusatory eyes, which only angered her cousin.

"Do you have any idea how worried I was about you? Why don't you rely on me?" Daffodil asked.

"I had no idea where you were. How could I have? You kept moving. All our letters to you came back because we didn't know your address. The postal charges added up, and even Gramps started to worry that you were dead," Karan said.

"Th-that's not my fault. I was busy... And raising a child is really hard... Have *you* reached out to Gramps and Dad since you got here?"

"Well..."

Daffodil and Karan both fell silent.

Bond turned to Nick and whispered, "Family, am I right?"

Nick wanted to smile, but it didn't show on his face.

"Excuse me, can I please order?" Nick called to a server. "I'd like a coffee and donut set—classic chocolate for the donuts and black coffee. Another snack would be nice, too..."

"How about mini sesame balls?" Bond suggested.

"You got it...," the waiter mumbled lazily, then walked away.

"I didn't call you here to relax, Nick!" Karan said.

"You scared me, Karan. You interrupted some serious research."

Karan sensed that he was a little ticked off and stopped arguing. "Urgh, sorry..."

"Oh, I'm sorry about that, too... I'm glad you're here, though," Daffodil said.

"You are?"

"I've been wanting to speak to you. I've heard so much about you all around the Adventurers Guilds."

Daffodil's comment put Nick on guard. There was nothing shady about the Survivors. But they did all engage in...questionable hobbies. There was nothing immoral about Karan's gourmet habits or Bond's bibliomania, but the other three were another story. Nick was worried that Karan's cousin would think her friends were a bad influence.

"Thank you so much for saving my cousin," Daffodil said politely, to Nick's surprise.

He hurriedly shook his head. "We all help each other. That's what an adventurers' party does. I don't deserve any thanks."

"I don't believe that for a second," said Daffodil. "Karan's always been so gullible."

"Stop it, Daffy!" Karan shouted.

"I'm just speaking the truth... To be fair, though, all of us rural folk end up getting tricked when we come here," Daffodil said with a sigh.

"Did you have some trouble, too?" Nick asked hesitantly.

Daffodil shrugged and nodded. "That's an understatement. But Karan and I were both lucky to meet people who were willing to teach us about the world. What was it you said you did, Karan? Abacus boxing?"

"Bare-knuckle math," Karan corrected her moodily, and Daffodil giggled.

"She's always been capable. She just didn't have the opportunity," Nick argued.

"She had every opportunity. She would always run away from her parents to go play when it was time to learn," Daffodil said.

"Daffy!" Karan shouted.

"Girls like her often dream of moving to a city, and then they get scammed and can't read job postings and get tripped up by the silliest things. There aren't even schools in the countryside, hard as that might be for you to believe," Daffodil said.

"I'm not from here, either, actually," Nick replied. "I learned to read and write and do math 'cause my parents were merchants."

"Really? That's interesting. It's uncommon for people like you to become adventurers," Daffodil observed.

"You're right about that."

"Is that true?" Karan asked.

"Why *did* you become an adventurer?" Bond asked.

They appeared even more surprised than Daffodil.

"Karan. Why do you think an adventurer would choose to study or act like a merchant?" Nick posed.

"Um, to win duels?" Karan guessed.

"I'm not talking about bare-knuckle math. The answer is simple—so they can eventually quit working as an adventurer."

Karan seemed troubled. "...Oh. I've seen some adventurers quit, both by choice and not."

"People who want to work as an adventurer their whole life don't study at all. There are plenty of adventurers who are strong enough to be hired by nobles, but are illiterate and clueless about etiquette. Those are poor traits to have, but people overlook it because it's expected of adventurers," Nick said. He hadn't answered their questions.

"You seem like you could handle a lot of different jobs. Have you ever thought about quitting the adventuring life?" Daffodil asked.

"Hmm... I did work a part-time job at a trading company once because a party member got hurt and we couldn't take on jobs," Nick answered with a bitter expression. "All I did was manage warehouse stock, help unload carriages, and write receipts. I was pretty good at it, but...I couldn't settle in."

"Why not?"

"I worked with a lot of newly hired employees who told me to do some physical labor and miscellaneous tasks along with the part-timers. They were all from Labyrinth City, the same age, and had just graduated school."

"That's pretty common. Schools will hold their graduations at the same time, so a lot of young people get hired together."

"They all asked me where I graduated from, and they were shocked when I told them I never went to school and that I worked as an adventurer. They never put me down for it; they actually seemed to think it was cool. It's just... I always wanted to tell them something."

"Tell them what?"

"That going to school and graduating made them much more impressive than me. It's like the difference between walking down paved roads and cutting your way through rough, overgrown animal trails. Anyone would rather spend life doing the former."

"Nick...," Karan said worriedly, but Nick laughed it off.

"Oh, don't get the wrong idea. They were all good people. I just found myself feeling inferior," he said.

"There are a lot of good people in this city. After living here for a while, I actually became more scared of other outsiders like me. Many of them adapt to the city in all the wrong ways and try to trick people who came from the same place as them," Daffodil said.

"Cafés like this are a common spot for scammers to target people who look like they came from the countryside. They'll pretend to be friendly while sitting around their victim so they can't escape."

"Yeah, seeing those people makes me want to punch a hole through their stomachs!"

"Okay, you two, this tangent's gone on long enough," Karan chided.

"Ah, my bad," Nick responded.

"Oh, sorry about that," Daffodil apologized. She cleared her throat, uncomfortable under the weight of Karan's glare.

Nick took a second to collect himself. "Anyway, I just couldn't settle in there. The Adventurers Guild suits me better. There are a lotta jackasses, but there are good people, too. Adventurers have definitely earned their dicey reputation, but I want to think they're not all bad."

"Is that why you told Karan not to judge people just because they're an adventurer or an outsider?" Daffodil asked, and Karan looked at Nick with surprise.

"We've been through a lot, okay?" Nick snapped, looking away. "I don't mind continuing to tell my life story, but what do you think? Have I earned your approval yet?"

"Your leader has trust issues, Karan," Daffodil said, amused.

"Yeah. That's exactly why I'm able to live without worry," Karan responded proudly.

Daffodil's eyes narrowed suspiciously. "I need to ask you something... Where's the dragon king gem?"

Karan visibly jumped in response. "I—I, uh...don't have it with me right now," she stammered.

Nick glanced at her awkwardly. The dragon king gem was a treasured possession of hers that was stolen by Callios, the leader of her first adventurers' party. It was a large ruby that Karan's father, who was the chief of the fire dragonians, spent a year filling with mana. It was very valuable and would fetch a high price on the market. It was also a source of gossip that spread when Karan returned alone from the labyrinth where her party had abandoned her.

"I know a man tricked you and stole it, you dummy! I want to make sure you're not thinking of trying to get it back!" Daffodil chastised.

"You're not mad it was stolen?" Karan asked, baffled.

Daffodil sighed deeply. "Haah... You don't get it at all. Criminals who steal relics and magic items are dangerous. I've heard rumors of terrorists and demon-god worshippers. You're lucky you weren't killed by a professional thief."

Nick knew she had a point. He might have even agreed if Karan were a total stranger. But when he thought of the pain she had suffered and the road she'd taken to recovery, he couldn't bring himself to say anything.

"Hey, Nick," Karan said quietly, drawing Nick out of his thoughts.

"What is it?" he asked.

"I think Callios fled somewhere he won't be found. He's still on the loose."

"Yeah... Probably."

"That means I'm better off than him. I don't have to live in fear of the Sun Knights. I can go to restaurants and donut cafés and eat delicious food. I'm free to do what I want."

The dwarf waiter reappeared just as Karan finished speaking and set a tray of colorful donuts and sesame balls on the table. A child's doll was included as a freebie.

"Here, Ares. Try this," Karan said, offering him a donut.

"Okay," Ares responded.

"You're supposed to say 'thank you.' Dragonians say that and put their hands together before they eat," Karan instructed.

"Thank you," Ares said. He timidly bit into the donut. He must have liked the flavor, because he quickly took a second and third bite.

"And this is what you do when you see a relative for the first time in a while," Karan said, rubbing the boy on the head. Ares squirmed ticklishly, but he accepted her hand.

"But I hate the idea of never getting back something that was stolen from me. I don't think forgetting about it and moving on is the right thing to do... Is it wrong to feel that way?" Karan continued, speaking her mind.

Fury twisted Daffodil's face. "Have you not been listening?! I'm not here to have a philosophical debate about life and what's worth doing! I'm telling you those people are dangerous and you shouldn't go after them! Got it?"

"No, I don't." Karan crossed her arms and looked right at her cousin. "Not fighting back against dangerous people might be the right thing to do for most. But I'm an adventurer who makes a living by killing monsters and catching wanted criminals. It's my job to do the right thing, whether it makes sense or not. Any adventurer too afraid to fight someone who pulls a knife on them is an idiot. I'd rather shove my face into a box of donuts and die."

Daffodil's glare turned even more intense. "Are you following the dragonian mission? Do you want to find a hero and save the world?"

"There's a dragonian mission?" Nick asked, surprised.

Karan blushed slightly. "Yes... Dragonians have a mission to serve a hero and save the world. That's why a lot of us leave home to become knights or adventurers."

"That's the first I've heard of it," Nick said.

"Well... It's embarrassing to tell people that I'm 'searching for my hero,'" Karan responded shyly.

Nick was confused and didn't notice the way Karan's eyes flicked to him. "Is it? Bond's always pestering me to become a hero."

"Are you implying that it's embarrassing for me to say that?!" Bond protested indignantly.

"You're different, Bond. You're just telling him to think and act like a hero," Karan said with a self-deprecating tone.

"Yeah, I suppose," Bond replied.

"I, on the other hand, used to think there would be a hero somewhere in the world who would rise up and save everyone. But the adventurers and knights in Labyrinth City... None of them are very heroic," Karan continued.

"You have that right," Bond agreed.

"There are so many adventurers who drink away their rewards as soon as they're paid, or reek because they never bathe. Others will trick their companions and steal precious treasures from them. We even met an adventurer who cheated at gambling and a respected doctor who kidnapped children on the side. There are no heroes in this world."

"Karan...," Nick said. She was trying to poke fun at the painful experiences she'd been through, and he wasn't sure how to feel about that.

"Nick has taken down some wicked adventurers, but idols are all he thinks about. The rest of us are obsessed with our hobbies, too. We're all too self-absorbed to be heroes," Karan said with a chuckle.

Daffodil looked exasperated. "That's exactly right. There are no heroes in this city. If you know that, why are you still working as an adventurer?"

"Hmm... So I can eat good food, I guess."

"That's just a hobby."

"Yeah. All I want to do is wake up in the morning, venture out with my party, kill monsters and catch bad guys, get paid, relax with a bowl of good food, and return to the inn to sleep."

"That sounds fine to me. You don't need to be an adventurer to live that lifestyle."

"Yes, I do." Karan sadly shook her head. "I'm too stupid to do anything else."

"No, you're not. You've gotten much wiser since you left home," Daffodil insisted.

"Maybe, but I still need to learn so much more about the world. I would fail the interview for any normal job. I think I'd still be easy prey to scammers," Karan responded.

"Karan..."

"If I ever become smart enough to make calculations and strategize, I'll be able to find creative ways to keep doing the right thing without conflict. But until then, I want to do good in the way any idiot can. I won't be a coward."

"You have to be strong to truly make a difference in the world. As strong as the hero who defeated the demon god," Daffodil said, shaking her head sadly.

"I'm not dumb enough to try to be a hero on my own, and I know I might lose to a really strong villain. I don't want to count myself out, but I've already had a few close calls. That said..." Karan trailed off.

"Yeah?"

"I think everything will work out just fine if I'm with my other Survivors."

Daffodil seemed to rack her brains for what to say and sighed. "Fine. Do what you want. But think about how long you want to keep doing this."

"I don't know about that..."

"I won't tell you to quit the Adventurers Guild right now. But I want you to remember this. Your parents love you so much more than any stone."

"Okay," Karan said with a nod.

Daffodil turned to Nick next. "Nick. Please take this to heart. Work might be going well now, but adventurers always reach a day when they can't go on. The heyday of any physically demanding job is fleeting. Even if you avoid a major injury, your heart and soul may end up broken from the number of terrifying experiences you end up going through. Am I wrong?"

"No, you're not," Nick admitted.

"When that time comes for Karan, I want you to make sure she retires. I don't want her losing an arm, a leg, her life, or something even worse," Daffodil beseeched.

Nick felt there was more to her request than simple worry for a reckless little-sister figure. There was a weight to her words that only a person who had lost something could project. Karan seemed to feel that weight, too, and couldn't bring herself to interject.

"I can't tell you what you want to hear. As the leader, I can kick her out of my party, but I have no right to tell her to stop working as an adventurer," Nick replied.

"This is exactly why I hate adventurers," Daffodil said with an exasperated shrug.

"I'm sorry, Daffy," Karan apologized.

"Don't say things you don't feel. I've always known what kind of girl you were," Daffodil said, rubbing the guilty-looking Karan on the head. Karan's cries for her to stop went unheeded.

Nick spoke up to save her. "I will say this, Daffodil. We're called the Survivors for a reason—our number one rule is to come back from any adventure alive. If Karan ever finds herself in mortal danger, I'll tie her up and drag her to you."

"Okay. I'll hold you to that," Daffodil replied.

"You're so annoying!" Karan snapped, escaping from her cousin's hand and turning away with a huff.

Daffodil laughed innocently. "I'll let you go for today. You can eat as much as you want," she said, picking up Ares and grabbing the check.

"Daffy!" Karan protested.

"It's okay to rely on your elders now and then, Karan."

"We ordered too much. You should take some home, at least. Excuse me, can we please have a takeout box? Oh, and is it too late to use a coupon?" Karan asked after calling over the dwarf waiter. He complained that she should've given him the coupon earlier as he checked them out, and Karan apologized.

"She's really grown accustomed to this, hasn't she…?" Daffodil giggled as she watched Karan's exchange with the waiter.

"She's definitely not an idiot," Nick said. Daffodil nodded happily in response.

A few days later, when the Survivors were all gathered at the Fishermen Adventurers Guild, Nick said something that shocked the rest of his party.

The View on the Road Home

There was a trade route commonly known as the Maiden Highway that ran between the western side of Labyrinth City and the capital. The name was a reference to the shamans and minstrels who'd traveled the road in ancient times. It was said that during the war with the demon god, all the women who practiced at sanctuaries in the capital traveled to a base where Labyrinth City stood now and helped to bring peace by praying for the hero.

North of the Maiden Highway was a mountain range of labyrinths known as the Five-Ringed Mountains. The "five rings" referred to the five labyrinths that made up the range, each of them particularly difficult.

South of the highway—which meant southwest of Labyrinth City—was a sprawling, barren wasteland known as Hyena Waste. One might think the name originated from prowling packs of hyenas, but that would be wrong; in fact, there were hardly any animals in the area at all. Instead, the word *hyena* was used to refer to the excavators and looters who searched the ancient ruins scattered throughout the waste.

Entering these ruins meant putting oneself in mortal danger. The ancient security and the monsters that spawned within the structures saw any invaders as looters and did their best to eliminate them. And yet the promise of treasure continued to tempt people into risking their lives, and over time, people came to call the area and its labyrinths Hyena Waste.

"Ugh, I can't believe they make you take one of those," Tiana said angrily as the party walked through Hyena Waste. She was looking at a cloth bag strapped to Zem's back. It was folded like a camping tent.

"It's the rule," Zem replied.

"I know that, but it's in bad taste. There's nothing to inspire you like taking a *body bag* into a labyrinth," Tiana complained.

"This is a dangerous job. You come to realize that after enough labyrinth exploration," Nick said casually without turning around. Tiana just sighed as she followed behind him. "We have all the information we need. We can handle this place just fine."

"Yes, you are right. However..." Bond nervously glanced ahead.

Karan had been walking ahead of the group without joining in the conversation. "That's it... The hole in that giant stone is the entrance," she announced.

She pointed toward a black opening that looked like an enlarged anthill opening in a stone structure. It led into a labyrinth that had a simple layout that spiraled downward with no branching paths until it reached the bottom floor, resembling the rings on a vase left by a potter's fingers as they spun it on their wheel.

This labyrinth was called Pot Snake Cave, and it was a C-rank labyrinth infested with deadly poisonous monsters. The place had a special meaning to Karan; it was where her first party, White Heron, had left her to die.

Nick was the one who suggested taking on this labyrinth, for a couple reasons. The first was that the Survivors had been raised to D rank in recognition of their accomplishments at the Manhunt guild, and all they had to do to reach C rank was clear one C-rank labyrinth.

C was an important rank for adventurers. It gave a party access to the Pioneers Guild, where highly skilled advanced adventurers gathered. It was also the rank where ambitious adventurers competed most ruthlessly to keep going up the ladder. Reaching it was a goal for Nick.

The other reason Nick chose Pot Snake Cave was much more important.

"How do you feel, Karan?" Nick asked.

"The monsters won't be a problem. But I feel…queasy," she answered.

The main reason Nick suggested they challenge this labyrinth was because he feared Karan was suffering from an illness.

"I knew it. You have labyrinthphobia," Nick said.

Labyrinthphobia wasn't an official illness recognized by sanctuaries and hospitals. It was considered a variety of panic disorder at most, and it was never specifically mentioned in clinical records. But in Labyrinth City, where a lot of adventurers lived, everyone knew what it was.

The illness presented no impediments to daily life, but coming across a monster that had clobbered you once or thinking of a labyrinth where a party member died could cause extreme anxiety, tension, and vomiting. It was a disastrous—and potentially lethal—illness for adventurers. The emergence of symptoms in a critical situation would put not just you but your entire party in danger.

Labyrinthphobia needed to be conquered as soon after diagnosis as possible. Adventurers who did nothing to cure their illness were eventually kicked out of their party and given a notice by the Adventurers Guild, forcing them to retire. There were no exceptions.

Nick first suspected that Karan had labyrinthphobia when a guild employee handed them a list of C-rank labyrinths. The employee kindly explained that they would be promoted to C rank if they cleared even one of the labyrinths, and when she shared details about Pot Snake Cave, Karan developed a nasty headache and didn't get up from the table for a while.

Nick noticed it right away. Karan had developed a severe case of labyrinthphobia that would threaten her career as an adventurer if left alone. That's when he declared they were going to Pot Snake Cave.

"I think so, too," Karan agreed.

"Focus on taking deep breaths. Zem, do you have any medicine?" Nick asked.

"I'll prepare a calming decoction... But do we really need to rush this?" Zem said, sounding doubtful as he dissolved ground-up medicinal herbs in hot water.

"Yes, we do. I won't consider withdrawing," Nick answered frankly.

"Why?! Just look at Karan...," Tiana said, worried.

"I don't mind. Let's go," Karan said.

Tiana gulped. "You're really pale. This is reckless," she insisted.

"My heart feels cold just being near this labyrinth. My legs are restless, too," Karan said, speaking clearly despite her shaking voice. "I never thought something like this would happen to me. But I was wrong. I've been scared this whole time. I'm scared right now."

"Then let's leave!"

"No. I have to fix this."

Karan gave Tiana a brave smile, but the mage still looked distressed. Nick remained cool, not letting Karan's state throw his emotions out of balance.

"There's only one way to heal labyrinthphobia: rechallenge the labyrinth or monster that caused it and win. The longer you wait, the harder it gets," he said.

"But I've heard there's a way to heal labyrinthphobia by clearing easier labyrinths," Tiana replied.

It was the shared opinion of Labyrinth City adventurers that curing the fear required facing the labyrinth or monster that caused it. The only other option in their minds was to quit working as an adventurer.

The time to full recovery differed greatly depending on the person. For example, an individual who knew an advanced adventurer and was blessed with friends who were willing to help them could perform a drastic treatment that involved forming an overpowered party and quickly stomping whatever caused their illness. Not many people had that option, however. The most common and safest method of treatment was to repeatedly clear a lower-level labyrinth that was the same type as the place that triggered the symptoms and gradually reduce them before tackling the main labyrinth again.

"We'd end up having to come here in the end anyway. It's best to get it over with," Nick insisted, believing they should clear Pot Snake Cave as quickly as possible. It was rare for him to make such an aggressive choice. It would be fair to say he was being stubborn and reckless.

"What do you think, Bond?" Tiana asked, repressing her anger.

Bond creased his brow and answered. "Hmm... Honestly, I believe this method to be crude. It would be best to treat the illness over time with appropriate counseling. I cannot wholeheartedly agree with Nick's decision."

"Then—"

"But such counseling is not available in Labyrinth City. Asking a private physician or a priest for help would be pointless, and I don't have an alternate plan."

"This is ridiculous."

Bond's answer only ticked Tiana off more.

"That's enough complaining," Nick snapped.

"Who do you think you are?" Tiana asked.

"The party leader. If you have a problem with my decision—"

"Oh, I have many problems with it. But I get your reasoning. That's not why I'm mad."

Tiana was angry because of Nick's attitude, which was why she was pressing him so firmly.

"Why're you upset, then?" Nick asked.

"I don't like this dumb tough-guy act you're putting on," Tiana answered.

"Just follow your leader's orders. That's how we operate. An adventurer who's scared of labyrinths is useless. We need to do this. That's all there is to it."

"That's a lie." Tiana glared at Nick, and he met her with the same expression.

"What's a lie?" he asked.

"Do you not see it? You normally take a vote for even the smallest of decisions and ask for our input when planning. But you're not listening to us this time. We barely even took time to prepare. It's weird," Tiana said.

"There's no point in discussing this. We don't have the luxury of choice here. If you're that upset about it, you can leave."

"Oh, you're going there, are you? Let me say one thing."

"As if I could stop you."

"You know you're pushing Karan too far, and you're acting like a tyrant so all the blame rests on your shoulders. You're acting this way to *make* us hate you. Just like a certain adventurer who drove you away using similar methods."

Nick grabbed Tiana by the collar, enraged by her accusation. But she didn't stop there.

"The leader of your previous party didn't give you a reason you could accept when he fired you, and even worse, he didn't listen at all when you tried to defend yourself. Wasn't that infuriating? This Argus might have been an amazing adventurer, but he definitely hurt you that day. Are you trying to do the same thing to us?" Tiana asked.

"Why, you little…," Nick growled threateningly.

"Oh dear. Did I make you mad? Why? Because I brought up your past? Curing labyrinthphobia requires overcoming past trauma. If you're going to demand that of others, you shouldn't get so worked up when someone drags up your issues."

"That is enough, Tiana!" Zem called out.

"Hey, Tiana!" Karan shouted.

Karan watched Nick and Tiana, too stunned by their exchange

to move. The tension between them was so great, it seemed they would come to blows. Ten seconds of silence stretched to a minute, and then five. Eventually, the intense anger receded from Nick's face and he calmly let go of Tiana's collar.

"Sorry. I wasn't clear enough with you all," he apologized.

Nick *had* been acting like Argus. He couldn't deny it. Wounds of the past became a part of oneself, for better or for worse. Some wounds inspired direct growth, while others took time to overcome. The Survivors all had plenty of the latter.

"For goodness' sake... Care to explain yourself?" Tiana asked, breathing a sigh of relief.

"This place should be easy for us, considering our strength. But you never know what could happen in a labyrinth... If something goes wrong, I thought it would be easier for you all to handle if you had someone to blame," Nick said.

"That's ridiculous! You pick the worst times to act stubborn," Tiana replied with a shrug.

"I can tell you're probably thinking about what Daffy said," Karan began quietly. "But I'm the one who has to brace myself and overcome this illness, not you. There's no reason to torment yourself for my sake."

Zem, who had been observing the conversation quietly, spoke up next. "Nick. I understand how you feel, wanting to cure Karan's labyrinthphobia. I also agree with your general plan."

"Zem...," Nick said.

"However, you should have explained yourself to Karan. And Karan, I understand why you want to respect Nick's thinking. But you should talk to him before you blindly follow his orders. Have you forgotten why Nick made the rules we abide by as the Survivors?" Zem admonished.

"Urk..."

Karan's expression made it clear that she had forgotten.

"We are all equal partners. It is your duty to protect the safe and not let us touch it. You should apply that mindset to our adventures as well. If Nick is behaving in a way that doesn't make sense, you can confront him about it. In fact, as his comrade, that is exactly what you should do," Zem continued.

"O-okay."

"I'm not telling you to suspect Nick of nefarious intentions. I trust him as well. But he can have errors of judgment. He has a virtuous soul, but no one is perfect. Party members need to speak up and share their opinion when the situation calls for it."

"...Okay." Karan nodded meekly.

"It's time for you to speak up, Nick," Bond said.

"Since when were you in charge? Eh, whatever." Nick smiled with some chagrin. He stood up straight and began to speak. "Adventurers suffering from labyrinthphobia can do as Tiana said. Most actually do spend time clearing a labyrinth of slightly lower difficulty until they feel ready to take on the source of their trauma. It's an effective method if you want to save your career as an adventurer. But it's not good enough for Karan."

"Why not?" Tiana asked.

"White Mask is a demon-god worshipper. His comrades will target us now that we've defeated him," Nick said, sending a chill down the others' spines. "I don't have proof of that, but it'd be dangerous to assume they won't want revenge. They're good at hiding their identities, they've got a boatload of valuable magic tools, and worst of all, they've all got more than a few screws loose. We don't know when or how they'll come for us... Karan, do you think that Callios guy who stole your dragon king gem could be one of them?"

Karan's eyes went wide with surprise. "Callios...a demon-god worshipper?"

"Are you sure you aren't overthinking things?" Tiana asked.

"I'm obviously just guessing... I actually have no basis for that at all. But it doesn't matter either way. All the demon-god worshippers would have to do to trigger Karan's labyrinthphobia would be to use a disguise or an illusion and put her face-to-face with someone who looks like Callios. Labyrinthphobia announces your weaknesses to the world. If we really are being targeted, she'll be in mortal danger until we cure it," Nick continued.

Karan was shocked to hear this. She had already wanted to cure her labyrinthphobia as quickly as possible, but she hadn't considered any of that.

"Did you think telling her that would put too much pressure on her? I respect that, but your strange behavior was probably making her even more nervous. Something was clearly off with you," Tiana chided.

"It wasn't that bad," Nick protested.

"It absolutely was!" Tiana insisted.

Just when it looked like the two were going to start arguing again, Karan spoke up softly. "I thought you were hung up on the promise you made to Daffy."

"That was part of it. She was right that I should make you retire before adventuring breaks you. You'd be surprised by the number of people who refuse to admit their labyrinthphobia isn't cured only to charge into a labyrinth alone and die," Nick said.

He steeled himself and looked at Karan.

"Labyrinthphobia destroys adventurers' careers without exception if uncured. I'd rather kick you out of the party than watch you fail to cure it, push yourself too far, and die."

The rest were rendered speechless by his brutal honesty.

A fire burned in Karan's eyes. "I don't want you to kick me out of the party. I don't want to die, either," she said.

"Good," Nick replied.

"And I *especially* don't want to lose to a crook because they took advantage of my illness with a cowardly trick."

"I agree with you there."

"Let's not do this the slow way. Let's clear this labyrinth and kill the pot snake now."

"Got it."

"But I can't do this alone. I can't do it with people I don't trust, either. Give me your support," Karan requested, extending a fist before her. The others each put a fist to hers.

"Karan. You're just as brave as you think you are. You're just as strong as you think you are. And you're *much* smarter than you think you are. But we're here for you if you need us. You don't have to watch your back," Nick reassured her.

"Okay," Karan said.

"Let's move out, everyone," Nick said.

Karan sucked in a large breath, channeled all her anger and resolve, and bellowed.

"RAAAAAAARGH!"

Her draconic roar echoed endlessly in the labyrinth, stirring the monsters within.

The Survivors resumed walking.

"Karan! Take out that silver stag!" Nick yelled.

"Take this!" Karan screamed.

Silver stags were incredibly nimble and had hard shells, but unlike most monsters in Pot Snake Cave, they were not poisonous. They served a different purpose; if poison was this labyrinth's sword, their shiny silver bodies were its shield.

"Watch your surroundings, Tiana! Bond and I will cover you!" Nick called out. He was knowledgeable about the monsters in this labyrinth and stayed composed as he gave orders to his party members.

"I know! Icicle Dance!" Tiana yelled, sending icicles flying in all directions. She didn't shoot them at random; each one was carefully aimed to strike a monster lurking in the dark. The icicles didn't all connect, but they restrained the monsters and allowed Nick and Bond to finish them off.

"There are three new ones behind Zem! They're all underfoot!" Bond said telepathically.

The Survivors' strategy was simple. Bond used his excellent hearing and smell to find the enemies hiding in the dark and gave orders using Telepathy. The party was able to get through the labyrinth without significant injury or fatigue.

"I sense no more monsters in our immediate vicinity. The only one that remains is..." Bond trailed off.

"The one in the pot," Nick finished. The others nodded.

The Survivors had reached the bottom floor of the labyrinth. The giant serpent waited there, slumbering within its pot.

Nick laid out the strategy. "All right, let's review. Tiana will restrain it from behind. Heat and cold will be ineffective if it uses its pot as a shield, so lightning spells will work best. But you don't have to kill it. Don't move up to the front line."

"Got it," Tiana answered.

"I'm gonna wield Bond as a sword and fight it using hit-and-run tactics. We might have to use Union. Be ready for that," Nick said.

"Understood," Bond responded.

"Karan. You're gonna defend the group by fighting up front. Do your best to provoke the pot snake," Nick ordered.

"Okay!" Karan exclaimed.

"And Zem. You're the key to this assault," Nick said.

"I will cast anti-poison spells once the snake's color changes. I have learned quite a lot of new spells lately," Zem replied with a smile. It wasn't like him to boast.

"When did you learn that kind of magic, Zem?" Tiana asked.

"I found some useful spellbooks while sorting through Nargava's belongings. The residents there offered them to me as a reward after I gave them treatment. I also found a copy of a spellbook page for Restoration," Zem explained.

"Excuse me?!" Tiana yelled, surprised. The others were astounded, too.

"That's the spell that can regenerate a lost limb," Nick said.

Restoration was a very advanced healing spell that could

regenerate a body part lost to injury. There were limitations: It didn't work if the wound was closed, and it restored body parts while retaining any tumors, sicknesses, or scars. Even so, it was a powerful spell.

"The spell is too advanced for me to use currently, but I will learn it eventually," Zem said with quiet resolve.

"It was presumptuous of the Garbage Heap residents to think the spellbooks were theirs to give," Tiana commented, eliciting a bitter smile and a shrug from Zem.

"They have their own way of doing things there. Anyway...I believe I have a good understanding of the nature of the monster's poison. Please wait as I make an antidote," Zem said.

"Sweet!" Nick cheered.

Pot Snake Cave was considered a difficult labyrinth because of one unique characteristic: The nature of its monsters' poison changed over time. The components morphed along with the passing of seasons and years, requiring new antidotes to heal it. There was no shortage of labyrinths with poisonous monsters, but this one was infamous among them. Fortunately, given his knowledge of medicine, the variety of illnesses he encountered in the nightlife district, and the notes and books he had received from Nargava, Zem was more capable than the average priest.

"Most monsters here consume and store poison like puffer fish or oil-eaters. I found moss inside the stomach of a snake I caught. It's called blue-fire moss, which, unlike most moss, is poisonous," Zem explained joyfully as he made the medicine.

The others felt a sense of dread as they watched him; Zem was not the type to consider taste when making medicine.

"Urgh... This is disgusting," Nick grimaced after sniffing the medicinal tea Zem gave him. He held his nose and chugged the green, black, and pink liquid. "Blech... Don't just watch me, you two. Drink up."

Tiana and Karan reached for the medicine hesitantly...

"Run, everyone!" Bond yelled, and they all scattered reflexively.

A giant spear whooshed through the spot where they had been standing a moment earlier.

"Wh-what the hell just happened?!" Nick shouted, shocked.

He turned around and saw the dim shape of a giant snake. Its eyes shone faintly in the dark. It was undoubtedly the boss of this labyrinth, the pot snake.

"Hey, what gives?! I thought it only emerged when you disturbed it!" Tiana shouted.

"It's definitely not supposed to leave its nest! Adventurers have killed this thing hundreds of times!" Nick called back.

"Y-yeah! It didn't come out until I kicked the pot last time!" Karan said.

"There are always exceptions! We've seen mutants before!" Tiana said.

"There are records of mutants, but… Well, there's no point in discussing this now," Nick said.

The pot snake picked up another weapon in its mouth. Nick figured it had picked up a spear dropped by a deceased adventurer and chucked it at the party as hard as it could. The throw was surprisingly accurate, given the darkness of the cave.

"This is bad… It is using some kind of stealth ability or spell to negate its noise, scent, and body temperature. It is visible, but only barely." Bond sounded unusually concerned.

"Snakes primarily sense by detecting heat, right?" Nick asked.

"Yes. Snake monsters should be the same," Bond answered.

"Karan! Tiana! Disturb it with fire and lightning! Don't worry about drawing attention to yourselves!" Nick ordered.

Karan breathed fire and Tiana cast lightning spells, but the pot snake just calmly backed up. It used a long-handled spear like a crutch to lift itself off the ground, pot and all, and hop around the cave.

"We have a problem, Nick. The medicine…" Zem trailed off, looking at his pot and cups. They had been shattered by the spear.

The ingredients he used to make the medicine were on the ground as well.

"Shit... Did you all drink it?" Nick cursed, looking at his party members.

"I am mostly immune to poison," Bond responded.

"I drank it. However...," Zem said.

"Karan and I didn't," Tiana finished anxiously.

Karan was pale as a sheet.

"Karan, are you okay?" Tiana asked.

Karan jolted at the sound of her name, but she quickly put on a brave front. "We weren't even sure Zem would be able to make medicine. The plan was to avoid its poison and kill it. We'll be fine."

"We didn't account for a mutant, though. No one's ever seen it preemptively attack adventurers and use a weapon to move around, right?" Tiana asked.

"Yeah. Both of those are firsts. This is definitely a mutant," Nick answered. He looked unsure for a moment, but he quickly made up his mind. "We'll stick to the plan with one alteration— get ready to use Union, Bond and Zem. If anyone gets hurt, we'll heal them immediately and kill the pot snake."

Karan gulped. She clenched her fists to stop them from trembling.

"You're still gonna fight up front, Karan. We'll heal you with Union if you get poisoned, but we may not be fast enough. Keep that in mind," Nick said.

"O-okay!" Karan responded.

"Do you understand what we're asking of you? You'll have to fight very carefully," Tiana warned.

"I can't get cold feet now. Losing my concentration could get me killed," Karan said.

Tiana groaned. For once, she had no argument.

The Survivors' fight against the mutant pot snake began.

*   *   *

The final floor of Pot Snake Cave was expansive. The boss was strong, yet its sluggishness made it relatively easy to handle in close combat. At least, that was normally the case.

"Dammit, what's with this thing?!" Nick cursed.

"The pot is made of a light and soft material! It can contract like rubber or muscle, allowing it to jump! It's also using its muscles to push off the ground, so think of it as a full-body spring!" Bond yelled.

"Snakes aren't supposed to jump around like springs! That's just stupid!" Nick yelled back.

The Survivors struggled to keep up with the pot snake's shocking agility. It skillfully dodged each of Tiana's spells. She probably would've had no trouble hitting it if they were outdoors, but the dark cave had many stalactites the snake could use to hide behind and swing around on to change directions. Whenever the party lost sight of their quarry, the snake would swing its body like a pendulum from the ceiling and crash toward them pot first.

"The way it zips around reminds me of a weirdo I know. Now I know how annoying it is to deal with," Tiana complained.

"Hey, who're you calling a weirdo?" Nick snapped.

"What should we do?"

"I'm thinking."

The pot snake fell to the ground as they spoke, leaving a small crater. It jumped again, wrapping itself around another stalactite. The Survivors would be crushed if they weren't careful, and any contact with its poisonous fangs could be lethal, too. They had successfully avoided both so far, but they had been injured by the rocks the pot snake shook from the ceiling.

"It's wearing us down. If I pause to use healing magic, it will certainly target me," Zem said, giving Nick a look that communicated a clear message: *Should we use Union?*

"We can't lose Zem! Stop trying to protect me, Nick! Just do what you need to do!" Karan yelled.

Zem and Tiana looked at Nick with surprise. He had been protecting her throughout the fight by keeping an eye on her and covering her blind spots. Karan had taken some scratches but no real injuries.

"You need to tell us if you're gonna do something like that," Tiana said.

"That would've defeated the purpose," Nick grumbled.

Tiana looked at Nick with relief, but his expression was grim. It would've been best if Karan hadn't realized he was protecting her. Clearing the labyrinth wasn't important; the only goal was freeing Karan from the shackles of her past trauma.

"I'm not a helpless victim that needs to be protected! I'm a member of your party!" Karan yelled. She lifted her Dragonbone Sword overhead and swung it down as hard as she could.

"*Hsssss?!*"

"Wha...? I hit it?"

She had struck the monster as it fell toward her, scraping its pot. The creature beat a hasty retreat, shrieking all the while, until the cave fell so silent, it was as if there had never been a battle at all.

"Th-that was incredible... How'd you know it was there?" Nick asked.

"Hee-hee... That was pure luck," Karan said with a broad smile, deflecting his praise.

"Pure luck... Now, that I don't believe." Tiana was baffled.

"Yes, there's no need to be humble. Feel free to call it intuition," Zem added, equally surprised.

Karan continued to smile. "The timing was lucky. But you all were in danger. I had to do something."

The others fell silent for a moment, then reacted with astonishment once they realized what Karan meant.

"You're kidding. Was that whole conversation an act?!" Nick shouted.

"I meant every word. But I thought I might draw the snake toward me," the dragonian responded.

Karan was out of breath, and her complexion hadn't improved. She wasn't exactly in perfect shape at the moment. But Nick felt a strange sense of ease from her, and a conviction that told him she wasn't someone who would meet her end here.

"Karan. I'm gonna focus on locating it. Don't let it interfere, no matter what," Nick ordered.

"Okay," Karan responded.

"Bond, cut off your mana a little. Release your blade when I give the signal."

"What are you planning? You cannot use Magic Search or Search."

"I'm gonna use Magic Sense."

That was one of the few spells Nick had learned. It was a simple spell that allowed the user to detect the presence and amount of mana in objects they touched.

"Huh? What are you gonna do with that?" Tiana asked.

"The pot snake's stealth ability is why we're having so much trouble. But...I just sensed it," Nick said after taking off a gauntlet and touching the ground with his bare hand. "It's quietly moving along the ceiling using the stalactites. The ground and the room's mana shake subtly when it shifts its weight. There are limits to its stealth, even when it's out of view. I just felt it under my feet."

"You can sense that?" Tiana asked.

"It's easy when I touch a bare hand to the ground... All right, Karan. It stopped moving. It's gonna attack soon," Nick warned. Karan began to ready her Dragonbone Sword, but he stopped her. "Don't give it any indication we know it's coming. Keep your breathing slow and exhausted. Wait for my order. When I yell, strike as hard as you can."

"You've gotten a lot more reckless," Karan said.

"You were damn right before—we aren't helpless victims that need to be protected. We are the hunters," Nick declared.

Karan calmly digested his words and smiled. Her fiery eyes

and sharp teeth shone in the dark. Nick felt sweat run down his back.

"Don't get too excited, now," he chided.

"Oh, whoops," Karan said.

They relaxed for a moment, and the pot snake began to move. It swung like a pendulum without making any noise and flung itself at the Survivors, using its giant body as a weapon.

"Wait, Karan! It's coming from your right... *Now!* Hit it with all you've got!" Nick yelled.

"GRAAAAAAAH!"

Karan's roar—which sounded just like an angry dragon—seemed to rise from underneath the ground as it echoed in the cave. White-hot flames surrounded her body, stronger than any she had summoned yet. Nick hadn't thought much of it when he'd called them hunters, but he felt like he'd hit the nail on the head. The dragonian before him was fearsomely strong.

"Take that!" Karan swung her sword down and cleaved the pot in two before it hit the ground. "...Did you all see that?"

The pot was used to store the snake's poison and as a shell, and it was a biological part of the snake's body that connected to its nervous system and skeleton. Karan's strike was lethal.

But the pot snake's vitality was something to behold. Its head snapped at her as she powerfully forced it to the ground. Its movement was greatly slowed once its body was severed, but...

"Don't let down your guard yet, you idiot!"

...the snake only needed to graze her with its fangs to take her down with it. Knowing that, Nick dashed forward and cast Light Body and Heavy Body in quick succession to give himself the strength to leap forward. That wasn't something he was taught; he'd learned it by watching and mimicking Olivia's Stepping. He slammed into Karan before he had a chance to celebrate the success of his gamble.

"Shit!" Nick yelled as a sharp fang grazed his breastplate. The

armor just barely protected him, but the snake shot venom at him out of its mouth. Sensing that death was near, Nick gritted his teeth.

The world went black.

The first thing Nick saw when he woke up was the setting sun.

He was riding on what he thought was his father's back, but it was surprisingly soft.

What highway was this? Why were they walking so late? Were they camping again?

Nick's parents were kind. They tried their best to teach him everything they knew, including how to read and write, how to do math, how to sing, what wild grasses were edible, how to haggle with a merchant, how to read and write a contract, and even how to negotiate with a people without written language.

If there was ever something he couldn't comprehend, his "teacher" would stay with him until he learned it. His teacher knew everything and didn't treat Nick like a child. She acted like an older sister to him.

But no one ever told Nick what he really wanted to know. His parents called themselves traveling merchants, but what was their real job? Who really was the teacher, and why did she only seem to appear when called for? Who were they running from?

Nick figured they didn't tell him those things because he was weak. He worked as hard as he could to not be a burden on their travels. He slept on his father's back when he was too tired to walk, but he hated slowing them in any way.

That was why Nick's dream as a child was to live in a city. He wanted to live in a wood or brick house with his family and sleep in a soft bed without fear of being pursued. It was a wish so meager, it could hardly be called a dream.

He wanted to go home, but there was no home to return to. Nick and his parents had been traveling from town to town as long as he could remember, so in a way, the highway was his home. And yet that desire never left his mind.

"I wanna go home…," he muttered.

"We're almost there."

The voice he heard from the person carrying him wasn't his father's. It wasn't his mother's, either. It was the curt voice of a girl.

"Where am I?" Nick asked.

"The road home."

Nick's consciousness slowly came into focus. He finally realized that this was the highway back to Labyrinth City from Pot Snake Cave and that Karan was carrying him on her back.

"Hey… Put me down…," Nick said, his speech weak and slurred.

"No. Don't move. You sound terrible," Karan commanded.

"Oww… My mouth hurts. My jaw hurts. Everything hurts…"

Nick was worse than sore; the moment he became aware of his body, it felt like he was being stabbed by a thousand tiny needles. He didn't even need to move to feel pain.

"You don't remember, Nick? You fell headfirst into a puddle of pot snake venom after you shoved Karan aside," Zem said with a small smile. He was walking behind them.

"I drank the medicine, right…?" Nick asked.

"You probably would have been unhurt if you inhaled poison in mist form, but you swallowed liquid poison and fainted immediately. It is thanks to the medicine that you are here. We were this close to having a use for that body bag," Zem answered.

"What were you thinking?" Bond muttered.

"Why should our leader be the most reckless member of the party? You need to abide by our name and 'survive,'" Tiana said.

"Now, now," Zem said to calm them down. He inspected Nick's eyes and throat without the usual gentleness a doctor showed an overeager patient. "You are fine. Do your best to bear the pain."

"Geez, this is so embarrassing…," Nick muttered.

"You're worried about embarrassing yourself after saving my

life? Stop talking. You'll bite your tongue," Karan chided, but Nick didn't listen to her. He was worried he would faint again if he stopped speaking.

"You took this road home alone last time," he said.

"Yeah," Karan responded.

"You really are amazing."

"Uh-huh."

"Do you want to keep working as an adventurer?"

"Yeah, I do."

Karan agreed without hesitation and stared at the setting sun. She wasn't watching the night sky or the stars that were blinking into view behind it but the sun itself, seeming to enjoy its beauty as it painted the sky red.

"If you do something that reckless again, Nick, *I'll* kick *you* out of the party," she said.

"Sorry. That was stupid of me," Nick apologized guiltily.

Karan laughed, as if she could see his expression without even turning around.

"I have to say, though... I kind of like it when you act stupid," Karan said. She blushed in the light of the evening sun, but Nick didn't see it. He just looked at the distant sky and smiled.

"You should follow your heart. If you want to do the right thing, do it. If you want to keep adventuring, don't let anyone stop you. I'll support you, even if you laugh at me for doing stupid things. I'll probably rely on you more than the other way around, though," Nick said.

"You've got that right," Karan responded.

"Here's to many more adventures. Let's live life to the fullest," Nick said.

The red evening sky slowly turned blue, and lights could be seen turning on in the distant city. The Survivors leisurely made their way toward them.

This was the road home.

The False Paladins

Zem told Nick to rest for a week and forbade him from going to concerts. He was calm but stern—there was no arguing with him on this. Nick had no trouble following the former priest's advice; he was injured all over, and the intense pain and exhaustion he felt from the poison left him little choice but to stay in bed for three entire days. His party members took care of him, and on the fourth day, he was finally able to get up.

"You scared me when you didn't come to the fan club meetup. I thought I'd visit and fill you in."

"Thanks, Jonathan."

Nick had received a visitor in his apartment during his period of rest. It was Jonathan, a boy who seemed to have been raised well. Nick had once saved him from being swindled by his girlfriend out of an expensive necklace, and when the boy was feeling depressed afterward, he invited him to an idol concert to cheer him up. Jonathan ended up becoming just as big an idol fan as Nick.

"Let's see..." Nick read the report Jonathan gave him. "'Thieves have been disguising themselves as fans and slipping into concerts to steal expensive new magic items being used for production and lighting. Security has been increased in response, and magic barriers are being erected before the stage.' What idiots."

"The lighting at the last couple of shows has been stunning. I heard some fans who are mages and researchers say they'd never seen anything like it," Jonathan informed him.

"I would've liked to see that. Man, I wanna get back to concerts as soon as possible." Nick sighed.

"Oh, I do have some bad news. The front row has been moved back from the stage a little," Jonathan said.

"Ah, I guess that's because of the barrier spell."

"The barrier's superstrong, too. Not just any mage could produce it. I'll bet it's strong enough to work as a shelter during a Stampede."

"That feels a little excessive, but…I guess it's warranted."

Nick flipped to the last page of the report. It displayed what looked like Wanted posters, complete with sketches of each person and their criminal charges.

"Restless Ironman Giuseppe, a D-rank adventurer. He was banned for life for repeatedly stalking idols' carriages… This other guy was banned for starting a brawl with spectators… This man was banned for disrupting a concert by howling at the full moon… Even a court mage got banned. That's crazy," he said, reading the page.

It was a blacklist for idol concerts. The venue staff and security guards could be trusted to handle ban-ees who were regular people, but some of them were adventurers and knights. That was why the fan club published a list of dangerous banned fans—many of whom had a criminal record—to help with security.

"Huh? I feel like I've seen this guy before," Nick said uncertainly after looking at one of the pictures.

"You mean that Eishu guy?" Jonathan asked.

"Yeah. I don't think I know him. Maybe I just passed him on the street. Hmm… His profile says he writes fraudulent and deceptive documents."

The man named Eishu had his crimes listed beneath his

sketch. He drew and sold moving portraits of idols without permission and sent cursed fan letters that played a voice when touched. He was also wanted on charges of theft, assault, and forging documents. There was a warning saying that anyone who saw him should stay away and report to the closest Sun Knight station.

Nick was taken aback by his description. "He's clearly skilled and blessed with mana. Why can't he use that to live a regular life?"

Jonathan agreed with an awkward smile. "And I don't want to cross someone like that at a concert..."

"If you do, let me or another adventurer handle it. The Hundredth Anniversary Concert's gonna be a blast," Nick said.

"Yeah it will! You have your ticket, right? Scalpers have been robbing people blind with the reissues, so you'll be in trouble if you lose it," Jonathan warned.

"Yeah, of course. I carry it around...everywhere... Wait, where is it?"

Nick had made plans to go to a special large-scale concert with Jonathan and other idol fans. It was the Jewelry Production One Hundredth Anniversary Grand Idol Appreciation Concert— which fans called the Hundredth Anniversary Concert for short— and the tickets were in high demand. Nick had waited in line for hours to buy his ticket, and after he got it, he'd wrapped it in oiled paper and placed it under a thin wooden board that he fixed to the inside of his breastplate so it would never leave his side.

His breastplate might have been knocked off during the fight against the boss of Pot Snake Cave. The thought sent a wave of anxiety coursing down his body.

"Eh, I'm sure it's around here somewhere. It'll be fine," he said.

"The concert can't come soon enough! Anyway, I'll see you later!" Jonathan said before leaving Nick's room.

Nick immediately began to search his armor, terrified he'd dropped the ticket on the bottom floor of Pot Snake Cave.

"Hey, Nick," Jonathan said, coming back to the door as Nick frantically looked for the ticket.

"Wha—?! O-oh, hey, Jonathan. Did you forget something?" Nick asked.

"Why do you look so panicked? Anyway, you have a guest," Jonathan responded.

"Thanks for the help, kid," said the man Jonathan brought to Nick's door.

"No problem. See you, Nick." Jonathan exited again, leaving Nick alone with the new visitor, who was in the hallway by the door.

"…What the hell do you want?" Nick asked.

"I thought you might've croaked when I couldn't find you at Fishermen," the man said.

Nick held the door open only a little, wary of his new visitor. He would shut the door even more if the man told him to open it.

"I see you're still breathing, too," Nick said.

The visitor was a skinny man with long black hair tied into a rough ponytail. He wore a kimono and had a long blade called a katana at his hip. He looked more like a wandering vigilante than an adventurer, the type who would be more likely to hunt bounties in the Garbage Heap—or be pursued by bounty hunters himself—than to fight monsters in a labyrinth.

"The exit's that way, Garos. It's down the stairs and to the right," Nick said.

"I'm here to see you, man… This is quite the room you've got here. You can't see the wall behind all the posters. So you're an Agate fan. I'd expect a virgin like you to be more of the Diamond type," Garos commented.

"Mind your own business!" Nick snapped, slamming the door in his face.

"I'm not makin' fun of you, man! I'm sorry!" Garos yelled through the door.

"I don't care. I've got no business with you. Don't ever show your face to me again."

"I came to pay you back!"

"...Huh?"

Nick was stunned. He reopened the door slightly. Garos put down his sword, sat on his knees, then put his hands together and bowed.

"I stole from the party wallet and framed you. I'm sorry!" he said.

"Don't bow to me out in the hallway unless you want my foot in your face!" Nick yelled.

"If that'll make you feel better, then—"

Nick kicked Garos in the jaw before he could finish his sentence, and Garos glared at Nick reproachfully.

"God dammit, man! That hurt! I didn't think you'd actually do it!" he shouted.

"How the hell did you think I'd react?! You can't treat people like that and expect to be forgiven with a simple bow! You should've come here ready for me to kill you!" Nick ranted.

"Now that's just unfair!"

Nick kicked Garos's sword down the hallway and lunged, while the ornaments on the sheath rattled like bells. Garos reflexively kicked up at Nick from the ground. Nick dodged it, but a thin blade on the edge of Garos's shoe cut him on his chin.

"Oh shit, I'm wearing combat shoes. Sorry," Garos said.

"You're not supposed to attack back!" Nick yelled.

And so a fight broke out.

"Oww... Did that make you feel better?" Garos asked some time later.

"Oh, shut up. That's what you say after letting someone hit you without hitting back," Nick retorted.

There was a large red bruise on Garos's face where Nick had hit him. He was also gingerly patting his side. That spot seemed to hurt more than it should have, given how lightly Nick had hit him. That might have meant that Garos had an existing injury, but Nick couldn't be less concerned. He had basically won, but he'd taken a few punches and kicks, too.

"You're still as fussy as ever," Garos said.

"Oh, fine... You can come in. I'll give you five minutes to talk. Don't touch your sword," Nick relented.

"What if someone takes it?"

"There's no one here dumb enough to steal an adventurer's weapon. Besides, you're the one who taught me to be cautious of anyone who can kill you, even if they're a friend or a lover."

In addition to being Nick's former party member, he was also an older apprentice of Argus's. As the senior, he'd taught Nick a number of lessons, most of them involving practical techniques one couldn't learn from formal sword or martial arts training.

Garos once took Nick to a dojo in the dangerous southeastern part of Labyrinth City to train, luring out thugs with money and attacking them. The point was to teach him how to deal with being surrounded, how to flee in a city, the subtleties of wielding a blade in tight spaces, how to immobilize a foe with a blow or a joint lock, and when to flee when someone was looking for a fight.

Nick still made use of those skills now. His success in the Garbage Heap had even more to do with the knowledge he'd gained from Garos than from the fundamental combat techniques he'd learned from Argus.

"Oh, I did say that, didn't I?" Garos mused.

"You were always taking me places and teaching me skills you said would be useful for guard work. Do you have any idea how many times you made me pay for your booze?" Nick said.

"Why would I remember that? Well, that's what I'd like to say, but it's kinda why I'm here."

Garos picked up a bag and tossed it at Nick. It was full of gold coins. Each one depicted the sailor saint Braun from the creation myth and was worth ten thousand dina in this kingdom. Judging from the size of the bag, it probably contained at least three hundred thousand dina.

"You didn't obtain this doing some dangerous job, did you? Are you working as an assassin?" Nick asked.

"Of course not! I got this doin' guard work. My client took a likin' to me after I ran off some thugs who attacked their carriage. They gave me a special bonus," Garos explained.

"So you're working freelance now?"

"Yeah. Argus doesn't much like guard or bouncer work."

Nick knew Garos as an alcoholic, a gambler, and a philanderer, but he was also an elite swordsman. He was a master of a weapon called a katana that was imported from a ruined country called Nozomi, and he could even slice through steel and the hardest of monster shells. He was even better at fighting people than he was at fighting monsters; that was apparently what the katana was designed for.

"If you have time for side gigs, you should go to a labyrinth," Nick chided.

"Combat Masters was only barely holding together because of the prep work you did for us. You know how important you were," Garos responded, causing Nick's anger to flare again.

Combat Masters couldn't take on the difficult labyrinths they did without careful preparation and sufficient funds. Weapons and armor were necessary, of course, and the work didn't stop with buying and equipping them—they had to be maintained and eventually replaced. Food and medicine were essential as well, and they needed to buy magic tools and talismans for especially challenging labyrinths.

Nick was saddled with taking care of all that preparation. He managed their funds and items and made sure his party members, who never saved any money, were ready to go. And yet he was kicked out of the party.

"Says the guy who got me kicked out," Nick snapped.

Garos groaned. "At least let me clear up that misunderstanding."

"What're you talking about?" Nick asked suspiciously.

"Argus didn't just abandon you, and he never believed my lie."

"...Really."

"You always had the wrong idea, Nick. Argus is a freakin' powerhouse. He'd be a match for any S-rank one-on-one. But he has no interest in rank. The only reason he runs Combat Masters is to look after lowlifes like me."

"Who calls themselves a lowlife?"

"You're the only one who wasn't. I actually always thought we were holdin' you back."

"Seriously?"

"You know Argus's history, right? He was a mercenary in the Demon War. I was, too."

The Demon War was a war between human countries and demon countries that had ended ten years earlier. Demons were a race created by the demon god in ancient times, but they split from their master after deciding they didn't want to keep living as puppets. They did not make peace with humans, however, and there had been many wars throughout the ages.

"When wars end, it's always sudden. Even the most skilled mercenaries end up unemployed. Argus started Combat Masters to look after people who can't do anything other than fight," Garos said.

"...Wait. This is news to me. He was always talking our ears off about how he chose to be an adventurer and how adventurers should behave. Are the other members of the party former mercenaries, too?" Nick asked.

"Yep. He always fed us those lines 'cause we didn't start as adventurers. A few of us prolly would've ended up with bounties on our heads if he didn't tie us down like that... Oh, that guy's a perfect example."

"Who?"

Garos pointed at the blacklist in the fan club report.

"That Eishu guy. He's the son of some grand master painter or calligrapher, and he made a name for himself makin' talismans for the army. Then he got carried away in Labyrinth City and ended up as a wanted criminal," he said.

"Don't tell me he was a member of Combat Masters," Nick asked timidly, but Garos shook his head.

"Nope, he wasn't. He worked alone 'cause he hated takin' orders... He did try to force us into buyin' some talismans once, and Argus got so mad, he threw him out the door. Eishu already had a bounty on his head by that point. You were small, so you prolly don't remember."

A vague memory resurfaced in Nick's mind after hearing that. He could see Argus arguing with a grizzled talisman salesman.

"Anyway, Argus always wanted to set a good example. He told us to forget our pasts when we moved to Labyrinth City and to work as adventurers, and made me swear to never talk about it," Garos said.

"Then why're you telling me all this now?" Nick asked.

"'Cause Combat Masters ain't gonna be around much longer. I don't need to keep his secrets anymore. You're independent now, and we're all about to retire. I'm gonna earn money as a body-guard and move to the countryside," Garos responded, standing up.

"Hey, wait! What's Argus doing?!"

"He'll have no trouble findin' work if he goes freelance. It's nothin' you gotta worry about... How long do you plan to work as an adventurer?"

"What's that supposed to mean?"

"I ain't sayin' you're not cut out for it. But we humans can't do violent work like this for too long. It breaks your body and your mind."

"That's just your opinion. Plenty of decent adventurers have stayed healthy."

Garos smiled coldly, as if he knew Nick was bluffing. "That may be true, but never assume the man before you is a decent person. You'll end up knockin' on death's door before you know it."

"Huh?" Nick said blankly. He didn't immediately process what Garos said, but then he noticed something. Garos was somehow holding the katana that Nick had kicked down the hall. He had his right hand on the hilt and was ready to strike at any moment. Nick hadn't thought he'd let his guard down at any point during the conversation. "Try m—"

Garos swung the blade at him before he could finish his sentence. The blade traveled a perfect arc for his neck, bringing certain death.

"Man... You've gotten a lot stronger," Garos said.

"Shut the hell up," Nick seethed, glaring at him and sweating.

Nick had realized he had no chance of dodging Garos's swing. The man's overwhelming speed rivaled Olivia's, and Nick was in a disadvantageous position sitting down. So he'd put his hands together and caught the blade. He'd first cast Light Body to significantly increase his speed, then once he stopped the blade between his palms, he cast Heavy Body to give himself strength far beyond Garos's expectations. As Nick caught the katana, he realized he might be able to use that technique to replicate what Olivia did when she threw him out the window.

"I thought I'd give you a little more instruction, but I guess that won't be necessary," Garos said.

"You think I'm happy to hear that from you? You just went easy on me, didn't you?" Nick asked.

"Yep. But I won't hesitate to kill you if my next job requires it. Got that?"

He reached for his weapon, but Nick slapped his hand away and threw it out of the room. They heard it stab into the wall of the hallway.

"Hey, what gives?!" Garos shouted.

"Don't think this money is enough to make us even. You'd better hesitate if you ever end up with a chance to kill me. You'll carry that guilt for the rest of your life," Nick warned.

"What?!" Garos responded, clearly unsure of what to say. After a short silence, he began to snicker. "Man, you haven't changed at all. You're not still givin' guild receptionists and merchants a hard time, are you?"

"Better that than being as careless as you! Are women still swindling you out of your money?!" Nick fired back.

"Shut up! Look around you, bud! Your room is covered in Agate posters and merchandise!"

"I'm not being swindled! I *chose* to invest in her!"

"That's even worse!"

"Excuse me?!"

Their argument devolved into another fistfight, until Nick ran out of steam and Garos slipped out of the room like smoke, leaving the bag full of coins. Nick stared at them silently without pocketing them.

Something about this farewell seemed final. If they ever did see each other again, it wouldn't be as former comrades. Neither would hold back in a fight, even if it meant killing the other. Nick knew it.

That was their last interaction as fellow apprentices.

One week had passed since the Survivors' adventure in Pot Snake Cave. Nick had finally recovered enough for the party to go to the Adventurers Guild.

"What took you all so long to make your triumphant return? Who do you think you are, cabinet ministers? You should've come sooner."

The woman facing the Survivors was Vilma, a guild employee. She was a white-haired old woman, but her dignified manner and sharp eyes gave her an intensity that many active adventurers lacked. She was a former adventurer herself and was truly strong.

Nick didn't argue in response to her slight provocation, surprising everyone. "I don't wanna be here... Can I go home?" he asked.

"Nick, please show a little more enthusiasm," Zem said with a strained smile.

Nick was the perfect picture of the phrase "down in the dumps." He was hunched over, despite his usual good posture, his eyes were lifeless, and his gloom seemed to pervade the whole space.

"When did you become so spineless? You just cleared Pot Snake Cave," Vilma said. She wasn't trying to provoke him; she was genuinely confused by his behavior.

"He has been this way since he realized he might have dropped a concert ticket in the labyrinth," Zem explained.

"You're always so careless," Karan said.

They both stared at Nick with disbelief, but he just sank back into the conference room's couch.

"It was an S-tier ticket for the Hundredth Anniversary Concert. And I can't have it reissued 'cause a bunch of assholes have been making forgeries... Argh! Damn it all! I'm so stupid!" Nick complained.

"Hmm, I see. I don't know if that makes you lucky or unlucky...," Vilma muttered.

"Huh? What could possibly be lucky about losing my ticket?" Nick asked.

"Never mind. Save your hobbies for after work. You've already gotten your reward, so the only thing left to do is the report," Vilma responded.

"Oh, right. Let's get it over with...," Nick said gloomily,

making an effort to collect himself. He faced Vilma and told her about the mutant pot snake they'd encountered.

"You all are finding mutants on every adventure," Vilma commented.

"You've got that right. How do we keep getting so unlucky? Does the world just hate us?" Nick complained.

"Stop thinking that you're special. That mindset is so typical of young people. Fourteen mutant monsters have been sighted over the last three months. Your encounter rate is rather high, though," Vilma said gravely.

"So mutant numbers are increasing after all. Do you think it's coming?" Nick asked.

"Yes, I think so. Estivation is almost here, though, so it's more likely to happen in the winter," Vilma answered.

The other Survivors were confused by their ominous exchange. Tiana spoke up for the group.

"What's coming?" she asked.

"A Stampede," Nick answered.

Nervous comprehension dawned on his party members' faces. A Stampede was a disaster-grade event, when a massive number of monsters spawned and left their labyrinths to attack human settlements. The abundance of monsters out in the world enriched the ground with miasma, which fed life to the demon god. That meant it was a sign of the demon god's resurrection.

"That's really bad!" Tiana shouted. She started to jump to her feet, but Nick stopped her.

"Calm down. Most Stampedes are small in scale, just like earthquakes and storms. As long as it isn't a massive, once-in-a-few-centuries Stampede, there's no risk of the demon god being resurrected," he reassured her.

"Really? I've never heard of Stampedes happening around the capital," Tiana said.

"That's 'cause there aren't many labyrinths around the capital, and the mana in the ground is stable. Here, we're surrounded by labyrinths and much less stable ground, so small Stampedes are pretty common. There was one three years ago, right?" Nick asked.

Vilma nodded. "Yeah. There were three monster hordes. One was made up of over five hundred goblins, one had golems, and the other consisted of tree monsters. Some traveling merchants fell prey to them on the highways, but they were stopped before they reached any farming villages or towns."

"Oh, that's not as bad as I thought... I expected a nationwide emergency," Tiana said.

"It would be if the Stampede was big enough to reach the capital, but that only happens once a century or so... Oh, wait. You might be in for a hard time, Tiana," Nick mumbled.

"What do you mean?" Tiana asked suspiciously.

"When the Stampeding monsters leave their labyrinths, they mostly emerge onto expansive plains and highways. Dragon knights are more suited to taking them out than adventurers. It's best to crush them with mobility and numbers."

"What do dragon knights have to do with me?"

"You don't know? The dragons and their jockeys that compete in dragon races are recruited to fight as dragon knights. Races will be canceled for around a month until the Stampede is suppressed."

Tiana's face went blank until the meaning of what Nick said set in. "No! I don't want that to happen!" she screamed.

"Sorry, but—"

"There are a lot of important cups in the winter, like the Big Dipper Memorial and the Pumpkin Stakes! Do something about it!" Tiana whined.

"Calm down, Tiana. There's no guarantee that'll happen!" Nick said.

Vilma put a hand to her forehead and sighed for the umpteenth time. "Nobody'd ever know you high-strung kids were on the cusp of C rank."

"Oh yeah, I wanted to confirm the promotion," Nick said, relieved by the change of topic.

"That's fine with me. You all are free to go to Pioneers and take on more lucrative jobs. You can also take on more dangerous labyrinths. I wish you luck in continuing to increase your rank. Well, that's what I would say, but..." Vilma paused. "First, I have a job for you. It's a bodyguard job. You all have never done one of those, right? Want to give it a try?"

"Oh yeah, I've heard of that." Karan sounded interested.

"Bodyguard and escort jobs are typically handled at the Travelers branch of the Adventurers Guild, but this place and Manhunt also handle ones that stay in the city," Nick explained.

"Have you ever done one?" Karan asked.

"We did a decent amount of them in Combat Masters. Argus and Garos were really good; everyone wanted to hire them...," Nick replied with a mixed expression. He had just remembered what had happened with Garos.

"What's wrong?" Karan asked.

"N-nothing. The clients are usually rich, so the jobs become a real pain if you upset them in any way."

Vilma smiled at Nick. She reminded him of a witch taking delight in a suspicious nightly ritual.

"Oh? Are you sure you want to talk about a job from this client that way? I can picture you a few minutes from now kneeling before me and begging, 'Please let me take this job!'" she teased before handing a piece of paper to Nick.

Though suspicious of Vilma's attitude, he began to read it.

"I couldn't tell you why, but the client chose you all for this job. If you don't want it, though, by all means, tell me. I'll give it to a different party," Vilma said playfully.

Nick didn't even hear her. His eyes darted across the page,

hands shaking. He read it multiple times, ensuring the words would stick in his head.

"Wh-what is it, Nick?" Bond asked.

"Is this...real life?" Nick finally said.

Sensing that they weren't getting anywhere, Tiana snatched the paper from Nick's hands.

"Hey, what're you doing?!" Nick complained.

"Let's see here... It's a weirdly long job. I don't love the idea of being tied down by guard work until the end of next month. We probably won't be able to explore any labyrinths," Tiana said.

"Yeah. I figure the job will last until after the concert," Nick said.

"Concert? What?" Tiana read the document again. "The main locations for the job will be the client's office, Starmine Hall, the southern town hall, and other event venues within Labyrinth City. The client is...Jewelry Production."

"That means we'll be working as bodyguards at idol concerts," Nick explained, his voice shaking. The other Survivors put their palms to their heads.

"So what'll it be?" Vilma asked.

"Please let me take this job!" Nick begged, fulfilling Vilma's prediction.

Broadly speaking, Labyrinth City got poorer and cruder the farther southeast one went. The most impoverished part of the city was the Garbage Heap, where residents settled down in abandoned buildings and expanded them with their own amateur construction. The people there led decadent and dangerous lives.

By contrast, the opposite side on the northwest of Labyrinth City was known for its sanctuaries, research facilities, aristocratic and magic schools, luxurious restaurants, and wealthy residential districts. The government office buildings and political agencies of Labyrinth City were located in the center of the city, so the most powerful bureaucrats and political leaders actually didn't live in the northwest, but the district still had a high threshold for entry. The wealth made it easy for any visitor to feel out of place, which served as its own form of security. That made it a perfect base for an idol agency, as long as it could afford the high property value.

"Should we really have come here dressed so obviously as adventurers? I feel out of place," Bond complained.

The Survivors didn't exactly fit in among the people walking the streets in the northwest district of the city, and the primary reason for that was their clothing. Most men wore a suit and tie or majestic robes, while the women wore blouses tailored specifically for them or glittering robes that looked like magic school uniforms.

"That's not our fault. Besides, armor is at least semiformal. These clothes would be appropriate to wear if we were invited to a noble mansion," Nick argued, but his party members could tell how happy he was to be here. The slightly higher pitch of his voice gave him away.

"Don't forget why we're here, Nick. This is a bodyguard job. If you start acting like a creep around the idols, you're gonna pay for it," Tiana warned.

"Yes, you should act naturally. I am worried that your image of these idols will be shattered upon actually meeting them," Zem said, giving advice of his own.

"D-don't worry, I'll take the job seriously," Nick said.

Nick had jumped on the job immediately when Vilma offered it, but Tiana and Zem quickly admonished him. He normally inspected the contract and asked question after question before accepting any job, to determine its legitimacy and the chances of actually receiving the reward, so the others were taken aback by his behavior. Nick regained his composure after that, but he didn't find anything wrong with the job's terms. Vilma teased them because she knew they would accept it.

"Make sure you stay focused, okay? They might ask us about the paladin. I doubt they would've contacted us in this round-about way if they found us out, though," Tiana said.

"I know. We never would've been able to take this job if it hadn't been given to us directly. We would've had to be really lucky if we applied," Nick replied.

The Survivors hadn't actually signed an official contract for this bodyguard job yet. They might have signed one at the guild if it was a basic escort, but this job involved working as body-guards for over a month. They would sign the actual contract after the client interviewed and tested them. The party was head-ing toward the office of the client—Jewelry Production—to gain their approval.

"Good. I don't want you getting nervous and fidgety. It would be rude to the people we'll be protecting," Tiana warned.

"That's enough, Tiana. He's already much better now than when he's in idol mode," Karan said to calm the mage down.

"Eh, I guess you're right. Whatever happens, happens. Are we almost at the meeting place? Where is it?" Tiana asked.

"We're supposed to meet a guide at the bridge, but…I don't see anyone," Nick answered, looking around. Just when he started to wonder if he had the wrong location, Karan tugged on his sleeve.

"Look at them, Nick. They're amazing," she said.

"Who?" Nick asked.

Karan pointed toward a river. A group of girls in casual attire was running and shouting on the riverside. They stood out in this district even more than the Survivors did.

"Quit dragging your feet! Raise your voices!"

"Yes ma'am!"

"I can't hear you! Yell loudly enough to reach the fans in the back row! Your voices should travel to the peaks of the Five-Ringed Mountains!"

It was a training session. A pink-haired girl in dark red athletic gear was calling to the girls with a loud, aggressive voice one wouldn't expect from her small physique. She seemed to be some kind of leader or trainer, and the other girls didn't complain—or couldn't complain—as they obeyed her commands and pushed themselves. Some of the girls were too exhausted to move a finger, while others were still running and exercising with ease.

Nick found the sight heartwarming. Argus had pushed him just as hard, and he didn't slack on his training now that he was independent. He would never think to train in a wealthy residential district like this, though.

"I wonder who they are. You don't typically see all-female knight or mercenary groups. This is a weird place to train, too," Nick said.

"Yeah," Karan agreed.

"Eh, whatever. We need to focus on finding our guide. They might be somewhere near the pink-haired girl," Nick said, looking around.

"You might want to look again," Karan responded. She pointed to the riverside a second time.

"Huh? Yeah, I see them. I don't think they're... Wait." Nick stared at the girls by the riverside, looking flustered. "Hey, that looks like Agate. And is that Topaz and Amber beside her?"

"How can you tell from this far away? Can you put that skill to use in labyrinths, please?" Tiana nagged.

Bond made a ring with his fingers and looked through it at the riverside. That was a habit of his when using Search to look at something in the distance. "That blue-haired girl is definitely Nick's idol— Oh, they noticed us," he informed the group.

The pink-haired girl turned around and smiled. Her face had a tranquil, statuesque beauty, and her smile had all the radiance of the sun. Even Nick's party members were captivated by her appearance.

"Yoo-hoo! Over here! You're the people sent by the guild, right?" she called out.

The Survivors could hear her surprisingly clearly even though she was on the opposite side of the river. Strangely, however, her voice wasn't ear-piercingly loud; it instead sounded as if she was right next to them.

"How is she doing that? That's crazy," Karan said, surprised.

"She's not yelling. She simply strengthened the directionality of her voice. We are the only ones who can hear her," Bond said.

"What do you mean, Bond?" Tiana asked.

"The sound waves of her voice are not spreading. She is using a strengthening spell on either her vocal cords or her throat," Bond deduced. He sounded impressed.

Nick offered a further explanation. "Sound crackles when you use a magic item to amplify a voice. That happens 'cause the sound collides with dust and other things inside the magic item. It's hell on your ears. But somehow, some of Jewelry Production's idols can use a technique to get around that. It's called Vocal Guidance."

"Can you stop trying to make it sound like it's some earth-shattering discovery?" Tiana said wearily, but Nick ignored her and looked at the pink-haired girl, who was beckoning them over despite their obvious bewilderment.

The history of Teran, the Labyrinth City, was at once long and short.

The name *Teran* dated back over a millennium. The land had once hosted a facility called the Teran Magic Laboratory. Later, it fell under control of the demon god vanguard and came to be known as the Teran Cluster. Mankind retook the land during the war with the demon god and built a defense institution called the Teran Distortion Agency. Many more destructive events ravaged the land, until a massive Stampede finished it off and turned it into a ruin surrounded by labyrinths.

Eventually, the region once again saw major development and

became what was now known as Labyrinth City. The destroyed and abandoned buildings were cleared away to create vacant plots, and adventurers helped grow the economy by collecting materials from monsters, which were either exported or processed within the city to create magic items. Some adventurers retired to work in commerce and industry—or if they were smart enough, to get involved in the city's politics.

One person named Diamond, the leader of an adventurers' party called the Adamantine Ensemble, had a major influence on the city's entertainment industry. Her party was the predecessor of the modern-day Jewelry Production, and unusually, every member could sing and dance. They eventually discarded their swords and staves, but not their music, and they performed live in the streets, at bars, and even outside the city as they devoted themselves to aiding Labyrinth City's development. That was how a unique music culture formed along with the development of Teran itself.

"So essentially, the original Diamond laid the foundation for modern idols," Nick said.

After they met her at the riverside, the pink-haired girl led the Survivors to a rudimentary building that looked like a warehouse. The mechanical atmosphere and ducts running along the ceiling made it look like a repurposed factory.

"That's why Diamond is a special name. Idols at this agency inherit a number of different jewel names, but only one girl every ten to twenty years gets the name Diamond, like you. Some get slightly different names like Pink Diamond or Black Diamond."

"Wow, you know your stuff! I'm impressed!"

The Survivors had been led to a reception room inside the warehouse-like building. Just like Nick said, the pink-haired idol's name was Diamond. She was petite and slightly taller than Tiana, and she was wearing dark red track pants and a T-shirt with a large word from the ancient civilization's language printed on the front. Her long pink hair was too glossy and soft to belong to a human, swaying and bobbing at the slightest movements.

Diamond's most attention-grabbing feature, however, were her eyes. They were large, full of energy, and most of all, extremely adorable.

"Thanks," Nick said, doing his best to remain composed before the most famous idol alive. If he wasn't on duty, he probably would've asked her to sign his armor by now.

"By the way, do you come to my concerts, Nick?" Diamond asked.

"Your solo concerts always sell out immediately. The only times I've seen you is when you appear as a surprise guest at Aggies's concerts," Nick explained, the words flying out of his mouth. His party members normally would've ribbed him for the way his speech accelerated when idols were involved, but they were overpowered by Diamond's mystical presence as well. It wasn't out of fear or awe, however.

"What's wrong? You're still nervous, aren't you? Come on, smile! Show me those pearly whites! It's an adventurer's job to smile!" Diamond said.

"No, it's not," Tiana commented.

Diamond gave her an enthusiastic wink and a thumbs-up. Tiana chuckled, then seemed to be shocked by her own behavior.

"Stop acting all stuffy and formal! Or would you rather join us and work as idols? You look like you have good balance, dragonian girl! Have you danced before?" Diamond asked.

"I performed the Dragon Dance when I was a kid. I don't hate dancing, but... I don't want to quit working as an adventurer," Karan said.

The Dragon Dance was a traditional dragonian dance. It involved dancing along to percussive instruments, and it was performed at summer and winter solstice festivals and to give a warm welcome to travelers.

Most dragonians left home to become adventurers or warriors, but some occasionally decided to try to make a living as dancers.

"Hmm. Okay. Well, you wouldn't be the only girl who performs as an idol on the side, so feel free to apply at the recruitment window anytime!" Diamond said.

"That's great and all, but it's not what we're here for. I want to talk about our job," Tiana interjected. She seemed just as overwhelmed as Karan.

Diamond had a natural knack for lifting others' spirits just by being around them. The Survivors all felt like she was a mirthful fairy who had jumped right off the pages of a novel.

"Yeah. I wanna hear about idol stuff, but we're here to discuss the bodyguard job. Umm... Can we consider you our direct client?" Nick asked timidly.

"Yeah, I am!" Diamond responded with an enthusiastic nod.

"No, she's not," a bald man in a suit who was sitting next to her answered at the same time.

"Hey, this was my idea! I should be the client!" Diamond whined.

"Miss Diamond. You need to leave backstage jobs and security to the staff."

"Oh, come on, that's just dumb. There's a lot I need to explain to them directly," Diamond complained, swinging her legs and clicking her tongue to show her annoyance. When she didn't protest beyond that, the bald man turned to Nick.

"Allow me to introduce myself. I'm Joseph Coleman, Diamond's producer," he said.

"I'm Nick from the Survivors. It's nice to meet you," Nick replied.

"Yes, I have seen your face plenty of times. I am also Agate's producer," Joseph said. Nick nodded with a troubled expression.

"Mr. Coleman. It sounds like you already know this, but this guy is a hard-core idol fan. Are you okay with that? Are you sure you want him as a bodyguard?" Tiana interjected.

"I appreciate the concern. This issue was hotly debated within the agency," Joseph answered.

"What do you...? Eh, that makes sense. It's definitely strange," Nick said, starting to argue but then nodding with understanding.

"Oh, do you think so?" Zem asked.

"Honestly, I half suspected this job was given to us by some criminal posing as the agency. And even if it was legit, I thought there had to be something weird going on," Nick admitted.

Zem's expression turned serious. "You should have said so sooner, Nick. I thought the prospect of working with idols might have driven all critical thinking from your mind."

"Sorry. I did get a little excited," Nick replied. Zem looked both exasperated and relieved. "It also occurred to me later that my friends in the idol fandom might shun me forever if they hear about this. I'm taking a big risk here."

"Are you afraid of learning all our secrets?" Diamond asked with a smile.

Joseph observed quietly; it seemed like he wasn't going to prohibit her from casual conversation.

"Trust me, I'd love the chance to watch you all up close, but I'd hate if I couldn't be a fan anymore," Nick said.

"I don't want to give up your ability to be a fan, but... You'll have to stop going to fan gatherings for a little while. At least while you're under our employ," Diamond responded.

"You both must want to know if we're fit for the job. This is business, not an extension of my fan activities. I think we should get to the point," Nick said.

"There are some idol fans who treat our concerts as business opportunities, you know."

"Huh?"

"Though I guess it'd be more accurate to say they pretend to be idol fans. Have you heard of scalpers?"

Nick grimaced. "Yeah. They're jerks who buy all the tickets

they can and try to make money off them. I've heard some people make fake tickets and try to force their way into the venue."

"It's a real headache. These people are hurting our image," Diamond said.

Surprise formed on Nick's face. "Hold on... Do you want us to catch these guys?"

"This isn't normally the kind of problem you'd turn to adventurers for, but we're afraid this might lead to a concert being disrupted or one of our girls being targeted."

"What do you mean?"

"Who do you think is buying the resale tickets?"

"The spoiled sons of nobles and merchants with too much money? Oh wait, I know where you're going with this...," Nick said.

"The biggest threat is fans who have been banned from concerts for life and can't buy legitimate tickets. Some of these banned fans are advanced adventurers, knights, and mages," Diamond told them.

"You can't be serious," Tiana said.

Nick pressed his lips together, thinking back to the fan club report Jonathan had given him. "Those idiots do exist, unfortunately."

"We need to determine if these people are just fools or if they are serious criminals with connections to demon-god worshippers," Joseph said.

That got the Survivors' attention.

"Why would you suspect that?" Nick asked.

Instead of answering, Joseph produced a slip of paper. "Jewelry Production's tickets are made with a special process. They are printed with ink extracted from particularly beautiful flowers that only grow in labyrinths, and the coloring and patterns cannot be achieved with normal printing equipment," he said.

The surface of the paper shone slightly and changed colors, depending on the viewing angle. The special printing had a sparkling, jewel-like quality to it. By contrast, the text was simple and easy to read.

∗   ∗   ∗

JEWELRY PRODUCTION ONE HUNDREDTH ANNIVERSARY IDOL APPRECIATION CONCERT

    BLAZING MOON DAY 30. 6:00 PM. STARMINE HALL. ROW C SEAT 15.

It was an idol concert ticket.

    "Wow, it looks like paper money," Bond remarked.

    "Oh yes, paper money was used in the past," Zem said.

    They both examined the ticket curiously.

    "Paper money still exists, actually. All the countries and banks that printed it were devastated by past wars, but what remains still has value. Very few people use it, though," Tiana said.

    "Wow, you know a lot!" Diamond exclaimed, surprised.

    "But this is the first time I've seen something resembling paper money that was made in the modern era," Tiana commented.

    "Hee-hee. The recent advancements in modern printing are incredible. This ticket costs ten thousand dina because of the anti-counterfeiting measures… Which would be fine on its own, but the problem is they're being resold for a million," Diamond said. This news was a shock to all the Survivors but Nick.

    "A *million*?!" Karan responded, shocked.

    "Yes, it's true. Some people have also begun to take advantage of the rising ticket prices by making and selling forgeries," Joseph added.

    "It takes only ten forged tickets to make ten million dina. Crazy, right? Look at this," Diamond said, picking up a slip of paper. She put it next to the ticket. Its luster and coloring appeared identical, and so was the writing.

BLAZING MOON DAY 30. 6:00 PM. STARMINE HALL. ROW C SEAT 15.

    "Is that a fake ticket?! It looks exactly like the real one!" Nick exclaimed. It was his turn to be shocked.

The iridescence of the ticket and its coloring were slightly different, but anyone who noticed that would chalk up the differences to slight variations in printing between each ticket. The design and writing were identical.

Nick found one aspect of the ticket strange. "Wait, this is a ticket for reserved seating. A general admission ticket would be way easier to get away with."

"I imagine the forgers made it a reserved seat ticket so they could sell it for as much as possible. And the larger the concert, the harder it is to catch duplicate tickets at the point of entry. It's also unlikely anyone who arrives with a fake ticket will follow orders and leave without a fuss. Some people simply want to enter the venue," Joseph explained.

"Do some people try to get backstage and into the dressing rooms?" Zem asked with a knowing expression.

"Yes, actually. We have had multiple guards assaulted and injured trying to keep fans out of dressing rooms. No idols have been injured yet, but neither have any criminals been captured or identified," Joseph answered.

"Do you think they'll come back?" Zem asked.

"We could handle any repeat offenders, but there is a chance a large group of people will storm the backstage area at once. The Hundredth Anniversary Concert next month is Jewelry Production's largest event ever, and I expect the risk of violence to be proportionally large," Joseph said.

"But where do demon-god worshippers come into this? I can't imagine why they'd bother with an idol concert," Nick asked.

"Oh? Are you surprised to hear me mention them?" Joseph said.

"How could I not be? They're a mysterious group plotting to resurrect the demon god." Nick seemed exhausted.

"Oh, I see. That's how you think of them," Joseph said.

"Huh? Who do *you* think they are?" Nick asked.

"We just perceive their real threat slightly differently. To us, they're an illegal organization that makes a massive profit by selling stolen goods and contraband. It wouldn't be wrong to call them a combination of a heretic cult, a gang, and a band of thieves."

Nick's mouth fell open in shock. "R-really?"

"Yes. Demon-god worshippers have attacked research facilities and artifact storehouses. Any other industry or business that deals in large sums of money must be wary of them."

"So you have to be more careful of them than the average person." Nick thought these explanation made sense.

"Of course, we currently have no reason to suspect them other than by the process of elimination. We have no evidence of involvement from other illegal organizations. But the threat posed by the counterfeit tickets is more important right now than identifying the criminals. That is why we want to hire capable, trustworthy people as guards."

"How can you trust us when this is the first time we've met? Doesn't the client normally perform a test for an extended bodyguard job like this?"

"Think of this conversation as your interview. I do already plan to give you an official offer, though."

"What?" Nick was surprised to hear that. He was about to ask for the reason when Joseph continued.

"You want to know why we chose you, right? It's because you fought White Mask," he said.

The tension in the room rose noticeably.

"...Guess we're celebrities now," Nick commented.

There were a few shady rumors associated with idol agencies. Some people suspected they were actually consulting firms that lent money. Others believed they obtained their talent through human trafficking. Yet more people suspected connections to major politicians or noble lords. Nick thought most of those rumors were unfounded, but he was beginning to believe some pieces of them might be true.

"In other words, your allegiances are clear. We know you don't work for demon-god worshippers," Joseph said.

"It's not like we chose to fight White Mask, though. Surely there are other people you can trust on that count. The Sun Knights, for instance," Nick argued.

Joseph didn't seem to care. "The Sun Knights are reliable, but I don't expect them to consider our every need."

"We've had knights start trouble with fans and even use their position to get close to idols. I don't do well with those types." Diamond sighed.

Nick nodded with understanding.

The Order of the Sun Knights worked to protect the peace in Labyrinth City, and deftly handled incidents involving violence and threats. Their authority gave them a difficult relationship with the populace, however.

"Your job will be to protect the idols. You'll help escort them from the office to concerts and guard them within the venues. Essentially, I want you to protect them every hour they spend working as idols. There are numerous events and concerts before the Hundredth Anniversary Concert, and I would like you to begin work today," Joseph explained.

"Huh? Today? We're not even waiting until tomorrow?" Nick asked, surprised.

"Our agency has twenty idols who have already made their debut. We have five carriages to transport them, each of which is operated and protected by a team of guards. We're still short one team, however. Multiple guards have been injured trying to stop fans who entered a venue using fake tickets and grew violent. We just don't have enough people."

"So you've already got holes you need us to plug."

"I'd like to hire a team that has reliable leadership and members who know how to divvy up responsibility. You had plenty of bodyguard experience in Combat Masters, didn't you, Nick?" Joseph asked with a glint in his eyes.

He was suggesting he knew a good amount about Nick's past. Nick nodded, trying not to react to that.

"We will prepare an ample reward," Joseph went on. "I cannot guarantee you personal interaction with idols, handshake tickets, or concert tickets, however."

"You have to take a break as an idol fan," Karan said with a teasing smile. Her eyes were determined, and she looked ready to crunch heads with her shining canine teeth.

"What do you think, Bond?" Nick asked. The holy sword had been unusually quiet.

"We don't have a choice. We have already fought White Mask. It was only a matter of time before we wound up in danger or a chance presented itself," Bond answered.

"Yep," Nick agreed.

"But this job will keep us busy for quite a long time. As our leader, you need to make sure we are properly rewarded. Specifically, we're going to need…," Bond said, lowering his voice and leaning in abnormally close to Nick's face.

"Hey, back off," Nick protested, bewildered.

"No. I don't want to be overheard," Bond said.

Nick noticed something in Bond's eyes, and he nearly gasped in surprise. They were small letters. One eye said "Don't use" and the other said "Telepathy." It was a warning.

"…Yeah, this is gonna be a really difficult job," Nick muttered.

And so the Survivors stepped into the world of conspiracy hidden behind the brilliant idol facade.

The rhythmic clopping of horse's hooves on stone pavement echoed within the carriage as Tiana drove it through the city. Nick was sitting next to her.

"Haah, I never thought I'd find myself working as a coachman." Tiana sighed.

"You should just be grateful we're not fighting with veteran guards over deployment like you normally have to on jobs like these," Nick responded.

Joseph Coleman had placed the Survivors in charge of a carriage shortly after their conversation. It was rare for the deployment of adventurers on bodyguard or escort jobs to be decided so smoothly. Coordination with veteran guards was normally an issue, and there was no guarantee that the person who needed protection would follow orders from the newcomers. Nick had been prepared to receive a less-than-warm welcome.

Contrary to his expectations, the veteran guards relaxed when they saw the party, relieved to have received reinforcements. The injuries had left them understaffed and overworked. Joseph had apparently spoken positively of the Survivors' accomplishments and told the guards that they'd caught the Iron Tiger Troop, so they got off on the right foot.

Nick was beginning to realize that guarding idols was an exploitative and thankless job that didn't pay enough for how exhausting it was.

"I'm glad one of us is good with horses. That's a huge help," Nick said.

"Don't mention it," Tiana responded.

Tiana was the one who had the most experience with horses. Nick and Zem had both ridden and taken care of horses plenty of times, but they weren't experts like her. Karan was terrible at riding, which was true of all dragonians; horses were spooked by their dragon scent and sizable mana. Bond had absolutely zero experience and was so curious about them, it would have been dangerous to have him drive the carriage.

As such, they had stationed Zem and Bond behind the carriage, Karan inside the carriage with the people they were protecting, and Nick and Tiana on the coachman's platform.

"Hey, Nick. You're free to use Telepathy now." Bond's voice echoed within Nick's mind.

Telepathy was a spell that allowed one to transmit their voice into another person's head without making noise, regardless of distance. It could be used to communicate in labyrinths while avoiding detection from monsters or to speak to comrades without being overhead during a negotiation. It was highly convenient.

Bond had never told the party not to use it before.

"What was that back there?" Nick asked.

"I can customize my skin and eye color to an extent, which lets me..."

"Not your eyes. That was the first time you've ever told us not to use Telepathy," Nick interrupted.

"I think the office was being monitored," Bond answered.

"Monitored? You mean someone would've noticed our Telepathy, like we did when the Iron Tiger Troop used it?"

"Yes. That is what I felt. They would not have been able to hear our conversation, but they could have used the process of elimination to figure out that we were the ones who used Telepathy."

The party gulped in response.

"Who was it? Someone from the agency? Or was someone monitoring us from the outside?" Nick asked.

"It felt like something was set up within that room. I do not think it came from outside," Bond answered.

"Why would someone do that?"

"They were probably being careful. There aren't many people who can use Telepathy,"

Zem began to speculate. "Perhaps our initial suspicions were correct, and the agency offered us this job after guessing that we might be the paladin. They could have set a trap in that room to detect the usage of any ancient spells such as Telepathy."

"...I could see that," Nick said.

Nick and Tiana had actually used the ancient spell Union to save a Jewelry Production idol. The idol was even inspired by that incident to write a song called "The Lovely Paladin."

"But what would they do after finding the paladin? Like you said, Tiana, they wouldn't have used this roundabout method if they just wanted to say thanks," Karan said.

"Hmm... Maybe they're being cautious. They could see us as a threat similar to White Mask," Tiana guessed.

"If they were cautious of us, they never would have met with us in the first place."

"That's true... Oh, I don't know. My brain feels like mush." Tiana sounded exhausted.

"How do you feel about all this, Karan?" Nick asked.

"Like you are all overthinking this job," Karan replied. She didn't sound nearly as gloomy as the others. In fact, she sounded confused about why they were so down.

"Really?" Nick asked.

"All we have to do is protect the idols from anyone who might target them. And protect ourselves, too. Can't we just do our jobs like normal?" Karan responded.

"Sure, but...I think they're still hiding information from us," Nick said.

"That's normal. Just because they trust us enough to meet with us doesn't mean they trust us enough to reveal everything. We just have to do our jobs and report. If they like what they hear, they'll tell us what we need to know. If this job still feels wrong then, or if they don't tell us anything, we can quit."

The others were struck by Karan's composure as she spoke. She had grown since their adventure in Pot Snake Cave.

Before, Karan probably would have spent her time in this wealthy residential district glancing around anxiously and having a hard time focusing on the job. She would have been more flustered when Diamond tried to recruit her as an idol, too. She was showing a new level of calm, not letting the unfamiliar perturb her like it used to.

And now she was remaining composed, despite the strange nature of this contract.

"If this job was a trap, they could have poisoned our tea at the agency. Maybe they have a trap planned for us in three days or in a week, but we have no way of knowing that now," Karan said.

"Th-that's a good point," Nick responded timidly.

"What do you think? I don't know much about idols yet, but I'll do my part to protect them. You should do whatever it is you want to do. I'll...give you my support," Karan said, finishing weakly.

"...Thanks," Nick replied with a bit of embarrassment.

The Survivors all relaxed, their anxiety fading as their secret conversation ended on a surprisingly peaceful note.

"Make way, make way! I'm coming through!" a coachman called out as he raced past the Survivors' carriage.

The party had reached the central street that separated Labyrinth City's northern and southern halves, and it was packed with carriages and pedestrians.

"Whoops, wasn't paying attention," Tiana said, quickly grabbing the reins and directing the horse to move the carriage out of the way. The horse whipped its tail indignantly, but it obediently pulled them to the side.

"Sorry, horsey. I didn't forget about you. Let's go," Tiana

apologized. It proceeded smoothly down the street while avoiding carriages and pedestrians as if it understood what she said. "It's easy to lose track of what's in front of you when you're focusing on Telepathy. I don't really want to use it while driving. I already have mixed feelings about working as a coachman."

Nick looked confused. "Do you not like driving? You seem fine with horses."

"That's not what I meant."

"Maybe we should demand we be escorted along with the idols. Diamond did recruit us, after all."

"Don't be stupid."

The Survivors were transporting two idols to a concert. They were inside the carriage along with Karan and a few staff members. One of the idols was going to perform at the concert, which meant she was the primary person they needed to protect. The other idol had come to support her. She was speaking to her to help calm her nerves.

Nick was a little relieved he wasn't sitting with them. It would be awkward if they spoke to him while he was using Telepathy, and even if he wasn't, he wasn't confident he'd be able to keep a cool head. One of the idols in the carriage had that effect on him.

"It's not the driving that I dislike. It's just that I don't want to be seen by old acquaintances," Tiana explained.

"Ah... That seems pretty unlikely," Nick responded.

"Sure, but this area reminds me of the capital. It's putting me in a bad mood."

"Are there idols there, too?"

"No. Only regular minstrels. The music culture here is pretty unique."

"A lot of people say that, but that's not quite right. Idols come from a legitimate form of music entertainment that originated in the ancient civilization. Diamond says we're reviving an ancient and honorable custom," a girl said after clattering open the carriage window. She was one of the idols the Survivors were protecting.

"Seriously?! Hey, that's dangerous. Get back in the carriage and close the curtain before someone sees you," Tiana ordered.

"Do I have to?" the girl whined.

"I can't believe you picked us on our first escort job, Agate. Are you not scared?" Tiana asked.

The girl's idol name was Agate. It had been less than a year since her debut, but her striking performances had gained her a large following. She was also the person who had saved Nick from the depths of despair after he was betrayed by his ex-girlfriend Claudine, getting him hooked on idols in the process. Later on, in a curious twist of fate, Nick and Tiana ended up using Union to save her life. It was as if they were bound by an invisible string.

"I feel better having guards that I've met. I prefer you to random people that my producer happened to approve after a test and interview. Oh, wait. I should hide that I know you, right?"

"Don't ask me. It's a little late for that anyway. You already shouted, 'Oh, it's the stray dog! Long time no see!' when you saw me," Nick said.

"Oh yeah. Ah-ha-ha," Agate laughed.

Once the Survivors were assigned a carriage, the question then became who they would escort... Though it didn't remain a question for very long. Agate approached the party immediately when Diamond and Joseph introduced them to the idols present at the agency, making it more than clear she knew them.

"Agate," Tiana said. "This guy's a hard-core idol fan. You know that, right?"

"I'm kinda the one responsible for that," Agate responded.

"That's a terrifying thought," Tiana said.

"Anyway, I had been wondering if you two were in the same party," Agate said.

"You know each other? That's news to me," Nick commented, looking at them questioningly.

Tiana seemed to be searching for words.

"Is that something I'm allowed to say?" Agate asked.

"Don't make it sound like we know each other more than we really do," Tiana replied irritably. "I have to ask... Did the agency choose us for this job because of the casino incident?"

"Hey, you don't trust me! I haven't said anything!" Agate insisted.

"Huh? Really?" Nick responded. He'd assumed Agate must have given them away somehow.

"Even I can tell what I should and shouldn't say... I think!" Agate said.

"That sure inspires confidence." Nick sighed.

Agate glowered at him, but her expression quickly softened. "Honestly, I also wondered if management hired you all because they found out... I can't say for sure that I was never caught by a leading question. I'm sorry!"

"Don't worry about it. I really would rather you keep it a secret, but sometimes you can't prevent someone from finding something out," Nick said.

"What will happen if they find out for sure? Will that cause you trouble?"

"Quite a bit, yeah."

"Then you'll have to be careful about unleashing your full strength..." Agate lowered her head, her expression serious.

"What is it?" Nick asked.

"...There have been a lot of people at shows recently with strange looks in their eyes. The number of fights has also increased significantly in the last two or three weeks. Some people have even deluded themselves that they're the paladin and going crazy," Agate said.

"Seriously? I haven't heard about that."

Nick had been busy with his work in the Garbage Heap and their trip to Pot Snake Cave during that time, necessitating a break from idol concerts. He made a mental note to ask his idol fan friends about this later.

"I want this show to go well for Amber, so...it would be reassuring if I knew the real paladin was there to cheer her on," Agate said.

Amber was the other idol in the carriage. She was going to perform at the venue they were traveling toward.

"Protecting the idols and making sure the concerts go off without a hitch is the job. Leave it to the real deal," Nick said.

Agate's expression relaxed. "I'm counting on you, stray dog and stray cat!"

"Who are you calling a stray cat?! Geez, I don't remember you being this bold...," Tiana grumbled, but she had a soft smile on her face.

The horse's hooves continued to clop along the road under the bright blue sky.

The concert was at the town hall in the commercial zone of Labyrinth City's southwest district. It was the same venue as the first concert Nick went to.

Fans were lined up outside, eagerly waiting for the doors to open. Amber—the star of today's show—had suffered a number of unfortunate setbacks, and a lot of fans had shown up to cheer her on and help make the concert a success.

Amber's first solo concert was originally supposed to be held over half a year before, but it was foiled when the owner of the venue they had booked skipped town overnight. The next attempt at the concert fell through when that venue was shut down due to an outbreak of yellow demon fever among the staff. Such unfortunate incidents continued, perpetually delaying her solo debut.

Amber's image as an idol was defined by an unyielding spirit and a bright personality. Those were true aspects of her character; she was always taking the initiative and encouraging others. But her bright personality coexisted with a sensitive nature. She was frustrated when Agate, who had entered the agency at the same time as she had, made her solo debut first. But she didn't let it break her.

She applied herself to practicing and improving her dancing skills, polishing her natural sense of rhythm. Having her debut delayed actually lit a fire in her heart. Topaz, another idol who'd started around the same time, also debuted before her, but again, she let that motivate her even more in her training. Her contagious effort galvanized other idols as well, and while it was later than she initially envisioned, her solo debut was finally set.

As tough as Amber was, though, the continual delays had begun to break her spirit. Any further delay could do serious damage to her mental state and her future career. She was becoming known as a popular yet unlucky idol who would never get a solo concert, and she had even gained the nickname "Miss Cancellation."

This was Amber's chance to redeem herself, and she couldn't afford for it to fail. She was determined to catch up to her contemporary idols.

Unfortunately, she fainted before the show.

"Amber collapsed?! Help her, Zem! Please!" Nick pleaded with Telepathy.

"I did. She just had anemia. She's fine now," Zem responded.

The Survivors got right to work after arriving at the town hall. They stationed Karan in the waiting room and split up so the other four members could each watch a different part of the venue, but it wasn't long before Karan told the others that Amber had collapsed and dragged Zem to the waiting room. Nick panicked with concern for Amber, but Zem quickly calmed him down.

"Th-thank goodness! A friend of mine named Jonathan is a huge Amber fan. He's really looking forward to this show," Nick said.

"I understand your concern, but please focus on your job. You're losing your composure," Zem chided.

"Sorry... I'm a little worried about something. We need to be careful."

"Worried about what?"

"The fake paladins. Agate said people are convincing themselves they're the paladin and getting violent."

"That is...definitely concerning. The venue's doors are about to open. Take care."

Nick focused on his surroundings after he finished talking to Zem in his head. This kind of job had a surprising amount of downtime, which meant the ability to stay focused was even more important than fighting strength.

Shortly afterward, Bond used Telepathy to inform the group that he sensed someone suspicious within a passageway that led into the venue, accessible only to staff. Nick was closest, so he went right there.

"You can't use this entrance. I'm going to have to ask you to leave," he said sternly when he found two men by the door.

They were both Amber fans, which Nick could tell by their cheaply dyed jackets that were closer to reddish-orange than to amber. They clearly weren't working together, though; one man was unconscious and bleeding from the nose, while the other was dragging him by the collar. It was obvious the one on his feet had assaulted the other man.

"Let him go. Put your hands up and face the wall," Nick commanded.

"Take me to Amber," the man growled.

The man was a bigger threat than Nick had thought. He

seemed deranged. "Bond! Tiana! I need support! This guy's dangerous!" he called out with Telepathy, and leaped at the man.

"What the...?" Nick muttered.

The assailant must have been either an adventurer or a knight, as he was a good enough fighter to knock a person out with one blow and quickly enter a defensive stance when Nick jumped at him. Nick had surmised as much, however, and when the man instinctively raised his arms to protect himself, Nick used Light Body to leap off them and land behind him.

"Time for you to take a nap. I'll hear what you have to say later, after I've given you to the Sun Knights," Nick said. He wrapped his arm around the man's neck, blocking his carotid artery. That was his signature move. Something felt wrong, though; the man's neck was hard, as if he was wearing thin, invisible armor that clung to his skin.

"I'm Amber's paladin! *Me!* I was chosen by the ticket!" the man shouted. A black fog-like substance that was barely visible drifted from the ticket in his chest pocket and wrapped around his body, and he ripped Nick's arm from his neck with impossible strength.

"What the hell—? Gah!" Nick grunted after the man punched him hard enough to launch him into the air. He thought he was going to crash into the ceiling, but someone caught him.

"You're...much lighter than you look. It's uncanny."

"Bond! Thank you!" Nick exclaimed.

"Who is that man?" Bond asked.

"An idol fan," Nick responded, just as the man swung at him with tremendous force, the black fog around his arm increasing its weight. "This is bad... Wait, that looks *familiar!* Doesn't that *fog* look like White Mask's armor?!"

"That *fog* is one stage before cognition armor! It's not manifesting, because he does not have enough mana, but its power will increase and make him impossible to handle! We must incapacitate him!" Bond replied.

The moment he was almost killed by White Mask flashed in Nick's mind, and he cleared it away by glaring at the man before him.

"Yeah. The concert could be canceled if we don't stop him here. We need to take him out as quickly as possible," Nick agreed. Not an easy task. This man was out of his mind. Nick didn't know if that was due to the man's nature or to the influence of a dangerous drug or spell, but either way, he was totally unpredictable. He might hurt Amber or a fan or wreak havoc on a much larger scale if they let him get away.

"I'm here!" Tiana said breathlessly as she ran up behind Nick, holding her staff.

"Tiana! Bond! We're gonna take him out in less than three seconds! Don't let him see us!" Nick commanded.

They all knew what they had to do.

""Union!"" Nick and Tiana yelled.

A white light blazed out against the black fog in the narrow corridor.

There was a festive mood in Amber's waiting room. The paladin who was rumored to have saved Agate had reappeared to protect another idol. That had to be a good omen. Amber, who had suffered anemia after being overwhelmed by the pressure ahead of her debut concert, had made a full recovery.

"U-um, Ms. Paladin! You're the real paladin, right?!" Amber asked.

The person was as beautiful as a fairy and had fine golden hair that flowed like water. Their body was supple, and they were more beautiful than most idols and models. No one in the room had seen this person except for Agate, but Amber knew who it was right away.

""Yes. I am the real deal, my lady. I caught the fake paladin, so you can relax,"" they answered.

"I-I'll do my best!" Amber said. She was struggling not to cry as she shook the paladin's hand. It seemed like she had come to think of the paladin as a real hero after hearing that they saved Agate. "Thank you so much, Ms. Paladin."

""I'm cheering you on. Good luck with your concert,"" the paladin responded. They said good-bye and left the waiting room. Then, after checking to see if no one was in the hallway, they entered an empty room and dispelled Union to split into Nick, Tiana, and Bond.

"You have to be more careful! You're gonna give us away!" Tiana complained immediately.

Nick and Tiana had quickly incapacitated the intruder after activating Union. They had used a slightly dangerous spell called *Steal Heat* to cool his body temperature and had taken the strange ticket that had given him strength. He'd been knocked out almost instantly. The only problem was they were seen by a part-time janitor who happened to be passing by.

Zem and Karan had warned Amber and her staff not to leave her waiting room, but Nick, Tiana, and Bond had missed the presence of the janitor. The janitor had screamed upon seeing Nick and Tiana in their combined Union state, but fortunately Agate had heard him, rushed over, and calmed him down ("You came back to support us, Ms. Paladin! Thank you so much!").

"We didn't have a choice. That guy could've easily killed a fan or a staff member if we didn't stop them," Nick argued.

"That's true, but...it's only a matter of time before people find out we're the paladin," Tiana said.

Bond tried to calm her down. "That Agate girl was quick on her feet. I don't think we have anything to worry about. Even if someone does figure us out, I am sure idols and their staff are strict about keeping secrets. If we keep their secrets, they will keep ours. Anyway..."

Bond pulled a slip of paper out of his pocket. It was the fake ticket they had taken from the assailant. The ticket looked completely different from the one they were shown at the agency; the paper had turned a dark color, as if it was soaked in venom.

"This is one of the fake tickets... It seemed to act like a talisman," Nick observed.

"I've never seen one like this, though. Even the way he used it is totally different," Tiana responded.

Talismans were one-use magic items that activated a spell when broken. Some expensive types automatically cast a healing or poison-curing spell when the owner's life was in danger. Most talismans were light-brown pieces of paper with a magic circle drawn in black ink, but the paper itself didn't change color after being used.

The piece of paper Nick was holding didn't resemble a normal talisman. When he held it to the light, it was possible to see densely packed hieroglyphic characters that were a slightly different shade than the rest of the dark ticket. This design and the sinister color it turned after use were like nothing they had seen.

Someone knocked on the door as the three of them examined the ticket.

"Excuse me! Is anyone in there? Can I come in?"

"Yeah, go ahead," Nick answered, and Agate walked into the room. She sighed with relief when she saw the three of them.

"That was my second time seeing the paladin, but it was still shocking... Is that some kind of ancient spell?" she asked.

"Hmm-hmm, actually—," Bond began, but Tiana slapped a hand over his mouth.

"Let's keep that a secret. I want no part of any scandals between you and the paladin," she said.

"Hey, I wouldn't tell anyone!" Agate sniffed. "Thank you, though. Seeing the paladin really cheered Amber up. She was worried about a stalker, too... That was probably the guy you just caught."

"I don't have a clue what you're talking about. We're not the ones who saved her," Nick said bluntly.

"Of course. My lips are sealed," Agate said with a smile.

"Was that guy really a stalker, though? A few things aren't adding up for me," Nick said.

"Really? Umm, he did seem pretty weird." Agate wasn't sure what Nick was getting at.

"I'm not talking about the man. His strength and this ticket he had on him are what feel off. Have you ever seen one of these?" Nick asked, showing her the ticket.

"What is that? It's creepy...," Agate said. It seemed like she had never seen a counterfeit ticket turn black. "Is this what the fakes look like? It doesn't look anything like the real ones."

"I think it looked like a normal ticket at first. It turned black when some strange mana appeared from it, and that's when the man attacked me," Nick explained.

Agate went pale for a moment as she realized they were in much more danger than she had imagined.

"Bond. Agate's not hiding anything, is she?" Nick asked with Telepathy.

"Hmm. I detect no heart palpitations or variation in her breathing that would suggest lying... Do you suspect her?" Bond replied.

"I don't want to, but we can't forget to keep an eye on our employers, too. Tell me if you notice anything."

"Understood."

Agate observed the ticket seriously, completely unaware of their conversation.

"I'll ask my producer about this later... Oh yeah, I came to tell you the concert is starting. You can catch a glimpse of the performance from the wings of the stage. Everyone but Nick, that is," she said casually.

"Huh? Why everyone else?!" Nick asked, shocked.

"Because there are friends of yours in the front row," Agate explained. "The fans don't have the angle to see the wings of the stage, but someone might be able to sense you anyway. Beastmen have good hearing and there are some idol fans with a sixth sense for noticing people."

Nick gasped and fell to his knees.

"Ah-ha-ha, that's such a shame, Nick. You behave yourself as we enjoy the show," Tiana said teasingly.

"Yes, we'll keep a very close eye on her," Bond agreed, chuckling.

Nick was white as a sheet, lacking the energy to even argue.

The concert was a roaring success. Amber was in top form—her voice was clear and her choreography was perfect. Her performance had never been sharper. The encore sent the crowd into a wild frenzy, and the crowd's thunderous cheers continued long after the show ended. Fans called it the best concert ever as they filed out of the venue.

"Agate! Topaz! I did it! I performed my own solo concert! Whoo-hoo!" Amber cheered.

"You were amazing, Amber!" Agate responded.

Agate and Topaz, who'd rushed here after finishing another job, were waiting for her backstage. They hugged their fellow idol as she cried a little.

"Hey, that hurts! Let me go! I'm sweaty!" Amber protested happily as they mobbed her.

Amber's manager and other staff members who'd devoted themselves to this concert all had tears in their eyes as well. The joy in the room was palpable.

But the Survivors' job wasn't done yet. They still had to escort the idols by carriage back to the Jewelry Production office through the nighttime streets of Labyrinth City.

Just when Nick was about to start preparing, he noticed that Karan was acting strangely.

"What is it, Karan?" he asked.

Karan watched the idols blankly, not hearing Nick.

"Hey, Karan," Nick said, putting a hand on her shoulder. She jolted and turned around.

"Oh, sorry. I didn't hear you," she said.

"What's wrong? Are you tired?"

"No. It's just...amazing."

"Right? Amber was stunning. She put her own spin on all the cover songs, and that last original song was out of this world. I wish I could have seen the dancing... I heard that Aggie and Topaz gave her advice on the lyr—"

"That's not what I'm talking about."

"O-oh."

"It's amazing that this kind of place exists. They're all following their dreams. They get along and cheer each other on, but they're also fiercely competitive. They all want to be the best."

Karan watched the idols with a distant look in her eyes. It was as if there was an invisible wall between her and the celebrating girls. There were always walls between fans and idols, or between clients and adventurers, but this wasn't the same.

Nick was about to continue that conversation, when a town-hall employee entered the room.

"Excuse me. We're about to turn out the lights...," she said apologetically.

Amber clapped her hands and addressed the room. "All right, everyone, that's enough fussing over me! Let's go home! Thank you for today!"

Everyone in the room thanked her and hurriedly got ready to leave.

"We've got one last job tonight, Karan. Let's get to work," Nick said.

Karan collected herself and nodded. "Okay. I wish we could use a dragon-drawn carriage instead of a horse-drawn carriage, though. Horses are such cowards."

"I prefer horses, personally. They're friendlier than dragons," Zem said.

"That's a tough one for me... I definitely prefer watching dragons," Tiana said.

"That's a nice way to say 'gamble on,'" Bond quipped.

"Shut up, Mop."

The Survivors got started on their last job of the day.

"We are calling this man and all others like him false paladins," said Joseph.

The Survivors went back to the Jewelry Production headquarters the next day. Joseph and Diamond invited them into a conference room, and they wasted no time getting to the main topic.

"That name sounds way too dramatic for a bunch of idol fans who have lost their marbles," Nick commented.

"I wonder if the real paladin would be offended by that name," Diamond said with an awkward laugh.

Nick decided not to let that slide. "They would," he said bluntly.

"S-sorry. I didn't mean anything by that," Diamond said timidly, shrinking away. She was usually easygoing, but Nick had successfully intimidated her.

"Let's drop this charade. We have our secrets, and I'm sure you have yours. But you're asking us to fight for you. If you hold back information we need to know, we're going to quit," Nick declared.

"That is understandable. Allow me to explain and offer my apology. I see now that is how we must begin," Joseph said. He wiped sweat from his brow with a handkerchief. "We know you are the Lovely Paladin. We obtained a list of everyone who was at the casino when it was attacked, and ninety percent of them said they thought it was you. The incident in the Garbage Heap only strengthened our conviction."

"Okay. Go on," Nick urged, speaking for the group.

"We wrote a song about the paladin, and despite being reasonably sure about their identity, we never considered reaching out and paying you a copyright fee," Joseph said.

"That's not the problem!" Nick shouted. He and his party members looked astonished.

"It's not?" Joseph replied with genuine surprise. It seemed he truly thought the Survivors were angry that Jewelry Production hadn't shared any of its earnings.

"We don't want people to know we're the paladin. Asking for money would've given us away. Do you want us to give you an invoice under the name *The Lovely Paladin*?" Nick retorted.

"Um... Why are you keeping it a secret? That ability of yours is very unique, but surely you are not doing anything illegal. Are you afraid of catching the attention of the Sun Knights?" Joseph asked.

"That's part of it. This secret getting out would cause a lot of problems for us," Nick responded. He didn't intend to elaborate on that.

"You guys are heroes, but you're living in obscurity. Wouldn't the Adventurers Guild make you S-rank adventurers immediately if you told them that you're the paladin and shared what you've done?" Diamond asked

Nick wasn't sure how to respond. The Adventurers Guild itself was the problem.

"Oh, do you have a bad relationship with the guild? Or are you hiding something from them?" Diamond asked.

"No, of course not," Nick said.

Diamond narrowed her eyes and grinned. "I can tell you're lying, Nick. Your breathing is giving you away."

"If that's what you want to talk about, we're leaving. Thank you very much for the job. We look forward to working with you in the future," Nick said bluntly.

"Hey, wait! I'm sorry!" Diamond apologized.

"Let's move on and talk about the false paladins," Nick said. "That really does sound wrong..."

Joseph seemed relieved that the conversation had returned to work. "This all began about three weeks ago, when people began to appear calling themselves the paladin."

"Why would they do that? I don't get it," Nick asked.

"That we don't know... But we have finally found something to connect them," Joseph said.

"What's that?" Nick asked.

"All the false paladins have had special counterfeit tickets. They seem to have some impact on their mental state. I never would have thought the tickets were quite so dangerous...," Joseph answered.

Tiana spoke up for the first time since entering the room. "Did you not realize the tickets are talismans? You have some of them, don't you?"

"The counterfeit tickets are deceptive in two ways. Not only do they imitate the design of the real tickets, they are also made so that you cannot detect that they are talismans," Joseph explained.

"Talismans have mana. Couldn't you detect that?" Tiana asked.

Joseph shook his head. "We checked, but the tickets barely contain any mana. There is so little that not even Magic Search can detect it."

"What?"

"The counterfeit tickets contain only the smallest speck of mana. The special paint used on the legitimate tickets already contains a little mana, so such a tiny amount cannot be used to identify a counterfeit ticket."

Joseph looked at the black strip of paper on the table. It was the ticket Nick had taken from the man they'd captured.

"The assailant is a D-rank adventurer known as Restless Ironman Giuseppe, who works primarily from the Travelers Adventurers

Guild. He suffers insomnia and excels at taking the night watch," he said.

"Can he use magic? Has anyone heard of him giving shape to his mana and wrapping it around his body?" Tiana asked.

"No, he seems to be an ordinary swordsman... Do you all want to know more about him?" Joseph asked, acting strangely hesitant.

"Can't we visit him in prison?" Tiana asked.

"...I don't want to put them in our debt. Some of our idols have been followed, and they might interfere with our concerts, claiming a need to increase security," Joseph said.

"Who's 'them'—?" Tiana began to ask, but she was interrupted when a staff member entered the room.

"Mr. Coleman. She's here," they said timidly.

Joseph made a rare sour expression. "Oh, great... Let's get our stories straight, everyone. This will be best with Nick alone. It may turn into something of an interrogation."

"Whoa, I don't like the sound of that. What's going on?" Nick asked, mirroring his expression.

"A Sun Knight is here," Joseph answered.

Diamond quickly said, "I've got training! Bye!" and fled the room with catlike agility. It was a truly impressive escape.

"I didn't expect to find one of the adventurers who distinguished themselves in the Garbage Heap here. Today's my lucky day."

"R-really? It's nice to meet you," Nick stammered, speaking with unusual politeness.

He was at a simple table set up next to the building's reception rather than in a conference room. Joseph chose this spot because he said he didn't want to let the person they were meeting any farther inside the building. Nick and Joseph were at one end of the table, and the new guest was sitting opposite from them.

"You're so formal. That's not very adventurer-like of you," she said. She appeared unoffended by Joseph's brusque treatment.

The guest was a beautiful woman with short blue hair and a demeanor so cheerful, she could have passed for an idol, though her eye-catching clothing—which consisted of a shiny silver breastplate and a white cloak—made it clear she was not. A hexagon with flames at each point was etched onto the cloak. It was the emblem of the largest order of knights on the continent—the Order of the Sun Knights—which made catching criminals and maintaining the peace its goal, rather than fighting monsters or warfare.

"Everyone's heard of the famous beautiful woman who serves as a Sun Knight captain. Any adventurer worth his salt would be nervous around you," Nick responded.

"I find that reputation flattering. Nice to meet you, Nick," the beautiful woman said, reaching out for a handshake. Nick gave his hand to her, trying to hide his surprise that she knew his name.

"I'm Nick of the Survivors," he said.

"I'm Alice Burrows. I'm the captain of the Gauntlet unit, which belongs to the Northwest Company of the Sun Knight Teran Defense Battalion," the woman replied, smiling at Nick.

Alice the Sun Knight was well known among adventurers, bounty hunters, and wanted criminals in Labyrinth City. The Burrows were a famous family that produced many people who assumed important roles in the Order of the Sun Knights. Alice could have joined the order as a captain, but she rejected that to sign up as a regular knight.

Alice quickly proved that she was not just a noble having fun. She captured criminal after criminal with bounties totaling over one million dina each and earned her position of captain on her own merit. Wanted criminals spoke of her with fear on their lips. Too many ruffians to count underestimated her before she became famous and were nearly killed for it, and adventurers came to fear her, too.

Once introductions were out of the way, they got down to business. Alice wanted to station Sun Knights at concerts to catch assailants, and Joseph objected, because he was afraid they would disrupt the shows. Their argument gave Nick a stomachache.

"But there have been frequent incidents. I'm going to station Sun Knights around the venues even if you won't let me place them inside. Are you okay with that, at least?" Alice asked.

"That would be reassuring. I really don't want to trouble you all, though," Joseph responded.

"Are you afraid of troubling knights you don't know? Do you want to join the Sun Knights, Nick?" Alice offered.

"Very funny. I'm not remotely qualified," Nick said.

Facing a Sun Knight with your employer in this manner was a common occurrence for an adventurer. The Order of the Sun Knights protected the populace, but they didn't consider the financial concerns of those they guarded. They also prioritized catching criminals over saving victims. Many people decided to hire adventurers as guards, instead of Sun Knights, for those reasons; adventurers had to safeguard the interests of their employer.

Nick had thought this meeting was an extension of some kind of turf war. He figured that Joseph would act angry at first and then look for a compromise. But he had been completely wrong.

"Don't be humble. We're grateful for your cooperation. You heard about the identity of the assailant, right?" Alice asked.

Nick answered while counting off on his fingers. "He's a D-rank adventurer, an idol fan, and he was caught having assaulted a victim. Now he's in prison, eating slop."

"He says he bought the counterfeit tickets from a hooded man in a back alley in south Labyrinth City. His memory of when he committed the crime is hazy, so I think the ticket either triggered a state of extreme excitement or placed him under hypnosis."

Nick and Joseph visibly reacted to Alice's words.

"So if we can just capture that hooded man...," Nick said.

"It'll be case closed. The dangerous nature of the tickets points to the seller being a demon-god worshipper. They're quite knowledgeable when it comes to special magic items and lost magic and technology. I want to get this counterfeit ticket dealer into custody," Alice said.

Nick breathed an internal sigh of relief. He realized why this knight was so passionate about her work. There was no greater achievement for a Sun Knight than capturing demon-god worshippers, who were known to work in the shadows. She wouldn't give them much trouble as long as they didn't get in the way of her efforts to distinguish herself.

But just as he was starting to get comfortable, Alice gave a warning. "We can't relax yet, Nick of Combat Masters. We barely have any leads on the seller."

"That's my last party. I'm a member of the Survivors now," Nick said.

"Do you know any demon-god worshippers?" she asked.

"Of course not. I'd arrest them if I did."

"You know a man named Garos."

"...He's a C-rank adventurer. He wields a katana and fights on the front line for Combat Masters. He spends his free time on booze and women."

"I heard he went to your apartment recently. What did you talk about?"

Nick looked down, wondering why she was asking that. Deciding he wouldn't be able to fool her with a lie, he braced himself and told the truth. "He brought money to repay a debt."

"Interesting. Where do you think he earned that money?" Alice asked.

"I was kicked out of Combat Masters. If you want to know about Garos, you should ask him or current members of the party," Nick said.

"Combat Masters filed for a break from the Adventurers Guild," Alice replied.

Nick felt his heart rate quicken. That news made sense, given what Garos had told him, but hearing it now only gave him a bad feeling.

"We're unable to locate them. The whole party disappeared shortly before you all defeated White Mask. You met with Garos after he moved out of his inn and vanished," Alice said.

"I don't see where you're going with this. Do you think Garos is the one selling the tickets?" Nick asked.

"The rate of demon-god worshipper activity decreases the more active Combat Masters is. As soon as they took a break, White Mask began wreaking havoc in the Garbage Heap."

Nick barely held back a gasp of surprise. He had never heard anything of the sort, and he didn't believe for a second that his former comrades were demon-god worshippers. But he couldn't deny they were suspicious. That wasn't just because of what Alice said; looking back, Garos's behavior during his sudden visit was very strange.

Nick pressed on with the conversation, not knowing what to believe. "But...that would make Argus and the other members suspects, too. Don't you have any other potential demon-god worshippers? No one in Combat Masters can even use magic. They're too simple to worship a demon god."

"A person without magic can still use a magic item or a talisman. In fact, wouldn't a less magic-oriented party be even more accustomed to using them in combat?" Alice retorted.

Nick had no response. What she said was true.

The Survivors didn't use many talismans or magic items because Tiana, Zem, and Bond could all cast their own spells, but Nick had spent plenty of one-use talismans when he was in Combat Masters. Even Garos and Argus, who were skilled with weapons and hand-to-hand combat, didn't mind relying on magic items and talismans. They actually made good use of them.

"Garos is the last member of the party to be seen, and he chose to meet with you," Alice said.

"But...I defeated White Mask." Nick was unable to manage anything but that excuse. He knew it didn't prove anything, though. White Mask's holy armor copied the skills of its past users and enabled the current wearer to use them. If Garos held back from using his own skills and only used capabilities given to him by the holy armor, Nick would have had no way of knowing it was him.

One of the purposes of White Mask's armor was likely to hide the identity of the wearer.

"That's right. You defeated White Mask and brought peace to that area of the city. You should be proud of that accomplishment. Many adventurers have faced White Mask and failed. How did you do it?" Alice asked with a captivating smile. She wasn't leaving without an answer.

"Strategy. Ability. Resolve. Luck. It all came together at the right time," Nick replied bluntly.

"Did White Mask let you get away because you're a former party member?

"No. Shouldn't fighting White Mask be enough to make my affiliation clear?"

"You must have some kind of special power to fight demongod worshippers without any connection to them and come out alive. Does it come from your lineage? Is it innate ability? Or could it come from an ancient artifact that you excavated from a labyrinth? I don't know which it is, but you must have some kind of power that most people don't."

Nick felt sweat run down his back. "Mind if I get my lawyer?" he asked.

"We're just chatting. Is your lawyer good at livening up a conversation?" Alice asked.

"My lawyer runs a cross-dressing bar in the southeast district. Beautiful and, yes, a good conversationalist."

Alice barked a laugh. "Good one. It takes guts to joke around in a situation like this. You're an adventurer to the core."

"Thanks," Nick said, keeping it to himself that what he'd revealed wasn't a joke.

Joseph gave Nick a look asking if he needed help, and Nick signaled back with a glance that he was fine.

"What kind of adventurer do you want to be, Nick?" Alice asked.

"I'm perfectly satisfied with going on adventures and spending my free time going to see idols," said Nick. "My instructor and my old party members taught me some skills, but I only use them to feed myself. I'm not gonna reveal those skills in casual conversation, and I wouldn't misuse them, either. All adventurers have one or two talents they want to keep a secret."

"Just one or two? Are you sure you don't have a few more secret skills than that?" Alice pressed.

"You think you know all about me, don't you? Are you a fan of mine?" Nick asked sarcastically.

Alice smiled. "Ha-ha, yes. I am a fan of yours. You joined the incredibly skilled party Combat Masters as a young boy with no family and became an adventurer. You then went independent, recruited talented adventurers, and defeated one of the demongod worshippers lurking in the dark underbelly of Labyrinth City. You sound like a hero out of a minstrel's story."

"You're giving me too much credit. I have no intention of becoming a hero."

"The citizens of this city are under threat. A day will come when people's ordinary lives are turned completely upside down. The weak will be preyed upon—that's the nature of this city. Don't you want a hero to appear to fight injustice?"

"Yeah. Of course."

"I do, too."

"Let's cut the chitchat and get back to work. The counterfeit-ticket seller is still out there."

"Yeah. Let's make it a competition."

"What?"

"Whoever catches the culprit first wins."

Nick had been trying to figure out what he had gotten himself into as he answered her questions. He didn't know if he was walking into the den of a lion, a dragon, or something even more dangerous. That was why he'd been avoiding questions he didn't want to answer, but he couldn't shake the feeling that she had a trap waiting for him at the end of the conversation. The thought made him anxious.

"Remember. You can listen to someone's breathing to tell if they're lying."

Nick heard Diamond's voice. He was sure he didn't imagine it, but he also knew it wasn't Telepathy. He clearly heard her voice in his ears.

"Hmm? Did I say something weird?" Alice asked.

"Yeah, you did," Nick responded.

Alice and Joseph must not have heard. Nick quickly realized how she had spoken to him—she'd used Vocal Guidance, controlling the direction and reverberation of the sound to send her voice directly to Nick's ears like a billiard ball.

"You don't need to respond. Keep your face straight and continue your conversation. She's not just after Garos—she's after you, too. I don't know why, though," Diamond said.

"Just to make sure we're on the same page...you want to compete instead of cooperate?" Nick asked Alice.

"Oh, do you want to work together? I'd welcome your transfer to the Sun Knights," Alice responded.

"Observe your opponent. No matter how perfect a script she's following in her mind, she has to speak using her lungs, throat, and mouth, just like any other flesh-and-blood human. Once you know her breathing, you know her rhythm. And grasping her rhythm will let you feel her emotions. Align yourself to those emotions, and you'll be able to win her over. Don't allow her song to rule you. Make this your own stage."

How do you expect me to understand all that idol lingo? Nick thought, but he did as Diamond said.

He strained his ears to listen for Alice's breathing. It was perfectly steady; he couldn't sense her emotion at all. It was discouraging at first, but then he noticed that something was off. Her breathing was *too* calm, as if it were following the perfect, mechanical rhythm of a clock. No person's breathing could remain that steady without special training. She was taking care to make herself look calm and prevent her emotions from showing. Just like a card or roulette dealer.

"That's it, Nick. No human is unbeatable. Good luck," Diamond said.

"What happens if I lose?" Nick asked Alice.

"I know a place where we can be alone," Alice said, smiling.

"So you want to interrogate me."

Alice was teasing him and pretending like this was nothing more than a pleasant chat. That was a sign that she was feeling anxious.

"But you can't tell what I know, so you're hesitating to bring me into custody. You're afraid that you might end up helping the demon-god worshippers by doing so. Is that right?" Nick said.

"I won't deny it," Alice replied.

Why was she anxious? It had to have something to do with his accomplishments. He had been intentionally avoiding certain topics, but those might be useful to get the upper hand now.

"I see what's happening here," Nick said. "The Sun Knights have been after White Mask for a while now, and it won't do your reputation any favors if it turns out he really was defeated by simple adventurers. You need to achieve something even greater than defeating White Mask to make up for it."

Alice's breathing was disturbed for the first time. Her goal may have been to catch demon-god worshippers, but that didn't explain why she was questioning him so persistently. Nick realized she wasn't fixated on him because he was a former member of Combat Masters; it was because he'd defeated White Mask.

"Did you make this a competition in order to set me loose and see what would happen? The demon-god worshippers are sure to come for me. They won't leave me alone after I embarrassed them like that," Nick said.

That was when he realized that this was the opportunity he needed. It was good that he discovered her weakness, but it wouldn't benefit him to rile her up further. Offering her some kind of compromise would be best. He was fine with letting the Sun Knights get the credit for exposing White Mask's identity and finishing them off.

But there was still something he had to say. Diamond's words echoed in his head. *Make this your own stage.*

"Are you sure you don't want to be a Sun Knight? You suddenly have me on the defensive," Alice said.

"I'll tell you everything we learn about the demon-god worshippers. I don't need credit or money. But I don't regret anything I did during that case. I won't apologize for beating you at your own game," Nick declared.

Alice's face stiffened. Nick knew he shouldn't anger someone of her station, but he couldn't stop himself.

"Martha Canning. She was a daughter of the Canning family, which runs an armor store on Blacksmith Street. She was ten years old. She had blond hair, a mole on her neck, and burn scars on her left wrist. Her parents were late to submit a missing persons report because she had a habit of running away from home," Nick began, counting off on his fingers as he reeled off facts about the girl.

"That's…"

"That's the name of a girl that the Steppingman—that Nargava—kidnapped. She contracted yellow demon fever in confinement and died. She was almost buried in a communal graveyard without being identified."

Nick had never had much love for the Order of the Sun Knights. That feeling was shared by most of Labyrinth City. The Sun Knights worked hard to catch petty thieves but did little to catch serious criminals. They also accepted bribes and did their best to please nobles and wealthy merchants.

That said, they were unexpectedly helpful when needed, and it was true that people had no choice but to rely on them. Nick had come to accept the Sun Knights' laziness for what it was, and he didn't think much of the adventurers who actively opposed them. He'd realized something recently, however.

He didn't just slightly dislike the Sun Knights.

He hated them.

"We searched for the missing children, and when we found one of them dead, we gave our all to saving the rest and bringing the case to a close. Isn't that what fighting injustice is all about?" Nick asked.

"That should be the desire of any knight," Alice replied.

"You said we should make this a competition. Whoever catches the counterfeit-ticket seller first wins, right? If you win, I'll do anything you ask."

"Are you sure about that?"

"But if I win, I want you to apologize to the girl who died. Tell her you're sorry for being completely ignorant of her."

Alice nodded silently, turned around, and walked out. Her easygoing, joking attitude had disappeared completely. Her footsteps were heavy as Nick and Joseph watched her leave the building.

"I've really done it now," Nick said.

"That is an understatement," Joseph responded candidly. "I've never seen an adventurer speak so aggressively to a Sun Knight."

Nick bowed his head in apology, belatedly realizing he had roped Jewelry Production into a fight. "S-sorry."

"Don't apologize. I understand what you're angry about," Joseph said. He didn't look upset; his expression appeared closer to satisfaction. "Now then, Nick. There are no events or concerts today, so you are free to do as you wish as long as you leave a few people to guard the building. I'll let you deploy guards as you wish."

"Huh... Are you sure?" Nick asked.

"Just make sure you catch whoever's selling the counterfeit tickets before the Sun Knights. Forget the competition—you can consider that an order from your client," Joseph said.

"Thanks... That's not something I should've done without consulting you. Sorry," Nick responded.

"I'm not nearly brave enough to jump into a conversation like that," Joseph said with a wry smile.

"Really? You look like you've been through more than a few battles to me."

"Ha. No. I get that a lot, but I assure you, I am no fighter." Joseph smiled and shook his head. "That's enough about me. You may have a hard time explaining this to your party members."

Joseph was exactly right. Picking a fight with the Order of the Sun Knights wasn't exactly the smartest thing to do.

"I don't think I'll be much help to you there. Good luck," Joseph said. He smiled, clearly amused, and left.

"Oh well... Better go confess and apologize."

Nick steeled himself and began to search the building for his party members so he could explain what had happened. He asked an employee where they were, and they directed him to the training room.

"Hey, guys. The meeting's ove— What are you doing?"

"H-hey! Don't startle me like that!"

"Oh, hey. We meet again."

Nick had opened the door and entered the training room to find a few familiar faces among the idols. Karan was there, having changed out of her armor and into workout clothes. She was with another female dragonian who was the same height as she was but seemed more put-together. Unlike Karan, she had blue hair and blue scales. It was Daffodil, Karan's cousin that Nick had met recently.

Zem was sitting in a chair behind them, watching over Ares, Daffodil's child.

"Umm, Daffodil? This is an idol agency," Nick said timidly.

"Yeah. I know. It's also my place of work. I told you I'm a dance instructor," Daffodil shot back, as if he'd said something stupid.

"Seriously?!" Nick exclaimed.

"I wouldn't be let in the building otherwise." Daffodil sounded a little annoyed.

"Wow... That's amazing. You're the real deal," Nick said.

"I'm retired from dancing, though. I was never as famous as the girls here," Daffodil admitted with a self-deprecating shrug. "But training promising girls and choreographing their dances is really fun."

She smiled kindly. To Nick, she seemed like a broad-minded, motherly person.

"It's a small world," he said.

"How did it go, Nick? I heard that a Sun Knight showed up...," Karan said, approaching Nick with concern.

Nick had decided to be careful and not use Telepathy during the conversation with Alice, so his party members didn't know yet what had happened. This wasn't the place to say he'd picked a fight with a Sun Knight, so he avoided the question.

"Those clothes look good on you. That style is perfect for tall people," he said.

"Aren't they great?! They're luxury workout clothes made by a sports apparel company! They're stylish enough that we could do her hair and makeup and send her out onstage as a dancer just like that!" Daffodil gushed.

"D-don't be stupid! I'm an adventurer!" Karan protested.

Amber, Agate, and another idol walked up behind her.

"Right? I knew it wasn't just me! When I saw her at the concert, I was confused about why an idol was working as a bodyguard," Agate said.

"She has such a cool silhouette. She'd immediately improve the aesthetics of any show," Amber commented.

"Yeah, I think she's ready for her debut already. We can be her mentors!" the other idol agreed.

The three girls talked excitedly about Karan while ignoring her protests. Nick couldn't help but smile as he watched her expression shift between troubled and embarrassed.

"Go easy on her, you all," he said.

"We're strict teachers, so we can't make any promises... Oh, I haven't introduced myself, have I? I'm Topaz. It's nice to meet you," the girl with Amber and Agate said. Nick didn't need the introduction; he was more than familiar with this blond-haired, carefree idol.

"N-nice to meet you, too," Nick said. "You can count on us to keep you safe."

Agate, Amber, and Topaz were popular as a unit who'd entered the agency together. They all had their solo activities, but they often performed together, too. Nick knew a lot of Amber and Topaz fans, and he began to sweat, knowing that he was learning secrets he couldn't tell them.

Nick also felt his irritation from the previous conversation fading. Karan was clearly having fun interacting with a world she'd had little contact with. He knew that as the party leader he should tell her to get back to work, but he wanted to watch her for a little longer.

"I won't tell you to stop dancing, but make sure you do it in moderation. We've never said members of our party can't have side jobs," Nick said jokingly.

Daffodil cheered, seeming to take his words seriously. "Yay! Your leader gave his permission! Is the makeup artist coming today?"

"He didn't mean it, Daffy! And you watch it, Nick!" Karan said hurriedly.

Daffodil calmed her down with a wink. "I'm joking, too. We should talk about this later, though."

"Ugh, I'm exhausted..." Karan sighed deeply.

"Is Diamond here, by the way?" Nick asked.

Daffodil looked around. "Huh? She was here earlier... Do you know where she is, Agate?"

"Nope. That's our elusive Sergeant for you," Agate responded.

"Sergeant?" Nick echoed.

Agate clapped a hand over her mouth. "Please don't repeat that to anyone. We all call her 'Sergeant' and 'Demon' because of how strict she is in practice."

"I'm pretty sure she can hear us... Eh, whatever. My lips are sealed," Nick said. He pivoted to walk away.

"Hmm? Where are you going?" Karan asked.

"I have a bone to pick with someone," he responded.

Nick walked the halls of the agency alone, looking for Diamond. Once he found a spot with no one around, he spoke out loud with a normal, conversational volume.

"Thanks for earlier, Diamond. I want to talk."

The hallway remained silent. But Nick could feel that Diamond had heard him.

Nick looked up at one of the ducts running along the ceiling. "You can hear conversations from any room with a duct running through it, can't you? They look like they're for ventilation, but they're actually there so all voices in the building travel to you.

Am I right?" he said. "Where are you hiding anyway? You've got a concert coming up. Do you really have time to mess with me?"

Nick's intuition had been good recently. Learning the spell *Magic Sense*, which allowed the user to detect mana in things they touched, had enabled him to sense faint presences and irregularities. Using it while fighting an opponent let him sense the flow of their mana and predict their next move. He could also sense the subtle flow of mana beneath the ground on which he stood.

Day after day we fought.

It was then that Nick noticed a mana-drenched voice coming from Diamond. It didn't travel directly to his ears like last time. It was more that he'd happened to pick up a sound wave that leaked out of the duct.

We were terrible cooks, even worse than we thought.

Nick started to walk, climbing staircases and moving through hallways as he searched for where Diamond's singing was coming from. He drew steadily closer.

On cold days it was a blanket; on hot days water.
We fought for the sake of fighting.

Nick could feel her rhythm, and from that, her emotion. He found himself wandering after Diamond's voice, forgetting why he was looking for her in the first place. He opened doors that were likely only meant for employees, climbed fire escape ladders, and ended up in an attic.

The attic had been repurposed into an empty room with acoustic foam wedges covering the walls and ceiling to absorb sound. The fine wooden floor was marked all over with tape, and Diamond was standing in the center of the inelegant room, intently practicing a song.

"Hey, here you—," Nick started to call out, but he broke off.

> *I cursed your name for being that way*
> *But now I see those were happy days*
> *I wish the right words had come to light*
> *I love you, please hold me tight*
> *I wonder if we'll ever meet again*
> *Once the journey's over and winter ends*

Diamond continued to sing, dancing on the old wooden floor, which looked like it should have creaked from the smallest amount of pressure. Sunlight streamed through a window in the ceiling, and her smallest movements kicked up dust that shone faintly in the light.

Despite all that, her dancing was modest and quiet, as if she were the star of her own little world.

"All right. Sorry about that. I wasn't ignoring you. I just wanted to focus on getting through that song," Diamond said once she was done.

"That was 'Undying Love Song,' the third song after your debut," Nick said.

Diamond smiled in acknowledgment. "It was actually my most popular song last year. How was that performance? I'm sure it felt different, hearing it up close like that."

"It gave me chills," Nick responded.

"Yikes, is that all you have to say? I wanted to see if you'd go full idol fan and gush over how amazing I was," Diamond teased.

"Shut up," Nick retorted, embarrassed. A hundred words of lavish praise would hardly be enough to convey his feelings after seeing her practice that song up close. That was how beautiful Diamond and her voice were as she sang.

His intention to deride her for slacking off and for interrupting meetings while she worked her junior idols to the bone had vanished like smoke. Diamond did practice. She took her job more seriously than anyone. She valued Jewelry Production and all its idols as much as she did herself.

"I'm pretty skilled, you know. And my hearing is superb. I hear nearly everything in this building, so I know if any suspicious people arrive or if any secrets are divulged. I know people call me Sergeant Demon, too," Diamond said.

"I believe it. You knew exactly where my conversation with the Sun Knight was going," Nick responded.

"I often prevent trouble at concerts when I go to support my fellow idols, too. Sun Knights are no match for me."

"I always thought you had a quick temper."

"I was a real troublemaker back in the day. I'm definitely in no place to judge you." Diamond giggled with an impish grin.

Her expression quickly turned calm again, and Nick felt himself drawn to her serenity. She looked like both an innocent girl and an adult woman who had tasted the sweetness and bitterness of life.

"I'm going to be spending a lot of time practicing from now on, so I won't be going to many meetings or training sessions," Diamond said. Her resolve was visible despite her nonchalant tone. "I'm gonna perfect my singing and my dancing. That's why I want you to protect me and the other idols at this agency."

"Why me?"

"Because you passed."

"Huh? So there *was* a test?" Nick asked. He was trying to sound upset, but he wasn't a good enough actor to fool Diamond.

"I wanted to know if you all could use Telepathy, but you all hid that from me. People who rely too much on that spell tend to get careless," Diamond said.

"I happen to know some people who paid dearly for that mistake," Nick agreed, thinking of the Iron Tiger Troop.

"Focusing too much on the conversation in your head can cause you to lose track of what's in front of you. There are also ways to mess with people who can use Telepathy."

"Huh? Like what?"

"You can remove the limiter on the spell and send a high-density thought into someone's mind to knock them out. It's terrifying."

Diamond was acting as if she was just remembering an old prank, but Nick could tell she was speaking from experience.

"I'm scared to ask how you know that…," Nick said.

"I learned it through this job. I once worked with a magic laboratory to see if we could dream up a new kind of concert that used Telepathy. They withdrew after saying it wouldn't be profitable enough."

"Whoa, that sounds amazing."

"Every now and then some naughty kid will use a telepathy orb to try to spy on the agency, too. Protecting the new idols from people like that is a full-time job."

"Is that why you don't use telepathy orbs? You're afraid of getting careless and being sensed by others?"

Diamond smiled painfully. Nick got the sense she was regretting something from her past.

"I want you to have this, Nick," Diamond said, tossing Nick a small jewel-like object.

Nick caught it suspiciously. "What's this? I'm guessing it's not just a gem…"

"It's a severance orb. It casts Discommunicator on yourself. Use it when you want to prevent someone from reading your mind or if someone sends you dangerous thought waves," Diamond said.

"That sounds really valuable," Nick replied hesitantly.

"If there's anything else you want, just ask for it. To protect others, you have to protect yourself first. We don't know where the demon-god worshippers are. You can't be too careful."

Nick pocketed the severance orb while feeling the weight of her words.

"I appreciate it. It seems like I've got the Sun Knights to worry about now as well as the demon-god worshippers," he said.

"That Alice girl is interesting. I don't know if our interests align or not, but she has more integrity than I expected. After you denounced the Sun Knights for their systematic dishonesty and indolence, I felt shame rather than anger from her voice and gait. This is just instinct, but I think you'll be able to rely on her," Diamond shared.

"...That kinda sucks to hear after picking a fight with her," Nick replied.

"Debating ideals is not fighting. It's like a pair of lovers sharing a kiss," Diamond said, putting a finger to her lips. It was a beautiful gesture, fitting for the most popular idol in the city. Nick felt a rush of admiration for her.

"If I'm being honest, you're scarier than that Sun Knight," he said in awe, but Diamond didn't respond. Instead, she changed the subject.

"All I want is for everyone to smile," she said.

"Yeah?"

"That includes people who feel trapped in life. People who are buried in regret. People who have been hurt by others or have hurt others without meaning to. I want more fortunate people to smile as well. I hope that, at least while they listen to our music, they can forget all the difficulties in their life and be happy."

"I definitely have fun when listening to your songs."

"But we had to do so much to reach this point. It's been really hard... Making it to our one hundredth anniversary is a big accomplishment."

"Yeah, it's really impressive."

"I need to narrow my focus so I can give my all to this moment. And that means rendering myself defenseless," Diamond said, performing a spin. That simple movement was executed with a flawless, crystalline beauty. "I have connections to stronger adventurers than you, of course. But sometimes you need more than strength. I want someone with ideals, who I can count on to get up and keep going when those ideals prove insufficient and carry them directly into a wall. Just like idols. That's the only way you'll gain my trust and that of my girls. I admit you've had plenty of reason to complain, though."

"I excel at complaining and fussing over details. Guild employees tell me how annoying I am all the time."

"That's just what I want. You'll stand up to the Sun Knights and fight injustice... I love that. It's so cool. It even makes my heart flutter. You pass the test."

"Geez, I had to make your heart flutter to pass? Talk about pressure."

"You should consider that an honor. I'm the most popular idol in Labyrinth City, if you can believe it."

"Trust me, I know."

"Oh, are you a fan of mine?"

"Of course. Aggie's my fave, though."

"That's a bummer. I'm gonna be jealous."

"I'll catch whoever's selling the counterfeit tickets. I won't let any false paladins ruin your concerts, either. The demon-god worshippers and the Sun Knights won't get the best of me. You just focus on making your own stage."

"I'm counting on you, my bodyguard."

Nick nodded in response to Diamond's affectionate words. The idol glided across the room and stood on a white X of tape on the floor. It was the center of the practice room, where she imagined herself onstage, surrounded by fans. Her presence here was proof that she stood above all the other hardworking idols in the city.

"Can you listen to one more song? I want to practice it," Diamond asked.

She began to sing. Nick turned his back and listened, standing guard so that no one would interrupt.

A Fight Behind the Scenes

The bodyguard job from Jewelry Production had turned out to be much more complicated than the Survivors expected. They knew it would entail protecting idols from blacklisted fans who were buying counterfeit tickets to get into concerts, but now they had learned that the tickets gave their owners strange power.

"Are we good on that part?" Nick asked.

"Not at all, but whatever," Tiana responded.

The Survivors had gathered in Tiana's apartment after work for a meeting. Nick was going back over everything that had happened so far, step-by-step, and the others were listening with slightly annoyed expressions.

"The counterfeit tickets seem to be talismans made by demon-god worshippers," Nick said.

"I don't like that, either, but go on," Tiana said.

"That caught the attention of the Sun Knights, who are now poking their noses into this case to catch demon-god worshippers," Nick continued.

Alice, the Sun Knight who visited the Jewelry Production headquarters, thought that Garos, Nick's former party member, might be a demon-god worshipper. She was also suspicious of Nick because he defeated White Mask. Knowing that this would only lead to trouble, Nick relayed the conversation he'd had with Alice.

"...So yeah, I ended up picking a fight with a famous Sun Knight. I'm in big trouble if we don't catch the counterfeit-ticket seller before them. Sorry," Nick finished.

"If you knew it was going to be a mistake, you shouldn't have done it in the first place!" Tiana scolded.

"I'm really sorry. I know I messed up," Nick repeated, shrinking away from her.

The others chuckled; they all had a soft spot for Nick's quick temper.

"All right. I'm not actually that mad," Tiana said. "It's inevitable the Sun Knights were going to suspect us, given what we've done."

"Yes. We are all in the same boat. There is no point in dwelling on the past," Bond agreed.

"Hey, you're partially responsible for all this!" Nick retorted. Bond's supercilious behavior was getting under his skin.

Zem laughed. "So in short," he said with his typical calm, "we have to keep the concerts safe and find the counterfeit-ticket seller. We must accomplish the latter before the Sun Knights. Is that right?"

"I think I'm gonna look for the ticket seller myself. I might ask for your help in spots, though," Nick said.

Zem frowned. "I don't love the idea of you working alone. I am also uneasy about our chances of fighting off the idol fans with those counterfeit tickets—the false paladins, I suppose—without you. We would not be able to use Union."

"That's true..."

Nick and Zem both looked anxious. Bond had registered Nick as his owner. His sword form was optimized to Nick's mind and body, so transferring ownership would not be easy.

"That won't be a problem. We used Union last time without thinking, but I don't think we needed it," Tiana said.

"Yes, I agree. We can handle the assailants if we can just figure out how the tickets work," Bond agreed.

"How?" Nick asked.

Tiana answered, sounding free of concern. "All we have to do is steal or burn the ticket."

"That's easier said than done, especially if the false paladin is an adventurer trained in martial arts," Nick argued.

"You would think," Tiana said. "But the only thing that sets the counterfeit tickets apart is the special paint. They're made of paper."

"That is right. The fastest way to deal with a ticket might be to fill a bucket with water and drench the assailant," Bond said.

Zem looked surprised. "Could they not have waterproofed the tickets? That feels like a major oversight."

"They could have, but..." Tiana thought for a moment. "These tickets don't make any sense. They have incredible effects despite not having any mana, but it seems like durability wasn't prioritized at all."

"Perhaps that is because they were hastily made?" Zem suggested.

"Maybe. I have no idea. Would someone capable of making these tickets cut corners on something so important?" Tiana said, collapsing on her bed in resignation.

"No... I know the reason," said Nick. "It's simple, actually. Making the tickets waterproof would change how they feel. They wouldn't pass for legitimate tickets when entering a venue."

"Your useless idol knowledge is actually coming in handy," Tiana teased.

"Shut up," Nick snapped.

"Well, I think we'll be able to handle ourselves protecting the idols. But..." Tiana looked at Nick with concern.

"What is it?" Nick asked.

"It's just... One of your former party members is suspected of being a demon-god worshipper, right? Are you going to have to catch him and turn him in?"

Nick shrugged. "Don't worry about that. I got kicked out of my last party 'cause he stole money and framed me for it. I'm not gonna waste any sympathy on him if it turns out he's a criminal."

"Oh yeah... I remember you telling us that. This guy's caused you a lot of trouble, huh?" Tiana gave Nick a sympathetic look.

"You've got that right... But I don't think Garos is the one selling the counterfeit tickets," he said.

"Do you have proof?" Tiana asked.

"He came to my apartment the other day, and he didn't show much interest when he saw how obsessed I am with idols. If he was selling counterfeit tickets, he would've seen me as a customer."

"You don't suspect him because he didn't try to sell one to you."

Tiana, Zem, and Bond looked relieved. Karan, however, was lost in thought.

"Did you realize something, Karan?" Nick asked.

"N-no, it's nothing," Karan responded, shaking her head. Her hesitancy was surprising, given her recent calmness.

"What's wrong? If you've realized something, anything, you should tell us," Nick urged.

"U-um, it might be unrelated, but... Is that okay?" she asked Nick shyly.

"Yeah, of course," Nick answered.

"Daffy is working really hard. It surprised me how invested she is in Diamond and the other idols' dance practice," Karan said.

"Man, I wish I could've seen that," Nick lamented. The others snickered.

"I am ignorant of idols and their music, but even I could see how impressive their training is," Zem said.

"Diamond changed her entire persona just by adjusting her posture in front of the mirror and finding the rhythm of each song... It felt like she was onstage even though there was no lighting or audience," Tiana agreed.

"It was as if the idols were truly minstrels," Bond said.

"Huh? That's 'cause idols *are* minstrels," Nick responded.

"Modern idols, yes. In ancient times, idols were people who used music and singing to fight. They combined mana with sound and visual effects to amplify spells. They could also place an audience into a trancelike state to gather mana from them and perform special ritual spells. It was a support job similar to shamans."

The others were stunned.

"Idols? Fighting? What, did they bring guitars to the battlefield?" Nick asked.

"The strings would break in no time," Tiana said.

"Singing in a labyrinth sounds like a terrible idea, too. You might as well shout 'Hey, monsters! I'm over here!'" Karan responded.

"Their music is certainly catchy, but I would rather enjoy it outside of work hours," Zem said.

Bond recoiled from their differing negative reactions. "What's cooler than taking a guitar into battle?! And yes, they actually did that! I saw fighting minstrels!"

Nick turned away awkwardly. He just couldn't believe him.

"Hey, you aren't taking me seriously! If you don't believe me, look me in the eye and say it!" Bond demanded.

"Okay, okay! We were talking about how Diamond is as amazing as ancient idols, right?!" Nick said.

"That's better," Bond huffed.

Karan spoke up timidly. "Um, that's not it... Sorry, I wasn't very clear. I wasn't just talking about the idols. Daffy is working really hard, too... So hard that it was weird."

"How so?" Nick asked, confused.

"Daffy has always liked dancing in front of others, but she never had any interest in teaching. It's more her personality to see someone like Diamond and get competitive. I don't think she's the type to give up dancing and commit to a teacher role," Karan continued.

"Maybe she had a change of heart after she retired from dancing?" Nick guessed.

"That's not all. She won't talk about Ares's father or anything else related to her family."

"Has it just not come up?"

Karan shook her head. "It feels like she's avoiding it. She won't talk about her personal life at all, even when I ask. But then she'll ask me if I'm eating properly and tell me I need to 'take the dragon by the horns' and gain experience outside of adventuring... Something's definitely off with her."

"It is weird that she won't talk about herself. We've already seen her kid," Nick agreed.

"I'm worried Daffy has gotten herself involved in something dangerous," Karan said.

"We could look into it, but we have never performed a background check... Labyrinth exploration and searching for people in the slums have become our specialties," Zem said with a shrug and a weak smile.

"Actually... There might be a way," Nick said.

Karan's tail twitched in response.

"I know someone who specializes in that kinda thing. I planned to meet with him to ask him about Garos. There's no guarantee he'll learn anything, but... Do you want to go with me, Karan?"

"Really?!" Karan asked.

"All right, I'm gonna borrow Karan for tomorrow. We're gonna gather information. Does that sound okay?" Nick asked the group.

Karan looked doubtful. "Are you sure you don't need my help for more than one day?"

"Hmm? Yeah, I'll be fine. It won't matter when we're meeting with an acquaintance, but once I start actually searching for the criminal, it'll be easier to act alone."

Karan didn't seem to approve. "I don't like the idea of you going off by yourself. I know I'm not one to talk, but you're always the one to rush headfirst into danger."

"That's right. You have a sharp eye, Karan," Tiana laughed.

Nick winced. "S-sorry. I won't do anything reckless."

"Really?" Karan asked.

"We need you at the concerts anyway. The idols seem to feel more comfortable with you around."

"That...is true. You're also Daffodil's cousin," Zem agreed reluctantly.

"I would be uncomfortable being the only physical fighter there," Bond said. He seemed unsure, too.

"...Fine. But Nick...," Karan began.

"Y-yeah?"

Karan looked Nick right in the eye. He flinched slightly under her silent gaze. She had always been brave on the battlefield and easily flustered over private matters, but her personality was steadily changing.

"If you run into any difficulty, don't just press on by yourself. Rely on us when you need to," Karan urged.

"...Got it," Nick said, half to himself. He was wondering if he truly would do as Karan said.

"Is visiting an inmate in prison your idea of a date?"

"Some people apparently attend trials on dates."

"It's in bad taste to enjoy someone else's life as entertainment."

"Says the fraudster."

A wicked laugh echoed in the dim room Nick and Karan had entered. They were visiting an inmate in the Sun Knight prison. Fortunately, it seemed like the knights working here hadn't heard about Nick from Alice, and they happily let him through after some coins changed hands.

"Nick. I don't want to give this guy sweets anymore. We

should give them to the knights instead," Karan said, upset at the inmate's teasing.

"Calm down, Karan," Nick responded.

"This is my second time here. Please don't tell me he's the adventurer who specializes in background checks," Karan said.

"He's not. There's just a few things I wanna check with him. This won't take long," Nick said.

Leon snickered. "Are you tired of comin' to me for help? You should follow your party member's example and learn to use all the resources available to you."

"I don't want your advice," Karan said, turning away in a huff.

That only amused Leon more. "This is a deal, missy. You fulfill my request, and I answer your questions. It's fifty-fifty. Let's put the past behind us," he said flippantly.

"The one in jail doesn't get to say that," Karan said, sighing, before reluctantly handing him the sweets. "These were made from a puree of boiled southern sweet potato mixed with butter, cow's milk, and sugar. You add dried fruits and berries and slowly bake it in an oven. The taste is good enough for high-class restaurants."

"Wow, that doesn't sound so bad... So whaddaya wanna ask me? You still havin' trouble with that rare magic item?" Leon asked.

"The Steppingman broke the phantom king orb. We collected all the fragments," Nick answered candidly.

Leon raised his eyebrows and went silent for a moment. "Wait, before we talk any more about this. A magic sword called the Butterfly Sword and a staff called the False Root Staff should've been stolen together with the phantom king orb. Did the Steppingman you guys were after not have them?"

"No... He didn't. Are they dangerous?" Nick asked.

"Yep. The Butterfly Sword has two bells, one attached to the blade and one to the scabbard. They're called the dream bell and the reality bell. You can use those to fool your opponent about the position or trajectory of the sword and perform an attack they can't see. You can also use sound and light to overwhelm their senses. The False Root Staff can be used to control magic creatures and golems. They're both just as nasty as the phantom king orb. Be careful of whoever has them," Leon warned.

"You're being strangely open with this information. We didn't even bring you the phantom king orb like you wanted." Nick was confused.

Leon snickered again. "You're not the type to lie about something like this. And even if I can't read you, the girl behind you is an open book. I'll acknowledge that you fulfilled your end of the bargain."

Karan looked offended, but then she quickly realized the emotion she was showing and tried to bury it. "I'm easy to read, am I?" she challenged.

"You just got angry and tried to hide it. You're not good at this," Leon said.

Karan seemed embarrassed and unsure of what Leon meant. "Huh? Are there ways to be good or bad at hiding your emotions?"

"Yep. One way to keep your anger from showing is to fantasize about ways to kill whoever's pissing you off. Or you can pretend to be weak and bait your opponent into a slip of the tongue. You have to find ways other than your facial expressions and body movements to vent your emotions. Try too hard to suppress them, and they'll escape in unexpected ways," Leon said.

Those words surprised Karan. She had been reprimanded many times and told not to let her emotions rule her, but no one had ever told her to find a way to vent them.

"Understand what I'm saying? You don't control your emotions by trying to hold them back. You do it by deciding how exactly you want to release them. That's more important for races like you and me that have ears and tails that can give us away," Leon continued.

Karan sensed something in his words, and she stared at him. "Why are you telling me this?"

"I told you, dragonian. We had a deal," Leon responded.

"...Okay," Karan said.

Nick, however, was getting fed up. "You're hardly in a position to give life advice, man."

"You can't live here without a little hypocrisy... Who was the Steppingman, by the way?" Leon asked.

"A former priest named Nargava. He was using a phantom king orb given to him by White Mask. White Mask killed him once he realized their intentions no longer aligned," Nick said.

"White Mask?! What happened with him?!" Leon yelled suddenly.

"We fought and defeated him. The person inside the armor fled, though," Nick answered.

"You defeated White Mask...? Unbelievable. Well, I guess your sword's ability would make it possible," Leon said, surprised.

Nick found his reaction curious. "Is White Mask that famous? Do you know his real identity?"

"Of course I don't. No one does," Leon said.

"You clearly know about him, though. Give us whatever details you have," Nick urged.

"Hmm... People call him the Southern Saint, but he seems much more like a pawn of the demon-god worshippers and an inhumane thief. He tends to target antique magic items."

"Antiques... Oh yeah, didn't you mention a major magic item broker last time?"

"White Mask is really only known for his strength and cruelty. The broker, on the other hand, is a powerful person who manages the distribution of goods. They support crooks like White Mask but never step out from behind the scenes themselves. I might have brought them up on a whim, but I don't know their intentions."

"Really..."

"But man, that's great news that you defeated White Mask.

You know how many adventurers he's killed who specialize in excavating ruins? Their comrades would cry tears of joy if they heard that." Leon noticed that Nick wasn't smiling at the praise and said, "What's with that face? That's a good thing."

"The Sun Knights are watching me now 'cause I upstaged them. Whoever wore White Mask's armor must hate me, too. And I think there's more than meets the eye with this job we just started," Nick replied.

"Really? Sounds interesting. Tell me about it."

Nick told Leon about their current situation, including how they were hired by an idol agency to work as bodyguards and that Nick would be arrested if he didn't capture the person selling the strange tickets before the Sun Knights. When he was finished, Leon clapped a hand over his mouth and laughed.

"Pfft... Heh-heh. The price of fame is high! Your life is so damn funny!" he said.

"Don't laugh. My life isn't for your entertainment. Do you have any idea who the counterfeit-ticket seller could be?" Nick asked.

"Antiques are my area of expertise. I'm sure you and your fellow idol groupies would know more than me."

"I guess that's true... Do you know anything about Garos?"

"Why the hell would you need to ask me that? You were his party member."

"You had to have looked into him, though, and from a different viewpoint than me or the Sun Knights. Don't you remember when you guys swindled me? There's no way you didn't consider the possibility of my party members trying to get revenge on you."

Leon grinned. "That's a good point... As far as I know, Garos is a typical Labyrinth City adventurer. He's reliable when it comes to monster extermination in labyrinths, but a total slob in his personal life. He spends all his time on gambling and women and never saves money."

"All true."

"What stood out was his unusual fighting skill... And how comfortable he was with killing. I saw him outside a bar once and got chills. Thought he was gonna kill the guy he was fighting."

"You saw Garos fighting?"

"Not just him. He was with everyone from Combat Masters but you." Leon pointed at Nick, as if warning him about an ominous monster in the depths of a labyrinth. "I didn't wanna make an enemy of everyone in Combat Masters. I considered telling Claudine to back off, but luckily you were kicked out of the party."

Nick was annoyed by Leon's frankness, but Leon was probably telling the truth. Making an enemy of Argus and all his former party members would place you in mortal danger.

"You're definitely not weak, Nick. With that holy sword, you have the strength of an S-rank adventurer. But that doesn't matter when it comes to takin' a life. You can easily make up for a lack of skill if you're prepared to kill," Leon continued.

"...I'm sure," Nick said.

"You're naive. If your old party member turns out to be a demon-god worshipper, kill him."

"Excuse me?"

"Listen up, man. Your life is in danger. You need to be ready to find the truth and kill your enemies. Watch out for your former party member. It's also possible the person behind this is someone you'd never suspect... That Diamond girl who hired you is pretty suspicious. So hold on to your doubt. If you become sure that someone is an enemy, don't waver. It's kill or be killed."

Leon wasn't provoking Nick or making fun of him. He meant what he said, and his voice carried the touch of sympathy a doctor used when speaking to a patient.

Karan watched Nick with concern.

Nick and Karan left the prison to find the sun shining brightly. Carriages traveled along the street, and mailmen rushed from one destination to the next. The prison was located behind a Sun Knight station, beyond which cafés and shops lined the street.

Nick thought melancholically about the difference between places where darkness gathered and light shone. One small misstep in life could leave you in the shadows before you could blink.

"It's such a peaceful day," Nick said after stopping and scanning the street. Leon's words turned in his head.

You're naive.

"You shouldn't worry about what he said," Karan told him.

"Yeah," Nick replied half-heartedly.

"No one hears that and actually stops worrying, though," Karan said.

Nick burst out laughing at her overly honest words. "You've got that right. It's not like we really solved anything."

"I'm bad at this. I never know what to say," Karan said unhappily, looking away.

Her innocent behavior was washing away the dark feelings that had settled in Nick's heart.

"It's been a while since you've made that face," he said.

"I came to accept that it's okay not to know everything. That there's no use growing flustered over not knowing what to do or say... But it's still frustrating when there's something I wish I understood," Karan said.

"What do you wish you understood?"

"Other people's feelings," Karan replied dejectedly.

Nick responded with a weak laugh. "I have trouble figuring that out, too."

"But I'm even worse. Everyone else is smarter than me. I don't think dumb people can understand how smart people feel."

"Once again, Karan, you're not an idiot." Nick tried to console her.

"I don't know..."

"Besides, even if you can't read a person's mind, you can try to figure out what they're feeling by watching them."

Just then, a houndian delivery boy sprinted past them. A human boy on a bicycle chased after him. They were both in their midteens and holding a bag full of mail.

"Wait, you idiot! I'm gonna pass out at this pace!" the boy on the bicycle yelled.

"Shut up! I'm not gonna lose to someone who needs wheels! Whoever finishes last has to buy the other dinner!" the houndian shouted back.

"You're on! I'm gonna win this time!" the boy on the bicycle declared.

After making a game of their job, the boys rushed to a postbox and deftly shoved their letters inside. The houndian boy was in the lead at first, but the boy on the bicycle began to catch up.

"H-huh?" the houndian boy shouted.

"You're too easy to read!" the human yelled.

The human was watching the houndian's tail. The twitches would point to which postbox the houndian was aiming for next, which the human boy used to race ahead and throw his letters in first. An old man on the side of the road yelled at them to put the letters in neatly, startling and scaring away a napping cat.

"Having beast ears or a tail is a disadvantage. It's going to take me a while to learn how to do what Leon said," Karan muttered after watching them.

"I'm jealous, personally. It looks easier to get your balance, and they're sensitive to sound and wind," Nick said.

"That's true," Karan said, patting her tail.

"Does it really move involuntarily?" Nick asked.

"I think so. I don't really notice it. I don't think I can stop my tail directly, so I need to control my emotions instead."

"That sounds hard," Nick racked his brain for advice, but he couldn't think of anything beyond the generic platitude that practice makes perfect. "It would be fair if humans had tails and big ears, too."

"It really would."

"Then what if you imagine that? Look at a person and think about how their tail would move if they had one."

"Huh?"

Karan's eyes widened in amazement at Nick's advice. She looked at the delivery boys racing down the street. She turned to the angry old man next, then the cat, and then Nick.

"Wh-what is it?" Nick stammered.

"I...wonder if everyone has moments when they think simple things or zone out and think nothing at all," Karan muttered, seemingly to herself. There was surprise on her face.

"I'm pretty sure everyone does that," Nick replied.

"The boy chasing the other one looks frustrated... But he's actually having fun," Karan said.

Nick nodded in agreement. "There you go. I'm jealous of how much energy those kids have."

"You sound like an old man." Karan burst out laughing.

"Hey, don't say that. That hurts," Nick complained.

"Then start acting younger," Karan giggled. "I'm...always getting distracted by weird or interesting things I see."

"Yeah, I can relate to that."

"I wonder if smart people are able to think things are interesting or weird without getting distracted."

"Probably."

"They also get frustrated when they lose, excited when they win, and annoyed by loud people, don't they?"

"Uh, yeah. I think that's a safe assumption." Nick was unsure where Karan was going with this.

"Huh," Karan said, her expression suddenly changing. She

looked refreshed, as if her confusion had been cleared away. "Let's get going, Nick. We're meeting with the adventurer who's good at investigating, right?"

Nick and Karan arrived at a brick building located near Anemone Alehouse. There was nothing vulgar about the place, but the inside was messy, as if the owner had no expectation of receiving guests. It was Nick and Karan's destination, Woods Credit Check Office.

"I know why you're here, but I don't have a clue where Callios from White Heron is, either," a man inside the office said without standing up. He looked around thirty years old and was wearing a battered white button-down.

"What?" Nick said. He and Karan were both startled. "What're you talking about, Hector?"

It was the man's turn to look surprised. "Huh? You haven't heard from Vilma? She gave me a job to find out the identity of a thief who masqueraded as an adventurer. I thought you must've gotten impatient and come here to pester me about it."

"No, this is the first I've heard of that... So Vilma went to you," Nick said.

"I've hit a brick wall, though. I know he was a magic item broker for connoisseurs, but I've got no records on him whatsoever. He's either a real big shot, or 'Callios' is a code name used by multiple people... Ah, whoops. You're Karan, right?" the man named Hector asked, scratching his head.

Karan cocked her head, apparently unoffended. "I don't care about learning the identity of one thief. I just want my dragon king gem back. Anyway, who are you and what is this place? I don't know what a credit check is."

Hector chuckled and finally stood. "The name's Hector Woods. I'm currently looking for your dragon king gem. I've seen no sign of it on the black market, so it's probably been stored somewhere."

Karan didn't seem bothered by that answer. She looked like she had already accepted it as inevitable.

"Okay. So what's a credit check?" she asked.

"Ah, it's just a formal way of saying detective work," Hector answered.

Karan's tail began to wag. The word *detective* must have caught her interest.

"Most of my work comes down to looking for missing persons and performing infidelity investigations. I also look into financial affairs and loans," Hector continued. Karan's tail stopped wagging, signaling her disappointment. "Ha-ha-ha, sorry if that's not as interesting."

"Oh, but if you're good at investigating people..." Karan trailed off, looking at Nick. She seemed to have realized why he brought her here.

"That's right. Hector specializes in background checks," Nick said.

He explained that Hector was originally a lesser noble in the capital and had a job compiling social registers, but he had to flee to Labyrinth City after a certain incident. Karan felt sorry for him until Hector elaborated—he was chased away after he had an affair with someone's wife.

"Nick saved me when I came to Labyrinth City and got mugged. I started helping him out with Combat Masters problems after that," Hector explained.

"I scratch his back; he scratches mine," Nick said, eliciting a glare from Hector.

"You should've shown yourself sooner if that's how you think of our relationship. I was worried about you when I heard you were kicked out of your party, then the next thing I know you're making a name for yourself in a new one. I wanted to hire you as a part-timer and push all my busywork on to you," Hector complained.

"Sorry, sorry. And that's too bad for you," Nick replied with a wry grin.

"You two seem close," Karan said, sounding a little bored.

"Whoops, sorry, miss. What did you two come here to discuss?" Hector asked after clearing his throat.

Nick put on his work face. "We have two matters. First, we're looking for someone who's selling counterfeit tickets to idol concerts," Nick said.

"Do you mean a scalper? I wouldn't know much about that. Want to make it an official request?" Hector asked.

"...No. I don't wanna put you in danger. The seller might be a demon-god worshipper," Nick said.

"Why would a demon-god worshipper sell idol concert tickets?" Hector wondered.

"I know it sounds weird. I've heard this is a real problem for rich people," Nick answered, smiling awkwardly.

Hector shook his head. "I'm not doubting you. I'm just genuinely curious. It's hard for outsiders to enter the underground marketplace for this kind of entertainment and make any money. Ticket prices change all the time, due to shifts in popularity. You hear of robberies and kidnappings for ransom, but selling something with such short-lived value is unusual."

"So selling these tickets wouldn't be worth it unless you were a fan," Nick said.

"It could be someone who loved idols so much that their feelings turned to resentment. The kind who gets overexcited at a show and gets banned for life or a girl who tried to become an idol but couldn't make it," Hector continued.

Nick thought back to the idol blacklist. "That makes sense... I hadn't considered that. Thanks."

"What's your other matter?" Hector asked.

"This one is an official request. I want you to look into a

dragonian dancer named Daffodil, Garos from Combat Masters, and the idol agency Jewelry Production," Nick said.

"Jewelry Production, huh…? Well, I suppose I would want to investigate them if I'm doing an entertainment-related job," Hector responded. His grim expression gave Nick a bad feeling.

"Don't tell me Jewelry Production is actually bad news. They're not involved with gangsters or demon-god worshippers, are they?" Nick asked.

Hector shook his head. "The opposite, actually. There are rumors the company is tied up with nobles—influential ones close to the lord of Labyrinth City."

"Are you serious?" Nick exclaimed.

Most nobles living in Labyrinth City did not own territory. Instead, they were nobles of the robe who gained their high-society status from administrative or judicial posts. Even so, the average citizen saw them as lofty rulers who could not be opposed.

"I'm not saying this based on definitive proof. But there are other idol agencies that clearly have the backing of an armed organization or gang, and Jewelry Production is the biggest idol agency of all. I wanna tread lightly with them," Hector said.

None of this was surprising for Nick to hear; at the very least, he got the feeling that Diamond and Joseph were not ordinary people.

"I won't pressure you to do anything dangerous. You can consider Jewelry Production an extra, inessential request," Nick said.

"Got it. What do you want me to focus on exactly?"

"Daffodil's background and behavior. And whether she has a connection to the demon-god worshippers."

Hector's eyes sharpened, his casual attitude quickly disappearing. "Garos is an adventurer, so I know what he looks like. I already told you how difficult Jewelry Production will be. I don't know who Daffodil is, though. Tell me about her," he said.

Nick didn't know what to say, but Karan answered for him. "Her full name is Daffodil Tsubaki. Nick said she's a dancer, but it seems like she's mainly working as a dance teacher and choreographer. She's twenty-eight years old and has a son named Ares."

"Did she get married and have her child in this city?" Hector asked.

"Probably. And I don't think she would have a kid without a husband," Karan answered.

Nick watched Karan, surprised by how smoothly she was answering his questions.

"Got it. I'll do a quick check," Hector said.

"Right now?" Karan asked.

"The full investigation will take time, but I can do a quick profile right now."

Hector got up from his chair and stood before a bookshelf, scratching his head. It was packed with rough binders containing newspaper and magazine clippings.

"What are those?" Karan asked.

"Watch this, miss. **Bibliosearch**," Hector said, casting a spell.

He released a dim light from his hands, which wrapped around the bookshelf. The bookshelf shook slightly, but nothing else happened. Karan frowned doubtfully, but Hector didn't falter.

"I got a hit," Hector muttered as one of the binders left the bookshelf and floated toward him, opening and turning pages in the air. He caught the binder and read. "She was in a D-rank adventurers' party called Terpsichora. I have an application here for their disbandment. The leader was Jack Codeau, and the other members were Daffodil Tsubaki and Jane Wyald... They disbanded because their leader was declared MIA after a labyrinth expedition. Their final labyrinth was Thousand Sword Peak."

It seemed to be information from a time when Daffodil

worked as an adventurer. The pages contained information about her party's history.

"He went missing in action, huh...? It would've been easier for them if he just died," Nick said with a mixed expression.

"Missing in action? Does that mean he's still alive?" Karan asked.

"Ancient ruins that have become labyrinths often contain traps that warp people down to the bottom floor or send them flying out of the labyrinth. When a companion is lost in such a manner, you report their status as MIA, which stands for missing in action," Nick explained.

"So he could be..." Karan trailed off.

"Barely anyone who goes MIA in a labyrinth comes back," Nick said coolly. Karan's face hardened. "A lot of adventurers report a party member as MIA because they don't want to acknowledge their death. The guild allows it, though once enough time passes they are treated as officially dead."

Karan looked down sadly, but she quickly recovered and asked another question. "Was that a spell, Nick? Can you use it to quickly search documents?"

"Yeah. It's a special spell used by civil officials and librarians," Nick answered.

"The spell itself is simple," Hector added. "Putting together the bookshelf is actually the hard part. You have to build and manage the bookshelf yourself for the spell to work."

"You compiled all this yourself?" Karan muttered, surveying all the binders with surprise.

"As you can see, though, these binders mostly contain stuff you could put in a scrapbook, like newspaper articles and Wanted posters. It's just public info, so nothing exhaustive. But it's really useful," Hector said with a smile.

"This guy's well-connected. He's able to get his hands on registers and account books that are inaccessible to most people. He

also receives newspapers from cafés that they were planning to throw out and cuts them up to put in his binders," Nick said.

"That's a valuable way of collecting information. Plus, this stuff is perfectly legal to view and copy if you have the qualifications and status. Using it for unintended purposes can land you in deep trouble, but...I'd appreciate it if you could pretend you never saw that part. Let's see here..." Hector turned the page. "Is this a victim report? It looks like she was a victim of fraud."

"What's it say?" Nick asked.

"The real estate agent she was working with when she was trying to open a classroom scammed her out of close to five million dina. She's running a dance classroom now, though, isn't she? She has to be getting money from somewhere," Hector said.

"Are you implying she might be in debt?" Nick asked.

Hector nodded. "I highly doubt she got her money back from the scammer, so it's possible. If she is borrowing money, we'll want to find out how much and whether the lender is reputable."

Nick was getting worried. This was a lot of information for Karan to take in at once, and she might storm out to question Daffodil about everything directly. That was more trouble than he wanted to deal with.

To his surprise, however, Karan remained calm and asked Hector a question. "Can you find out if anyone bad is following her?"

"Of course. I'm just getting started here; the meat of my job is after this," Hector answered.

"And you didn't see anything about a marriage or a family, did you?"

"It's possible she just didn't submit a marriage certificate. Some people see submitting paperwork as unnecessary because of the marriage customs of their clan. I'll look into that, too."

"Please," Karan said, not letting herself get flustered.

"I should tell you it's more than possible this could turn out to be nothing. It's far from unusual for a business owner to take out a loan. The fact that she overcame her troubles and is working hard is actually a sign she's doing well," Hector said.

"You're a surprisingly good guy," Karan responded.

"Right?" Nick agreed keenly.

"Hey, what do you mean by 'surprisingly?'"

"Don't worry about it," said Nick. "What about the other two?"

"There's too much information about Jewelry Production to really glean anything. Finding the necessary information will be a challenge. Give me time. So...I'll start with Garos."

Hector cast Bibliosearch again, but only one binder flew toward him, bringing up nothing but adventurer files. There was much less information on Garos than there was on Daffodil.

"What in the world? There's barely any info about him at all," Nick said with some relief.

Hector looked grim, however. "...That's strange."

"Is anything bothering you?" Nick asked.

"I know about Garos. You complained about his bad habits with booze and women all the time, and how he would take out advances from the party wallet before you received your rewards," Hector said.

"Yeah, I remember," Nick replied.

"A guy like him should be mentioned in more records. I'd expect to see that he got arrested by the Sun Knights after getting in a drunken fight or that he failed to return a loan and hurt his credit score. But I'm not getting anything like that."

"Is that really so surprising? I wouldn't even expect the crooks living in the Garbage Heap would show up in many documents."

"The people in the Garbage Heap don't emerge if anything happens to them. There's usually a decent amount of info on them from before they move there, though. Garos is mentioned in my database even less than the average Garbage Heap resident."

"It still doesn't seem that weird to me..."

"Has he paid you any sudden visits recently? Strike it rich out of nowhere?"

Nick laughed awkwardly, but then he noticed something— Hector was serious. He wasn't joking around or trying to scare him. "Listen up, Nick. There are two types of people who have no public records: those who never go outside because of a sickness or some other reason and those who excel at hiding and falsifying information," Hector said.

"I wouldn't expect Garos to fit in that latter camp... But he is cautious," Nick admitted.

"I'm disappointed I have so little info on him. I thought my records on adventurers were exhaustive."

"Getting no information still tells us something, though. You just explained how weird it is."

"That doesn't make it any less frustrating. I pride myself on having a perfect library... I need more data," Hector said.

The word *data* reminded Nick of something. "Oh yeah, I have something interesting. I'll lend it to you for you to read," he said, fishing through his pocket and pulling out an item.

"What's that...? Oh, it's a knowledge orb. What's in it?" Hector asked.

A knowledge orb was a gem with information from books and documents stored inside. This was the one containing past issues of *Lemuria Monthly* that Bond had given him.

"Past issues of an occult magazine," Nick answered.

"Why would you waste a knowledge orb like that? Do you have any idea how much these cost?" Hector sighed as he took the knowledge orb from Nick.

"I know it sounds crazy, but there might be some legit information in there. Analyze it when you have a chance," Nick requested.

"Eh, I guess I don't mind. Anyway, are you gonna be okay? If Garos is guilty of what he's being accused of, you'll probably end up fighting him. Didn't you say he's a skilled fighter?" Hector asked.

Leon's words resurfaced in Nick's head.

What stood out was his unusual fighting skill...and how comfortable he was with killing.

"...Yeah. I can vouch for his strength," Nick answered.

"This is a shady situation you've gotten mixed up in. Be careful," Hector said.

"You don't need to tell me twice." Nick suppressed a shudder.

The sun was setting when Nick and Karan left Hector's office. Streetlights were beginning to pop on, but the scarcity of lights around the detective office, the red sky, and the shadows cast by the surrounding buildings combined to create a strange, dark atmosphere in the immediate area.

It was still early for dinner, as was apparent from the amount of pedestrian traffic made up of people leaving work. Nick and Karan had been on their feet all day, however, and couldn't wait for restaurants to open at night, so they bought food at a stall and ate as they walked.

They were both carrying a grilled octolegs as a snack. It was made by covering the legs in a mixture of wheat flour and water, then grilling them. The food was beloved by everyone in Teran, from the rich to the poor.

"Man, if you dunk one of these in some soup and smother it in cheese, it's so damn good," Nick remarked.

"Isn't it? A stall on Hammer Alley pioneered that recently," Karan said.

"Ah, that's hot...," said Nick, gasping as he burned his mouth. Karan laughed at him.

Nick could tell that Karan was worried about him. She was being kind, but not in the simple way she was earlier when she was worried about what she should say; she knew she didn't need to say anything and was comfortable with that.

"You've matured a lot recently," Nick said, causing Karan to choke. "Wh-whoa, are you okay?"

"Th-that was your fault! Don't say things like that out of nowhere! Geez..." Karan swallowed the rest of the octolegs in her mouth and collected her breath. She then timidly asked Nick a question. "How have I matured?"

Nick looked away, too embarrassed to answer honestly. "Uhh... Well, Hector comes across as kinda shady, but you were able to remain calm and give him what he needed to know."

"Oh, that..." Karan sighed, sounding both disappointed and relieved.

"I really mean that. Can you not tell how much you've grown?" Nick asked.

Karan put a hand to her chin and thought. She spoke slowly when she realized how to respond. "You told me to imagine humans having tails and think about how they would move."

"Yeah, I did."

"So I followed your advice and tried it. I thought about how his beast ears and tail would move if he had them. Imagining that as I talked allowed me to put off my feelings for later."

"For later, huh...?"

"I thought that smart people, and cunning people like Leon, were totally different creatures than me. But...then I realized that everyone has things they want to do, things they don't want to do, and things they want to do but don't understand. Once I figured out that everyone has that in common—even people who are nothing like me—I became able to picture how humans' ears and tails would move. I was focusing all my attention on watching Hector's."

Karan's words sent a chill down Nick's back. He'd had a similar feeling at Pot Snake Cave—that Karan was breaking out of her shell. He wondered at the mystical moment when she would finally cast it away entirely; would she emerge as someone brilliant and promising or as someone strong and terrible?

"How did Hector's ears and tail move?" Nick asked.

"He had the tail of someone who was disappointed their hunt failed but didn't want anyone to know it. He was trying to keep it high but couldn't stop the tip from drooping," Karan answered.

"You're making him sound weirdly cute," Nick said, chuckling.

Karan wasn't trying to be funny, though, and she continued speaking. "I think...he felt a little embarrassed, too. You helped him in the past, right? He saw a chance to repay the favor, and when his search failed, he was hiding his disappointment."

"I dunno if Hector's that considerate of a person...," Nick said. *But I don't feel like she's that far off the mark.*

Karan might not have been right about every detail, but Nick thought it was likely that some unconscious part of Hector did feel guilty. He'd complained to Hector about Combat Masters a decent amount, and the literary-minded detective had always agreed with his feelings. It was probably true that Hector felt sympathy for Nick when he was kicked out of the party and thought about either offering help or trying to place him in his debt.

But then something unexpected happened—Nick formed a new party with surprising speed and resumed work as an adventurer.

"We'll have to make good use of him, then," Nick said.

"Yeah," Karan agreed.

"So, Karan. How's my tail...?" Nick trailed off, deciding that no good would come of asking that question. Would he be able to lead Karan if she saw his feelings of hesitation? His feelings didn't matter anyway; they knew what they had to do. Find the demon-god worshipper selling counterfeit tickets and catch them.

Shit, that's exactly what Leon was talking about. My softness will get me killed if my goal is to catch them, Nick thought.

He couldn't show mercy, even if the demon-god worshipper

turned out to be Garos. No, *especially* if they turned out to be Garos. All he needed was the resolve to do what needed to be done. If killing was his last resort, he wouldn't get the job done. He needed to be like steel and make killing the goal.

How much damage would it do if he made Karan anxious because she saw his lack of resolve?

Nick felt a wave of embarrassment and looked away from Karan. "Never mind. Let's go back to the inn and rest."

"Nick," Karan said.

"I said it's nothing," Nick answered without turning around.

"Hey! Nick!" Karan called out, grabbing his shoulders and pulling him back.

Nick stopped walking but didn't turn around. "Hey, what gives? That hurts."

"I've...always wanted to know what you're thinking," Karan said.

"It's not anything important. Let's go home," Nick repeated.

"I act like an awkward, clumsy fool around you all the time. Not even my parents have seen that side of me," Karan said.

"Where the hell is this coming from?"

Nick didn't hide his irritation, and Karan faltered for a moment. But she didn't stop talking. "I'm telling you that I have nothing left to be embarrassed about. I was tricked and left to die, and even then I thought it must have been some kind of joke. Who would be that stupid?"

"Come on, Karan! How many times do I have to say it?! You're not an idiot! Don't use that as an excuse to justify the things you can't do!" Nick shouted.

"Then look at me!" Karan shouted back.

"What do you want?!" Immediately, Nick regretted raising his voice. He calmed down, afraid he might have hurt her feelings. "Wait, huh?!"

But as soon as he relaxed, Karan reached out and grabbed his arm. She was imitating Nick's signature move, which he'd used to lock Nargava's arm joints.

"Hey… Amateurs shouldn't try joint locks! You'll break something!" he yelled.

"Then teach me how to do it!"

"Is this really the way to ask me?!"

"*Please* teach me!"

"Okay, okay! Let me go!"

Karan released Nick, and he cursed. He took a breath and lifted his head to find himself looking right into Karan's eyes. They were beautiful, reminding him at once of jewels and flames as they quivered before him.

"I have nothing left to hide. Nothing I'm scared of other people learning about me. Are you okay with learning other people's secrets but not sharing yours? Do you suddenly think of yourself as some kind of hero?" Karan accused.

"You're the one who's been pushing me to become a hero all this time," Nick shot back.

"I only meant you should become a hero if you have the opportunity. I'm not searching for a hero anymore anyway," Karan declared. She startled at her own admission, but then she met Nick's gaze again and continued. "You're not a hero. You're just a regular person."

"…That's right. I'm just one fragile man."

"Yeah. You taught me how to lie. How to see through a lie, too. You even taught me how to cover it up when you get stubborn and make a mistake. You're a dishonest person who can't do anything on his own. You and everyone else."

"So?"

"Say something."

"Say what?"

"I don't know. I have no idea what you're thinking or hiding. Share something with me."

Nick's instinct was to tell her to back off, but he couldn't say it. Her eyes scared him as she stared straight into his.

"You always keep your worries inside. You try to do everything by yourself, even when Tiana gets mad at you and I tell you not to charge ahead alone. I was wondering why you do that. So I wasn't trying to act mature just now. I was thinking about how I want to know more about you," Karan said.

Nick had a realization at that moment.

"I don't want you to just lead me around by the hand all the time. I want us to be true partners," Karan continued.

He knew that Garos, Leon, Nargava, and all the other liars he had met wouldn't have been able to withstand those all-seeing eyes Karan was giving him.

Nick also realized he was at a fork in the road. There was a line on this dark and shabby street where they were standing right now, snacks in hand beneath an evening sky changing from blue to red. If he crossed that line, there was no going back.

The road to becoming a true liar was so tempting. He could ignore the things he didn't want to see or excuse his way out of dealing with any kind of undesirable situation by saying he simply didn't notice it, that it wasn't his problem. If he put all the skills he'd cultivated to use, he could race off into the night and continue turning a blind eye to his own pitiful flaws.

"...I know I've always talked a big game with you. But that doesn't mean I'm gonna share everything. There are things I don't want to share, specifically because of our friendship," Nick said.

"How could I have known that?! Actually, I've known that for a while!" Karan responded.

Like Karan said, Nick had no right to act this way after all he'd said to the party. He'd never had any qualms in the past about setting aside his pretensions and showing them the most pitiful sides of himself.

"I figured... I think everyone's the same way," Nick said. "We

all have something we try to keep to ourselves, no matter how obvious it is to others. Even if our secret's exposed, we keep lying and pretending we're doing just fine. We even take pride in our ability to get by with lies. Life is easier that way."

"I don't want you to become that kind of person, Nick. I don't want you to be like Leon and Nargava. The only reason I didn't turn out like them is because of you," Karan said. Her fiery eyes welled up, and the tears finally spilled down her face.

"Don't cry, you dummy. It's not worth that," Nick said.

"Don't call me a dummy. You're always getting mad at me for calling myself stupid," Karan complained.

Nick hugged Karan. It was a little too rough to be a lover's embrace, yet too gentle for simply consoling a friend. That was how things often felt between them.

"I only call you a dummy when you do something reckless or when you cry. But I would never call you that for not knowing something. Everyone grows smarter over time as they become aware of the things they don't know," Nick said.

"So you're making fun of me. You must think I'm a fool who knows nothing of the world," Karan responded.

"I wouldn't expect you to stick by someone who makes fun of you without realizing their own stupidity," Nick said.

"You're right about that," Karan agreed.

"Okay. I was acting like an idiot," Nick admitted.

Karan wiped her damp eyes, and Nick quietly comforted her until she was done crying.

"Listen up, Nick. Make sure to sharpen your knife yourself. Don't just perform the minimum upkeep and leave the rest to a craftsman. Customize your grip, too. Keep it in perfect condition and sleep with it at your bedside."

"Be just as cautious of people as you are of monsters. Some people pose as adventurers and attack others in labyrinths. It's real *easy to kill and erase all evidence that way. Take much better care than you would on the highway to remove all traces of any bonfires you make."*

"Lend me some money."

"When you enter a bar, be wary of anyone stationed in a spot where they can see every seat. That goes double if they're alone and not drinking."

"If you're alone in a street fight, knock them over and get on top of them. If multiple people attack you at once, do your best to fight them off and try to get away. Wait as long as you can to draw your blade. You wanna make them think they can't beat you even when you're barehanded."

"Never push yourself too far in a fight. Avoid fightin' at all if there's no one to mediate. If you've got no choice, make sure you give 'em a drubbin' they won't forget. You should consider killin' 'em, too. Wanna know how to hide a corpse? ...That was a joke, dummy. Of course I don't know how to do that."

"Hell yeah, I caught a camel bird! The fat in the hump is delicious."

"I'm gonna return your money, bud. I know everyone says that, though. I'll figure it out once we get our next reward. Don't sweat it."

"Come on, Nick! I need money! Please? Think of all I've taught you."

Nick and Karan found a bench in a nearby park, finished eating their now-cold grilled octolegs, and started to talk once they had calmed down. Nick was telling Karan about Garos. There were a lot of good memories and even more bad ones. Karan listened calmly at first, but she was slowly losing patience as he spoke.

"...Anyway, he was the first one to look after me after Argus brought me into Combat Masters. Once I gained some skills and made myself useful, though, he started to ask me for money and force me to accompany him to bars. I had to take care of him, more than the other way around... And in the end, he framed me and got me kicked out," Nick said.

"That's terrible," Karan responded.

"You've got that right... But he brought me money and apologized. Hector warned me about Garos suddenly finding money or coming to see me, and he's already done both," Nick said.

Karan's anger turned to surprise. "...Yeah, he did say that."

"His visit scared me. I didn't know what he was doing there. His money could've come from anywhere, so I'm hesitant to use it," Nick said, looking tired. He didn't actually feel as much fear as he said he did, though.

"Nick... Do you respect him?" Karan asked.

"He's a scumbag who spends too much on booze and women, but in terms of pure skill, he's one of the best. He can cut through steel and avoid detection by monsters. I can't think of a better bodyguard." Nick wasn't really answering the question.

"It's hard to believe a drunk could be good at working as a bodyguard," Karan said.

"One of Garos's special skills is being able to vomit on command. If he was ever wasted when we received an emergency job, he could just throw up and be good to go. He could use that trick to save himself if he ingested monster poison, too. He's strong without having to rely on weird magic items or drugs. His instincts are better than beastmen's, too, so he can't be caught off guard," Nick continued.

Karan gulped. She could feel the praise and fear in his voice. "Do you think he's the demon-god worshipper selling counterfeit tickets?"

"I dunno. But he's definitely up to something."

Garos had visited Nick from out of nowhere with a large bag of money in hand. Combat Masters took a break at almost the exact same time the Survivors defeated White Mask. Alice, Leon, and Hector all warned him about Garos in different ways. It was all too much to be a coincidence. Garos was clearly involved in this case.

"I think I know why he's so good at bodyguard jobs. It's because he knows how killers think," Nick continued.

"You don't have to fight Garos if we encounter him," Karan said.

"Don't even try that. Garos wields his sword to kill people, not monsters. He'll kill you."

At least, he would if she didn't have the resolve to kill him. Nick didn't want to force the weight of taking a life onto Karan.

But Karan smiled his warning away. "But you're not alone, Nick. We accepted this job as a party. We can team up and kick his butt together."

"I suddenly feel bad for the guy," Nick said, bursting out laughing. She was so nonchalant about it.

Karan didn't join the laughter. Instead, her expression hardened. "Don't. There's no way he'll play fair when he attacks. Besides, don't get the wrong idea, Nick."

"Huh?"

"Fighting Garos is not what this is all about. We were hired to protect the idols and catch the counterfeit-ticket seller. No good will come of you getting worked up over this."

Nick winced. He was embarrassed; Karan's words made him realize he had become entirely focused on Garos.

"I feel like I understand what Tiana was saying. You can be a real airhead sometimes." Karan sighed with open exasperation.

"Excuse me?!" Nick exclaimed. He was shocked to hear that from Karan.

"There's no guarantee that everything you're afraid of will come true. Even if it does, you don't have to fight alone. The enemy is a demon-god worshipper who's stealing magic items and selling fake tickets. There's no way they'll fight fair. Do you disagree?" Karan asked.

"No... You're probably right," Nick relented.

"It's fine if you really want to resolve this yourself. But you'd better not leave us out because you don't want to get us involved. We're all doing the job we signed up for. You already abused your authority when you begged Vilma to give us this job," Karan said.

"S-sorry about that..."

"And don't make me keep telling you to confide in us."

This was the first time Karan had ever scolded Nick like this. He was embarrassed by it, but a part of him felt happy, too.

"I'll back you up if it comes to a fight. Ask Tiana and Bond if you need their knowledge, and rely on Zem if you need to win someone over. You formed the Survivors because you knew there were things you couldn't do on your own," Karan finished.

Nick couldn't argue with anything Karan said. But rather than frustration, he felt pride. Karan had become an outstanding adventurer.

"Well, damn. I've been in the wrong. I'll tell you everything," he said, resigning himself. He had no choice but to face the true feelings he had been keeping even from himself. That he was afraid.

"I...think I'm scared of fighting Garos," Nick admitted.

"Okay," Karan said.

"I don't want to have to try to kill a former party member. I think I'd have a seventy-to-eighty-percent chance of dying." He clasped his hands together.

The ridiculous speed of Garos's blade was still seared into his memory. He stood little chance of defeating Garos; it was much more likely his own head would be separated from his shoulders. If he did happen to win, he'd be rewarded with the dead body of a former party member. The only outcomes awaiting him were painful ones, and the idea filled him with fear and dread.

"I think anyone would feel the same way... There's no way to fight a former comrade to the death without forgetting about all the good times you had. I don't want you to become so broken that you can do that," Karan said quietly.

Nick had actually felt that he wouldn't be able to survive and protect his friends without sacrificing, like Leon or Nargava had. But Karan was showing him that wasn't the case. As an adventurer who had been through one of the darkest experiences imaginable without letting it corrupt her, she was living proof of that. He could see that true strength was the ability to recover when the world threatened to break you or send you into despair.

Nick suddenly felt his shoulders relax.

"...I'm gonna start going after the counterfeit-ticket seller tomorrow," Nick said.

"Will you be okay?" Karan asked with concern.

Nick let himself be more vulnerable than he otherwise would have. "I'm planning on asking my idol friends about the counterfeit tickets, but there's a chance one of them could be involved with the seller. I'll try to act casual so they don't know I'm performing an investigation. If a fight breaks out and things get dangerous, come help me out."

"You just can't stay out of trouble, can you, Nick?" Karan teased.

"Hey, I'm being serious. I'll help you if you find yourself in a crisis, too," Nick said.

"...Okay. I'll hold you to that." Karan gave a shrug and a laugh.

"I know I have you to watch my back. Whether we're together or working apart, that doesn't change," Nick said, looking Karan right in the eye. The darkness of night only emphasized the bright and honest beauty of her eyes, and he didn't look away.

The identity of the counterfeit-ticket seller was a mystery. Jewelry Production had given up searching, and the Order of the Sun Knights had yet to discover anything.

With Hector's advice in mind, Nick was beginning to grasp

the reason for that: It was because the buyers were all keeping their mouths shut. They weren't just staying quiet because they felt guilty but also because they felt a camaraderie with the seller and wanted to keep their secrets. He also figured the seller was being very careful to only sell to idol fans. The only people who could do that had to know how idol fans thought and how to pick them out of a crowd.

Nick had that ability, too. He also had friends who were just as capable and might be able to find the counterfeit-ticket seller.

"You can't tell anyone that I'm giving you this information. As a lover of idols, this seller offends me to my core, but I'm scared of them targeting me. I'm helping you because I owe you more than one favor. Please be careful. I mean that in all seriousness."

"I know, I know. Don't tell anyone the agency hired me, either."

But there was one problem—Nick was a traitor.

He had taken a job that involved speaking to idols directly and seeing them backstage. From an idol fan's perspective, that was a traitorous action. Nick had initially planned to gather information while not revealing that secret to anyone, but his conversation with Karan made him realize there was only so much he could do alone.

Actually, once he sat down and thought about it, he realized that finding the seller without giving himself away would've been impossible. The other idol fans definitely would have grown suspicious of his questioning. They were always quick to realize when one idol of their number was trying to get a leg up on the other in terms of information.

"I understand. I'm so ridiculously jealous, though. You have no idea!"

"I'm truly sorry."

After that realization, Nick turned to his friend Jonathan and shared many details about the case to get him on their side. He told him that they were hired by Jewelry Production to manage security, that idol fans were being brainwashed by strange counterfeit tickets, that the Sun Knights were watching him for some reason, and more. He kept his friendly relationship with Agate a secret, however.

Jonathan's expression was mixed when Nick finished. Actually, he was straight up angry. But Nick had saved him in the past when Claudine very nearly swindled him out of a significant amount of money. After much consternation, he decided to assist with the search for the counterfeit-ticket seller in exchange for the promise that Nick would get him a signed card from an idol.

"So you think they'll show up at the west ticket agency," Nick said.

"Yeah, I'm sure of it. That's where he's targeting idol fans who failed to buy a ticket," Jonathan answered.

Jonathan hadn't agreed to help on an empty promise. He was from a merchant's family and was on the wealthy end of the idol fan spectrum. The seller had contacted him before, and he had a good idea of when and where they would appear. He led Nick to the ticket agency in western Labyrinth City to lure them out.

"If you complain at this agency about not being able to get a ticket and leave without anyone with you, the seller will approach you," Jonathan said. "Even if he doesn't show up today, I'm sure he will after a few days."

"Do we have to wear these clothes, though?" Nick asked.

They were both wearing the uniform of a magic school in Labyrinth City. The loose, brand-new robes didn't have a single crease, and anyone who saw them would think they were apprentice mages.

"You're too muscular, Nick. He'd know you're an adventurer right away," Jonathan replied.

"Ah, they'll realize I'm a professional."

"That's not the problem. He'll assume you don't have any money."

Geez, he doesn't hold back, Nick thought, but he followed behind Jonathan without argument.

"Like we agreed, I'll be a magic school underclassman, and you'll be my supportive upperclassman. We don't want any idol fans to see us, so put up your collar and wear your hat," Jonathan insisted.

Nick ignored his tone and performed a final check on his appearance. "Got it. Let's do it, my underclassman."

Nick and Jonathan entered the ticket agency. This wasn't the branch that Nick visited regularly; instead, it was primarily used by nobles, merchants, and other members of high society. It also sold tickets for cultural events such as operas and theater productions.

While Nick looked around with interest, Jonathan lashed out at the employee behind the register.

"What?! You're out of tickets?!" he cried.

"As I said, the purchase period is over," the employee said.

"Are there really no available seats at Pazzy's concert?! What about canceled tickets?!"

"I am sorry, but—"

"That's impossible! You *must* have leftover tickets from people who canceled!"

"Once again, we don't have any! Reserved tickets that are canceled are put into a lottery! We won't know anything about that until we hear from management!"

Jonathan continued to harangue the employee as persistently as he could. It was an excellent performance of a fan who couldn't accept his tickets being sold out.

"H-hey... Calm down, Jonathan," Nick said, half acting and half serious.

"It's not my fault! I wanted to sneak out at night and line up for a ticket, but the superintendent at my dorm was keeping watch, and I can't afford to fail any classes," Jonathan complained.

"Forget about it, man. You don't wanna have to repeat a year 'cause you got too obsessed with idols. That would just be embarrassing," Nick said, soothing Jonathan and apologizing to the employee with a look and a quick bow of his head. The employee responded with an exasperated glance but seemed mostly used to this.

They left the ticket agency, Nick pushing Jonathan from behind. Jonathan played the part of being frustrated, but once they moved far enough away, his expression turned serious.

"A scalper has infiltrated the ticket booth. That employee is probably an accomplice," he said.

"Are they selling the tickets illegally?" Nick asked.

"I doubt they're putting unsold tickets on the black market, but they're probably leaking information on canceled tickets and customers. The scalper appears when customers plead at the ticket window like I just did."

"Do you think he'll bite?"

"Probably. But he won't approach me if we're together, so we need to split up."

"Yell if you need help," Nick said quietly before raising his voice for another performance. "Give up already, man. Let's hang out somewhere, then get back to campus. Oh, how about that café? The waitresses are really hot."

"Go back without me! I'm not going to go around *flirting*; I've devoted my life to idols!" Jonathan yelled back.

"Tch, fine then, weirdo. Make sure you get back before curfew," Nick said with an exaggerated shrug. He split up with Jonathan and walked to the café. He pretended to relax as he scanned the crowd for anyone following his friend.

"I'll have a coffee," Nick called to a staff member." I'd like it to go."

"Are you free, young man? Sounds like you had an ugly split with your friend," an amorous waitress asked Nick. She was a houndian, and her sharp ears must have picked up on the performance. "I'm so bored. I've been getting no customers today. Do you want to have some fun?"

"Ah-ha-ha! You're beautiful *and* a flatterer! You shouldn't tease kids like me, ma'am," Nick said, trying to laugh her off, but that only seemed to make the waitress like him more. She stepped toward him and smiled suggestively.

"I like kids. Do you hate adults?" she asked.

The woman softly traced an index finger from Nick's chest to his chin. His eyes darted around for some way to escape, and from the corner of his vision, he noticed Jonathan being led into a back alley by a suspicious man.

"S-sorry, miss. I'm worried about my friend," he stammered.

"Ah... I see that man around here sometimes. He really is suspicious. I wonder if he's some kind of gangster. If he starts trouble, get your friend and bring him here. I'll give him shelter," the waitress said.

"Thanks! I might take you up on that!" Nick called back.

He slapped money on the table to pay for the coffee and dashed after Jonathan. Fortunately, he didn't lose sight of them and was able to catch up. The man was wearing what looked like a black mage's robe with the hood up, and it was difficult to see his face.

"Would you be willing to take less for this seat? And this *is* a legitimate ticket, right?" Jonathan asked.

"I won't force you to buy it. I have other customers," the man responded.

"Huh? W-w-wait, I never said I wouldn't buy it..."

He's a natural actor, Nick thought, impressed by Jonathan. He was skillfully extending the conversation while acting like a stingy idol fan.

"O-okay, fine. I'll buy it... This investment is more than worth it for Pazzy!" Jonathan declared.

"Hmm? Are you a Topaz stan? I thought Amber was your fave," the man commented.

"W-well, there are a lot of people who support Amby, Aggie, and Pazzy as a group. Some people even throw in Diamond."

"...I guess that's true. Whatever. Agate's new song was sensational. I want the three of them to sing it together."

"I would die for that."

Nick was surprised by how talkative the man was. He seemed like someone whose hobby had grown until he found a way to make money off it. His customers became accomplices to his wrongdoing, and they didn't want to betray him, because they thought of him as one of them.

Nick couldn't tell if that was by design or if his love for idols was genuine.

"By the way, I have a tip for you. Have you heard the rumor about counterfeit tickets?" the man asked.

"I have, but... These aren't fake, are they?" Jonathan asked.

The ticket seller grinned, his mouth barely visible under his hood. "If you doubt me, hold the ticket tight and pray. If your love for idols is true, you will receive the strength of the paladin. That is proof that it is legitimate."

"The paladin? Do you mean the one that saved Agate?"

"Ha-ha-ha... You'll have to find out for yourself."

The man gave Jonathan his ticket without incident. Nick breathed a sigh of relief as he watched from the shadows.

Jonathan intentionally avoided Nick as he left the alley and grabbed a carriage to go home. The rest was up to Nick. He took off his robe and hat so that the rustling of his clothes wouldn't give him away, then entered the back alley to follow the seller. Nick didn't have much experience with tailing people. He did, however, know how to avoid detection in labyrinths by beasts and monsters with stronger senses than humans.

He was currently light as a feather, using Light Body to mute the sound of his footsteps. Not only did the counterfeit-ticket seller he was following not notice him, neither did the people who habitually gathered in the back alleys. He was like a ghost floating by without a physical presence in this world.

Back alleys were places of ambiguity. They lacked the light of the main streets, but they didn't have the decadence of the Garbage Heap, either. They were a zone where beasts maintained the reason to continue wearing their human skin. That final flicker of light before a person fell into total darkness either warped them or returned them to sanity. The back alleys were a crossroads where people were either tempted into deeper darkness or returned to the light of the city.

Nick continued to quietly follow the man. He wondered if he was Garos. He knew darkness awaited him, and he tried to keep the animosity down.

Eventually, the man dropped a strange piece of paper, and that was when Nick started having trouble keeping track of him. The more Nick tried to concentrate on him, the more difficult it became.

Crap, is he using a phantom king orb? Or is it another kind of illusion spell?

One way to break an illusion was to say the person's name. The technique strengthened your conviction about their identity, but it only worked if you got it right.

Nick asked himself if the man was Garos. Karan's words answered him—that there was no guarantee that everything he was afraid of would come true.

If he's not Garos, who is he?

Nick considered that as he carefully picked up the piece of paper the man had dropped. He was afraid the man might get away as he picked it up, or that the piece of paper was a trap and the man would attack him, but he pushed that fear aside.

It was likely a talisman, but the design was atypical. It somewhat resembled the design that was barely visible on the darkened counterfeit ticket. The paper was a useful clue, but it wouldn't help him figure out whether the man was Garos.

Or maybe it would. The counterfeit-ticket seller might have been a person who couldn't cover their tracks without relying on this kind of trick. Garos would have noticed he was being tailed with his own senses and shaken off his pursuer without leaving a trace.

After some thought, Nick decided to take a chance.

"Your name is Eishu," he muttered.

That was the name of one of the blacklisted idol fans and one of Garos's old companions. Eishu had been drawing and selling moving portraits of idols without permission and sending cursed fan letters that spoke when touched. He used to make talismans in the army but had become a wanted criminal in Labyrinth City.

He was definitely capable of making the strange counterfeit tickets, he was obsessed with idols, and he was connected to Garos. Nick said the name with confidence that there wasn't a better suspect, and the man's fading shape solidified.

Nick's suspicions about the paper were correct—it was a talisman that cast an illusion spell. It seemed to have a similar effect as a phantom king orb, though not as strong. He was both excited and nervous from successfully dispelling the illusion. He was growing steadily closer to the truth and to danger.

He continued to follow the black-robed man, who kept walking for about ten more minutes before suddenly stopping. Nick was afraid the man had noticed him, but fortunately, he hadn't.

"Yo. How's business?"

"...What do you want, Garos?"

An insouciant and familiar man emerged from within an alley. Nick was simultaneously shocked to see him and not surprised at all.

The man in the robes relaxed and lowered his hood, revealing a face that looked identical to the sketch on the blacklist. He had a writing brush and ink bottle at his hip instead of a sword. Sure enough, the man was Eishu.

"What has your panties in a twist? Didn't make the sale?" Garos asked.

"No. You and I had no plans to meet up," Eishu responded.

"Aww. Is that any way to treat a coworker?"

"I have to be careful. My face is compromised."

"I swear, you're way too careless to be a shadowy demon-god worshipper," Garos said with a snicker.

Eishu shrank back, as if something was making his skin crawl.

Nick thought the same thing as Garos as he watched the two of them. Eishu was much more careless than he had expected. Why would a person who had been fleeing from the Sun Knights for an extended period of time allow himself to become a wanted criminal with a large bounty on his head? Why was Nick able to trail him? He quickly received the answer to those questions.

"That's only because you took away my phantom king orb! I'm doing the best I can with my makeshift talismans!" Eishu responded angrily.

"I never felt this way, but he always hated you. Said you were too hooked on those girls' songs to even pretend to have a chivalrous bone in your body, or something like that. Well, that aside, it was our employer's decision. I was powerless to oppose," Garos said.

"But wasn't it broken in the end? You're as good as naked," Eishu responded.

It was all starting to make sense. Nick knew why Eishu had ended up on the idol blacklist and become a wanted criminal, even though the demon-god worshippers had shown no trace of themselves until now. It was because they had been using the phantom king orb to hide. The Survivors had robbed them of that tool when they defeated White Mask—or more specifically, destroyed his holy armor. Eishu never would have let himself be discovered if not for the showdown with Nargava.

"Back in the day, you never woulda been stupid enough to leave evidence and get a bounty on your head, Eishu, even without a toy like that. This hobby has robbed you of all sense." Garos sighed.

Eishu answered with an unsettling smile. "You wouldn't understand. Idols give light to those who must remain in the dark."

"Then why the hell're you harassing them, you dumbass? You were tasked with testin' the talismans and seein' if our client's hypothesis is correct, not makin' money and messin' with concerts. Your ancestors would weep if they saw how you're usin' the skills they passed down for talismans and woodcutting. Have you forgotten that you're a wanted criminal now?"

"I won't let bounty hunters or knights get the best of me. The idols will prove equally as strong. They will not let my obstruction break them. They will overcome this trial I am giving them and ascend to greater heights. There is nothing I want to see more."

"Oh, for the love of... You're being followed right now, you dimwit," Garos said. There was a malicious aura around him now.

Nick didn't know if Garos had discovered him or if he was about to kill Eishu, but it was time to get out of there. Just as he started to run, however, someone appeared behind him. The person jumped over Nick with incredible speed and landed right in the middle of the argument.

"This is over, Eishu and Garos!" the person yelled.

"Alice?!" Nick exclaimed.

Alice swung her sword forcefully to split up Eishu and Garos. Not willing to let her upstage him, Nick drew his dagger and slashed at Garos.

"A Sun Knight...and Nick?!" Garos shouted with astonishment as he blocked Nick's dagger. "When did you team up with the Sun Knights?!"

"This is a coincidence!" Nick yelled back, drawing close to

Garos. Facing this man with his blade drawn was terrifying, but he was ready. He was neither trapped by fear of killing him nor hardened completely with deadly resolve. The desire to learn the truth was all the motivation he needed to face him.

"You take care of him, Nick," Alice said.

"I'm not working for you," Nick responded, but a melee suited him. He stood a better chance in a chaotic fight in which flukes could happen than in a contest of proper swordsmanship.

"Who's your employer, Garos? Are they a demon-god worshipper?" Nick asked.

"Heh, I ain't tellin' you about my client," Garos answered.

"That's basically a yes! That makes you and Eishu demon-god worshippers, too!" Nick yelled, holding his dagger with a backhand grip and performing a compact strike.

Garos avoided it with incredible swordsmanship, smiling wickedly. "You've improved, but you're still not good enough."

"What's that technique you're using? You're either physically teleporting your katana or using illusion magic. When you visited my apartment, you made it look like I knocked your katana into the hallway when it was actually by your side the whole time."

"...Good eye. I'm surprised you're not rushing to finish me right away. You always had a short fuse."

"I've got no reason to stick around and die here. It's more important that I return with my eyewitness account that you're a demon-god worshipper. Time is on my side."

That was a lie. Nick actually had to catch Garos before Alice. He was pretending to be at ease, though, which he couldn't have done without a certain level of preexisting calm.

"Too bad for me... You've grown, Nick," Garos praised as he swung his katana up at Nick's chin. Nick kicked off the ground and wall and barely avoided it.

"Eishu's not White Mask. You are. Was the holy armor completely destroyed?" Nick asked.

"See if you can figure it out. Study the feel of my hands, my breathing, and my mana waves. That'll give you the truth even if I don't answer," Garos said.

Nick threw a punch, and Garos sneered and countered. Neither attack landed. Even so, they were steadily pushing their fight toward its conclusion, as if advancing pieces on a game board or solving a formula.

"You can tell if a person's lying by their breathing," Nick said.

"That's right. You know more than I thought," Garos replied.

"Once you know a person's breathing, you know their rhythm. And grasping their rhythm will let you feel their emotions. There's no doubt about it. You're White Mask. Your back and stomach are still injured."

"You should never hesitate to target a wound or a weakness. But if you focus on it too much, you'll get predictable."

"Why is Eishu selling counterfeit tickets?"

"'Cause he's obsessed with idols. Seems he's tryin' to support them by givin' them some trial to overcome. Are all idol weirdos that way?"

"Some do get carried away, but you can't manifest that by using deceptive talismans to attack them. That's just nuts. Why is he sending fans into a frenzy and giving them power anyway? Does he think he's some kind of ancient shaman? Those went out of style centuries ago."

"Oh, you know that part, too… Guess there's no reason to keep my mouth shut. Well deduced. A shaman can produce a boatload of mana by putting themselves or their followers into a trancelike state. What about you, eh? What's your game?"

"What are you talking about?"

"Huh? …Whoops, I said too much."

"What?"

Just then, Garos's breathing and rhythm shifted. He regained his focus slightly faster than Nick and slashed his katana at his neck. Nick forced himself back and dodged it by a millimeter, but Garos kicked his shins with such weight, it felt like an iron club.

"Ngh...!" Nick grunted as the blow knocked him off his feet and sent him flying backward. Garos's attack was even swifter and more brutal than when Olivia had knocked him out of the office building. He twisted his body as hard as he could to avoid crashing back-first into the brick corner of an abandoned house and landed gracefully.

"Crap... You can use Stepping," Nick cursed.

"You've gotten much better at tailing people, but you don't stand a chance against me in close combat." Garos smirked.

He didn't just use Stepping for movement. He could switch between Light Body and Heavy Body in a tenth of a second to control the subtleties of a fight and increase the speed of his attacks, or even apply the two spells to individual body parts including his arms, shoulders, back, and legs to produce a flow of strength and an abnormal speed that wasn't possible with muscle alone.

Nick knew just how complete Garos's skill was as he scrambled for distance.

"Tch!"

Nick normally fought by threatening his opponent with his dagger and pressing them with his martial arts skill and joint locks. That strategy worked against Nargava. Unfortunately, Garos knew Nick's signature moves. Nick had learned many of them *from* Garos, and his former comrade's skill at each surpassed his own. He had planned to make up for that by using Stepping, but it turned out Garos was proficient at that as well.

"Here's a tip for you, Nick. Don't leap around like a grasshopper against a superior opponent. If they catch you while you're in the air, you're finished. I'm bad at jumping but good at crossing blades," Garos said.

"You think you know everything, do you?!" Nick yelled back.

"All right, playtime is over... Try and dodge this."

Garos stepped back and sheathed his katana. He was about to perform his signature move—a draw slash. Nick had seen him sever steel-like monster shells using the deadly force with which he could whip his katana out of its sheath. But he was more than familiar with the extremely fast attack, and given that Garos wasn't disguising it at all, he knew he could dodge it. He had even figured out how Garos was able to manage such speed.

Despite Nick's confidence, however, a chill ran down his back. He heard an eerie ringing that seemed to be coming from vibrating air. Garos's katana was likely the source or, more specifically, a strange metal ball attached to its sheath. There was a straight gash cut into the ball, and it rattled with a hollow sound as it swayed back and forth. When magical light began to spill out of it, Nick could sense it about to explode in a torrent of power.

"Shit! He's about to do something! Run!" Nick shouted.

He glanced behind him and saw Alice cornering Eishu, who was trying to hold her off by throwing out fire and ice spells with reckless abandon. Talismans were single-use items that could be used to quickly cast spells by skipping the need for chanting or gathering mana. You could continue to use them as long as you had the stamina.

Talismans had drawbacks, however. They contained a limited amount of mana and drew from the user when they didn't have enough for a spell. They were also very expensive, and given their disposable nature, they cost significantly more to use as a primary weapon than magic items. Anyone who could overcome those disadvantages and make good use of them made for a formidable opponent.

At least, that should have been the case, but Alice was blocking each of the spells with ease. As far as Nick could tell, she was going to have no trouble arresting Eishu. He would be an extremely valuable lead.

Then the tremendous explosion of light that erupted from Garos's katana upended everything.

"Grk..."

Nick's mind went fuzzy for a moment, and it took a few seconds for his vision to return. He looked around and saw surprisingly little damage. Trash and rubble had been strewn across the alley, but there was no significant damage to the surrounding buildings and walls.

Unsurprisingly, Garos was gone. He had used the explosion to escape.

"He only intended to blind us with that explosion. It was bright and loud but did no damage. He got us good," Nick said.

"What do you mean?" Alice asked. She'd regained her vision, too, and looked around while rubbing her eyes.

"Garos killed Eishu. I should've realized that's why he was here," Nick answered, pointing at something. Alice looked in that direction and gasped.

Eishu's body stood there, headless and bleeding from the neck. His talisman pouch and head were nowhere to be seen. The corpse collapsed to the ground with a thump, signaling the end of the battle—and the start of a new case.

The Truth Behind the Scenes

While Nick was fighting Garos, Karan faced an unusual crisis of her own.

"Okay, we're heading out. Take good care of the agency, Karan," Tiana said.

"The idols will be safe with me," Karan answered.

The Survivors had established a work routine for while Nick was away. From morning until noon, Tiana, Zem, and Bond would protect the idols as they went out for events, and Karan would stay at the agency to watch over the idols while they diligently trained and attended meetings. Then from noon until night, all except Nick would join up to help with concert security.

Karan honestly wanted to go with Nick and help him, but she was well aware she didn't have the knowledge or experience required to search for a person. She would only get in the way. Shortly after she renewed her resolve to help by doing what she could, she heard Daffodil scream in the training room.

"What?! You can't reach one of the dancers?!"

"We went to her apartment, but it was deserted... We may not find her before the show," Joseph informed her apologetically.

The idols in the room listened with concern. Karan did her

best to avoid looking at them and pretend like she wasn't listening, but she sensed trouble.

"No... Dragonian dancers are so valuable," Daffodil lamented.

"We will have to look for a substitute in the meantime. It would not be hard to find a human dancer, but..." Joseph trailed off.

"I want the backing dancers on both sides to be a race with a big tail, like a dragonian or a vulpinian. They should be able to make full use of the stage," Daffodil said.

"Do you have anyone in mind?" Joseph asked.

"Hmm... I know of some dancers from the wind dragon clan, but their people don't get along with my family... Hey, do you all happen to know any beastmen who can dance?" Daffodil turned and asked the idols who were stealthily listening in.

"I know a squirrel girl, but she's not athletic..."

"I have a cat beastman friend, but she has a thin tail. She'd probably be too self-conscious."

"The beastman receptionist at the Adventurers Guild is super athletic. Ah, but they can't have side jobs."

No one had a good answer. Karan shut them out with all her might. Now might be a good time to slip away to the bathroom.

"The choreography isn't that difficult, right?" Agate asked.

"Yeah. We would only need them for the beginning and end of the show when everyone is onstage. Hmm... We need someone brave enough to go onstage with this little warning," Daffodil said. She and Agate glanced at Karan.

"...No way," Karan said bluntly, sensing everyone looking at her.

"Hey, Karan. You wore a costume the other day!" Agate said.

"I'm not doing it!" Karan insisted.

"Don't say that, Karan. Nick said it looks good on you, remember?" Agate said.

"Wh-what does Nick have to do with anything?! I'm working as a bodyguard!" Karan declared, flustered. She turned away, determined not to get dragged into this, but she had already fallen into

Agate's trap. She had no chance of winning an argument against a group of idols, all of whom were skilled in the art of conversation.

"Being with us will make protecting us easier. Pretending to be an idol will let you jump in at a moment's notice," Agate argued.

"I'd feel better about you filling in than someone I've never met. We've seen how hard you work," Amber agreed.

"I just want to see you dance!" Topaz said.

"Why are you asking me?! I'm an amateur!" Karan cried.

"No you're not. You danced a lot until you turned thirteen or so," Daffodil responded.

"That's true, but that was a long time ago!" Karan was getting upset.

Joseph intervened to calm them down. "Don't worry, Ms. Tsubaki. We are not asking you to actually go onstage. We just cannot visualize the show in practice unless we have the proper number of dancers. All you would need to do is fill in until we find a replacement."

Karan knew she couldn't outright reject a request from her client. If only she could turn to her absent party members for help. She had been through many hardships and grown as a person, but she had no choice but to comply.

And so Karan danced—and it was more fun than she expected. She was getting into it, actually. She stepped and turned to the music, matching her movements to those of the surrounding idols. There was a large mirror on the wall, and she couldn't help but think they were beautiful as they all danced in unison. She even found herself singing and giving advice to new dancers.

Nearly an hour had passed before Karan returned to her senses and realized just how long she had been slacking from her guard duty.

"No more idoling!" she shouted.

"But you were so good... Shockingly good," Daffodil said.

"I know you're not being serious, Daffy!" Karan responded.

"I was joking at first, but… The dancing came so naturally to you that I ended up training you like you were already a member of the team," Daffodil said earnestly.

The other idols, and even Joseph, seemed to see Karan in a different light. She realized they were becoming serious about this and panicked.

"I'm warning you, I'll—!"

"Sorry, sorry. I'm not going to use you in the real concert. You have the potential to be a good dancer if you keep working, but it would be a big mistake to think you're on par with fully trained idols," Daffodil said.

"When did this become a competition…?" Karan complained, but secretly, she was relieved.

"How are you this good, though? Is it because you used to be a dancer?" Agate asked.

Karan was unsure of the answer herself. "Maybe because the choreography resembles dragonian dancing. It felt natural. I also sometimes see idols dance at parks and outdoor events."

"Hmm…" Agate smiled meaningfully.

"What do you want?" Karan asked.

"Do you wanna take a quick break?" Agate asked. "I'll buy you a drink."

"I'm working," Karan said.

"I'm gonna borrow her for a bit!" Agate announced to the other idols and guards. They said not to worry and encouraged the break.

It was true that Karan hadn't taken much time to rest. She was the kind of person who didn't get tired from waiting and standing around, and the other guards and idols had come to trust her for that.

"I don't need a break!"

"Yeah, yeah."

Agate brought Karan to a break space on a staircase landing near the roof of the agency. There was a bench set before a large window with a sweeping view of northwest Labyrinth City. The cityscape was orderly and clean, and the tallest building in the city, Teran Hall, was visible in the distance. Schools with young students, knight training facilities, trading posts, and other spacious buildings could be seen as well.

Seeing this side of Labyrinth City affected Karan more than she would have thought.

"Do you want a coffee?" Agate asked.

"Sure, but is it really okay for me to slack off like this?"

"It's important to take breaks."

"...Are you not scared of me?" Karan asked timidly.

"Why would I be scared of you?"

"I often scare little girls and kids."

"Oh yeah, some people are scared of dragonians. Daffodil complains about that sometimes."

"Hmm...," Karan answered wordlessly. The truth was that *she* was scared of *Agate*. She felt an immeasurable...something from the girl that she couldn't figure out. "That's true, but adventurers probably scare people, too."

"A lot of them act like ruffians, but I like everyone from the Survivors."

"What about the false paladins?"

"I am scared of them. But I won't let them break me."

"Can you continue working as an idol, knowing they're out there?"

"Oh... Yeah, that is scary. I don't want to be followed by anyone dangerous. I also worry about how long I'll be able to maintain my skin, my voice, and my back. There's always a chance my fans could lose interest in me."

Agate laughed with an embarrassed smile. Still, her fear wouldn't stop her.

"But you're still going," Karan said.

"Honestly, I never set out to become an idol. It just kind of happened. I feel a little inferior compared to the girls who came to this agency with the goal of going down this path," Agate admitted.

"Really?"

"Don't say that to the other idols, of course. Some might use that admission to pick on newcomers or bully me. Everyone here works so hard, which leads us to have complicated feelings toward each other. We all act cute, but we're bursting with ambition. Especially the top idols and managers..."

Karan froze, wondering for a moment if Agate herself was plotting something.

"Oh, don't get the wrong idea! That's not why I brought you here!" Agate shook her head. She must have sensed Karan's unease.

"I'll pretend I didn't hear that. What did you bring me here for, then?" Karan asked.

"I wanted to make something clear. I'm not ever going to date Nick," Agate said.

Karan choked on her coffee. "Wh-what are you talking about?!"

"Huh? Are you not his girlfriend?!" Agate asked.

"No, I... I'm not!"

"You just hesitated. You seem closer than normal friends or coworkers. You look bored without him here, too."

"I'm not bored!" Karan realized how flustered she was and began to nervously explain herself. "Nick saved me. I want to repay him for that. I want to be helpful and do more things with him. But..."

"But what?"

"Nick has been lying to us recently."

"Let's go punch his teeth out," Agate said, shocking Karan speechless. "Oh, sorry. I didn't mean to say that out loud. Go on."

Karan laughed and continued speaking. She was touched that Agate was understanding enough to make that kind of joke, and before she knew it, she was pouring out her heart.

"He's not really lying, I guess. He's just not telling the truth...

And when he does lie, he does it for my sake or for the rest of the party. I was happy when he told me that but also a little sad."

"It's good he was willing to listen to you and share that," Agate said with a smile as Karan searched for the words to say.

"I always want to say something to Nick when he keeps his worries to himself. I get angry wondering why he won't rely on us. Then we get angry at each other and fight. I prefer that to not talking at all, but I want to understand Nick without having to get mad at him," Karan said.

"So you want to know what he's thinking without having to beat it out of him?" Agate asked. There was pain in her voice as if she was remembering something from her own past.

"That's all I know how to do. I want to help Nick without bothering him. I'm tired of getting worked up and then thinking about how stupidly I behaved. But I don't really know why I feel that way. I might've grown a little, but I'm still an idiot," Karan said.

"You don't know exactly what you're feeling," Agate responded gently. Karan nodded. "I think you'll understand someday. If you're brave enough to listen to his true feelings and share your own with him, you definitely will."

Karan was growing a little offended by Agate's responses. She sounded like an adult speaking to a child, acting like they knew everything while saying nothing at all.

"Hey, it's not fair if I'm the only one who has to open up this way. Do you have anything embarrassing to share?" Karan asked.

"Not really," Agate said, gloom coming over her face. "My job is a lot of fun right now. I practice, go to events, perform at concerts, hit a wall, realize how much I need to improve, then practice some more... There's so much I can't do that I want to become capable of. So right now I just want to focus on work."

The gloom faded as she spoke. She reminded Karan of an adventurer facing the dark depths of a labyrinth.

"There was a person I...used to depend on. I convinced myself that their dream was my dream, when I was really just hiding from my own emptiness," Agate said.

"I know what you mean…"

"I feel like if I find someone to replace them with, I'll end up making the same mistakes. I want to grow and become an adult so I can be part of a supportive relationship, rather than just depend on someone… I want to share a dream instead of committing myself to someone else's."

Karan was afraid for a second that Agate had read her mind. Her words reminded her of when she'd relied on Callios.

"Don't you think it would make you happy to pursue a dream together with someone like that?" Agate asked. Her smile was so bright, Karan had to look away.

"What is your dream? To become the most popular idol?" Karan asked.

"Hmm. I do want that, but only to help me accomplish my dream," Agate answered.

"Which is?"

"I'm just one small person without physical strength, mana, or lineage. I've lived a pretty weird life compared with most people. Not that I can say that to my fans. But…"

"Yeah?"

"I want my wonderful songs to reach into people's souls!" Agate declared, reaching out her hands as if she could literally touch the hearts of her fans. "I may be small, but my words can impact the world. I'll help great people like you and Nick recover from hardship and find the energy to work hard tomorrow and the next day. Even lowlifes will hear my songs and be inspired to change and do good."

"I wonder if that's true," Karan responded with a cynical smile. She wanted to support Agate, but the discussion was bringing down her mood. She didn't share that faith in humanity. People were too dishonest by nature.

Karan wondered if part of her reaction was born out of jealousy. She couldn't compete with Agate as she spoke confidently about her ambitious yet clear dream. Karan was well aware of her own ugly flaws.

Even so, Agate smiled at her.

"It is! Just you watch!" she said, clapping her on the back so hard it hurt. Karan was so surprised by the violence that she just gaped wordlessly. "Everyone who hears my songs will be heroes and saints! That goes for you, too!"

Those words shocked Karan. "...The dragonian mission to serve the hero."

"Oh yeah, Daffodil said that once."

"Did she say anything else?"

"Uh... Well, she was drunk at the time," Agate said evasively.

Karan smiled bitterly. "She probably said it was stupid to let yourself be tied down by that mission. She's always felt that way."

She had never liked that about Daffodil. Karan was always proud that dragonians were known for their bravery, but her cousin didn't think that way. She thought it was ridiculous that they should have to commit their lives to supporting someone else. She said everyone should be the main character of their own life.

That opinion had always irritated Karan. She was aware of her own strength, but never thought she had what it took to save the world or lead other people. Her idea of the hero didn't involve ability, talent, or motivation; she thought they would be an intelligent and just person who lived to guide the people of the world. She thought that by giving her strength to the hero, she and the dragonians would become just people as well, despite being known for nothing but their strength.

But she'd learned something after being deceived and hurt, becoming hopelessly addicted to gourmet food, and getting back on her feet. There was no single intelligent and just person who would rise up to lead humanity. The world consisted only of fools who searched for that hero person only to be deceived, fools who were ensnared by suspicion after being deceived, and fools who chose to deceive others.

Living an entirely just life and committing yourself to one person was not realistic. Karan was beginning to think if there was a hero, they would be a person who was conscious of their own flaws and insignificance but persevered in the face of hardship anyway.

Karan knew a person like that, and he didn't allow her to remain ignorant of the world. He kept telling her she wasn't an idiot and encouraging her to learn and grow as a person. When he made a mistake, he listened to his party members.

Karan had acknowledged that he was a regular person and not a hero. That was an important decision for working alongside him, and she would never forget saying those words. But it felt like a sad ritual she had to perform to grow up and leave her naive dream behind.

An epiphany struck Karan. Maybe you didn't have to be an all-knowing hero to do good in the world. Maybe you weren't born intelligent and just; maybe you reached that point by fumbling in the dark and making mistakes until you became the kind of person who could make a difference. If that was true, anyone who had people to support them and admonish them when they messed up could become a hero.

Even Karan, despite how foolish she was in her past and how foolish she still was.

"Ah, they're back," Karan said.

"Where are they?" Agate asked.

"Over there," Karan responded, pointing out the window at a carriage.

There was a silver-haired boy lounging on the roof. It was Bond. He had the bearing of a cat that could inexplicably land on its feet if it happened to roll off. He called out and waved when he noticed Karan and Agate, and they responded by turning to each other and laughing.

"Be careful at the concert this evening. Topaz's fans are pretty unique," Agate warned.

"You can count on me. I'm a hero, after all," Karan responded.

Take care of the horses. Travel. Watch for threats. Wait. Take care of the horses again. That was the typical loop the Survivors' bodyguard jobs followed.

"I'm exhausted," Tiana silently said to her party members. Working behind the scenes to protect the extravagant world of idols was more monotonous and boring than she could have imagined.

"Was the job this morning hard?" Karan asked.

"Not really... It was just really slow. I thought it would never end," Tiana answered.

Tiana, Zem, and Bond had been placed in charge of security at an event in the morning. As per usual, the job consisted of transporting the idols to the venue by carriage, watching for threats, and waiting for the event to end.

It was a quiet event at which the idols had been tasked with promoting a clothing brand targeted at mages, and it passed without incident. The attendees were all either mages or people who worked with the brand, so no one was there to see the girls, and there were no false paladins. That made for a slow, boring job during which they spent more time guiding lost guests than actually protecting anyone.

It was now evening, and Tiana, Zem, and Bond had joined up with Karan to run security at a concert. Tiana realized her desire to go home was showing on her face and rubbed her brow.

"I think you would've handled it well, Karan... I just can't deal with all the standing around. It makes me too sleepy," Tiana said.

"Now, now, Tiana. Don't say that... We can take a break once all the fans have entered the venue," Zem responded.

"The staff meals are delicious. They're using a quality caterer," Karan said.

"Eating a meal backstage really makes me feel like a celebrity," Bond added.

Tiana refocused on the scene before her after getting a little distracted by their conversation. She was standing by the entrance of the venue, watching as staff tore off fans' ticket stubs and ushered them inside. The venue was Labyrinth City's southern public hall, and Topaz was performing there tonight.

The evening had been surprisingly peaceful so far despite the significant traffic. Nearly all the attendees were men, which was typical of idol concerts, but there were even fewer female fans than Tiana had seen at other shows. Topaz's mature and tolerant nature, combined with her youthful playfulness, had captivated many of the opposite sex, resulting in an even greater percentage of male fans compared with the percentage at other idols' shows.

No small number of fans had actually allowed themselves to fall in love with Topaz, and her groupies had taken on the personality of a vigilante group. They often dealt with rude and misbehaving fans before venue security could act. This radicalization had caused many headaches for Topaz and her managers, but it made the Survivors' job as newly hired guards easier, and Tiana thought their intensity would help her stay awake, too. Even if it was a bit much.

Tiana hoped nothing would happen as she watched the idol audience stream into the venue with tickets in hand, but she knew how unlikely that was.

"Excuse me, sir. Would you mind showing me your seat number?"

"H-huh? Just let me in already!"

A staff member and a fan began to argue. The staff member must have had a good memory and realized that the fan had the same seat number as someone they'd admitted earlier. The customer was clearly suspicious—he was already agitated when he was called forward.

It was only seconds later that his ticket started to burn and black fog coiled around his body. He was a false paladin.

"Everyone! Grab the buckets! Quickly!" Tiana yelled.

The nearby security guards and staff working at the entrance quickly followed her orders and splashed the man with buckets of water that had been set nearby as if they were for a fire.

"What the hell was that for?!"

"Gah, that's cold!"

The water drenched other fans near the man, too, eliciting complaints, but Tiana shut them up with a glare. The realization that something weird was going on spread through the crowd.

"W-was that really enough?!" one of the staff members asked nervously, but Tiana could see that it had worked.

"Wh-why'd you do that?! I-I'm f-f-freezing…!" the man whined.

When he was drenched, Tiana cast the spell *Freeze* with very little force. That lowered his body temperature and froze the wet ticket, weakening its effect. The man then finished it off by accidentally crumpling it in his hand, causing the black fog to disappear immediately.

The transformation had failed, leaving the man with nothing but a counterfeit ticket.

"Now where did you get that fake? You're going to tell us everything!" Tiana demanded.

The man realized he was at a disadvantage and used what little strength he had left to get up and attempt to run. Tiana was worried he would harm other members of the audience, but he didn't make it far.

"Did I hear 'fake ticket'? How dare you try to get into one of Pazzy's concerts that way!"

"H-hey, you're on the blacklist! Have you learned nothing?!"

A group of surprisingly macho men wearing orange-tinged red jackets surrounded the man with the counterfeit. The Topaz groupies seized him.

"H-hey! Go easy on him! I want to question him later!" Tiana shouted.

"I underestimated you. You seem to be an adventurer of some renown," one of the groupies said, bowing his head to Tiana.

"Huh? Y-yeah, I suppose," Tiana responded.

"Wait a second... You're Lady Tiana from the Survivors. What are you doing here?"

Tiana didn't remember the man, but he seemed to recognize her.

"U-umm... Have we met at an Adventurers Guild?" she asked.

"I'm Willy. Oh, I never gave you my name, did I? I go to a lot of concerts with Nick... Wait. Is he working as a security guard here, too?" the man asked.

Tiana nearly cursed, but she held herself together and thought of an excuse. "I'm working a part-time job because we're taking a break from adventuring. There's no way they'd hire Nick, ah-ha-ha!"

"I guess so. Well, good luck. The show's about to start!"

Willy gave her a bright smile and a thumbs-up and gladly handed over the man with the counterfeit ticket. Tiana breathed a sigh of relief that everything had worked out.

"Hey, what's taking so long?! Let us in already!"

The fans at the gates grew impatient and began to complain. While Topaz did have a lot of diehards, ordinary fans still significantly outnumbered them. They needed to reopen the gates and restore the flow of fans into the venue. Unfortunately, the staff were taking a while to recover from the confusion of what had just happened. Fan admission wasn't part of Tiana's job, but if someone else with a counterfeit showed up right now, she wouldn't be able to handle them.

"THIS IS AGATE, HERE TO SUPPORT TOPAZ! THERE IS PLENTY OF TIME BEFORE THE CONCERT BEGINS, SO PLEASE BE PATIENT!"

A loud voice echoed in the venue, causing the area around the entrance to go quiet. Tiana looked toward the voice and saw Agate holding a voice-amplifying magic item. She had emerged from a staff passageway and used it to speak to all the fans in attendance.

"Hey, it's Aggie. She came to watch the show."

"I love Aggie, too. She's grown so much since her debut."

"Didn't you say Pazzy's the only one for you?"

That one statement was all Agate needed to calm the angry atmosphere at the entrance.

She's good, Tiana thought before thanking her.

Topaz addressed the crowd after singing a number of songs. The day's security work was about halfway done. A false paladin in possession of a counterfeit ticket had already been caught, and now that the show had started, it was unlikely any more fans would arrive. The entire staff was relieved.

"There are no problems at the entrance. What about you all?" Tiana asked the others using Telepathy.

"Everything is fine in the waiting room," Zem answered.

"There are no signs of trouble in the stands, either," Bond said.

"And nothing in the hallway," Karan answered.

Tiana heard Topaz's sweet and kind voice reverberate throughout the stadium as they spoke in their minds. She wondered what kind of singer Agate was. Tiana had been watching the girl practice while on guard duty. Agate was so much more lively than when they first met, and she seemed to emanate a strange passion.

Maybe I should go to one of her shows... Tiana thought, just before she heard a voice.

"Why...? Why did the show have to start already...? I finally got a ticket..."

The sun had set, and the streetlights around the venue were popping on to illuminate the area with warm color. A man emerged from the darkness beyond, his dimly lit face the picture of anguish. He was drenched in sweat as if he was being roasted over a fire, his eyes were bloodshot, and his breathing was shallow.

"Someone is approaching the entrance, and he looks dangerous. Karan, Bond, hurry over here for support," Tiana said. The tension in her voice sent a wave of nervousness through the others.

"Could you please show me your ticket?" she asked, holding her staff ready for a fight.

The man looked like he was too far gone to hear her. His eyes were unfocused yet hostile. A black fog began to wrap around his body, and this fog was much more distinct.

"Get down, everyone! Rushing Stream!" Tiana yelled, warning off the staff members who had sensed trouble and begun to approach her.

A torrent of water rushed from her staff. The false paladin didn't even try to dodge it. *He went down easier than I expected*, Tiana thought with relief, but that thought turned out to be premature.

"DON'T GET IN MY WAY!" the man shrieked.

"Wha...? It evaporated?!" Tiana exclaimed.

A tremendous heat protected the false paladin, turning the water to vapor before it could drench the ticket. The air turned as humid as a sauna. Each step the man took was accompanied by a sizzle as the heat beneath his feet burned the dust on the ground.

The black fog had now manifested into a set of armor that seemed just as formidable as White Mask's. A fire spell also protected his body; it was as if his armor was made from the black flames of hatred itself.

"Take this!"

"Hi-yah!"

Karan and Bond raced toward the false paladin and attacked him while protecting Tiana.

"Be careful! There's something weird about this guy!" Tiana warned.

The false paladin caught Karan's and Bond's blades in his hands, and Karan was astonished by his strength.

"Where is his ticket?!" Bond asked.

"Hidden under his armor!" Tiana answered.

"Then we'll have to tear the armor off!" Karan shouted.

The dragonian let go of her sword and grabbed the man with her hands. Meanwhile, Topaz's concert had reached its climax. The man's strength seemed to grow in proportion to the audience's excitement.

"Grk... It's hot...!" Karan groaned.

"Karan! Don't hurt yourself!" Tiana yelled.

"Zem can just heal me later!" Karan yelled back. She appeared to successfully lock the false paladin's arm, but then he flung her off.

"I'M GONNA MISS THE SHOW!" he screamed. He grabbed a pillar to try to climb to his feet, but he broke it when he pulled on it and lost his balance, falling back to the ground. Tiana realized that he couldn't fully control his impossible strength.

"He can't handle his armor! Don't let him get up!" she ordered.

Karan and Bond teamed up to keep him occupied with attacks. The false paladin's defense was so great that not even the sharpest strikes could scratch him; their swords might as well have been hammers.

They couldn't afford a stalemate. Tiana didn't know why, but this man was significantly stronger than any of the false paladins they had encountered thus far, and he was growing stronger still. They couldn't let this stretch on any longer.

"Urgh... No, I'm..."

Fortunately, the false paladin's strength suddenly began to bleed out. Bond and Karan realized that something was happening and stayed their blades. The protective flame vanished from the armor, and the armor itself dissolved into smoke and disappeared.

This left a defenseless would-be concertgoer lying on the ground.

"What happened...?" Tiana said.

She realized belatedly that Topaz's final song had ended and the crowd had quieted. Fans were streaming out of the venue to return home. Tiana was confused, but she pushed that aside; they needed to clean up.

"I do not know what happened, but we have him...," Bond said with a melodramatic and tired shrug. He took the ticket from the false paladin; it was blackened, just like the previous counterfeit ticket they'd obtained. Tiana thought it looked even darker.

The man was lethargic and unmoving. He resembled the Survivors when they dispelled Union. This was how people reacted when released from certain types of trances.

A thought occurred to Tiana. "...Hey, Bond. You were telling us about minstrels before. Something about how they could perform special ritual magic."

"Yes, I remember," Bond responded.

"Can you explain that again?" Tiana asked.

"Hmm. Minstrels fulfilled a support role by granting strength to their companions through song or by placing a crowd in a trancelike state to...gather mana..." An expression of surprise came over Bond as he spoke. "Are you saying this man is a minstrel?"

"Do you disagree?"

"...You cannot cast ritual magic without a ritual. The ritual is necessary for collecting mana. We can omit much of that process when casting Union, but normally a ritual requires preparation. You need a ritual implement for gathering mana, an altar for presenting offerings, a crowd of participants to offer prayer in unison, and a shaman or minstrel at the center of the ritual to ask for prayer..."

"Can someone steal mana that is being collected?"

"From where?"

"The concert."

Bond said nothing.

"I don't know what a ritual implement is," Tiana continued, "but the rest of the factors are in place. The venue is decorated with wreaths and other gifts in celebration of the concert. The fans are wearing jackets of the same color and waving magic glow sticks while the idol calls on them to sing and cheer. How is that any different from worshippers and a priest gathering in a cathedral and singing hymns?"

"...The idols in this city are performing rituals. And one concert gathered enough mana to give this man strength rivaling White Mask's," Bond said.

A chill ran down Tiana's back. A strange conspiracy larger than they could have imagined was occurring just underfoot. It was big enough to consume everything if they let down their guard.

"We need to do something about this before something truly terrible happens," Tiana said.

"Garos killed the counterfeit-ticket seller right in front of you, and you were questioned at a Sun Knight station?! That's way too much information for me to process at once!" Tiana exclaimed through Telepathy.

"Don't worry, they didn't hold me for long. Let's gather at a place called Woods Credit Check Office," Nick responded, leaving the station.

Watching Garos silence Eishu had made Nick a material

witness in the case, and to make matters worse, Alice, a Sun Knight captain, was there, too. He was preparing himself for the possibility of going a few days—or even a week—without seeing the light of day, but he was released from the station surprisingly quickly. When he tried to leave, thanking his luck for avoiding days of questioning, a slender yet muscular arm wrapped around his neck.

"Bwah," Nick gasped.

"Oh dear, Nick. Were you trying to leave without saying good-bye? You'll hurt my feelings."

"What the hell?! You can't just sneak up on people and put them in a chokehold!"

The person let go. It was Alice.

"I'm guessing you're surprised by how quickly we let you go," she said.

"Yeah, I am," Nick responded.

Garos had killed Eishu, who turned out to be the counterfeit-ticket seller. The murderer was Nick's former party member, and a knight witnessed the incident. Nick would not have been surprised if they'd confined him at the station and questioned him all day and night. He'd decided to tell Alice everything except for the truth about the Sword of Bonds in the hopes of avoiding that.

"You've told us everything you know, so there's no reason to hold you. Our time will be better spent investigating. Oh, don't mention that to the other Sun Knights. I'm not really supposed to tell you any of this," Alice said.

"You're a rotten knight," Nick commented.

Alice ignored the jab and continued. "Let's review the case. There's no doubt that White Mask is Garos. He's continuing his job even after losing his holy armor. We also learned Eishu was a fellow demon-god worshipper."

"Yep. Their conversation doesn't make sense unless we assume they had the same employer," Nick said.

"But Garos killed Eishu."

"Eishu was getting carried away with his hobby and endangering the demon-god worshippers. His carelessness enabled us to track him down."

Alice nodded. "Eishu let his guard down...and that's why he had to go. You're good, Nick. I was surprised when you broke his illusion."

"I had no idea you were behind me hitching a ride, though," Nick said.

"I helped you, didn't I? You would've died if you'd had to fight them alone," Alice replied with a flirtatious wink.

Nick sighed. "I know. Thanks."

"Anyway, Garos is our biggest problem now. He stole the rest of Eishu's tickets," Alice said.

"I don't know much about the tickets, either. Garos reacted to the word *shaman*, for some reason."

"We'll have to look into that. I'll start by putting Garos on the Wanted list. We need to speak to the rest of the members of Combat Masters, too."

"Go ahead. This is their own fault. I told you about the safe house Argus and the others use. But..."

"Yeah, the odds of finding them there are slim."

Nick had no choice but to accept that he had been deceived in a major way. He hadn't caught even a hint of Garos's true identity during the near decade he'd spent in Combat Masters. Argus almost certainly knew about it and kept it from Nick. It was even possible that Argus himself was a hit man for the demon-god worshippers.

"Discovering the truth is often painful. Do you still feel like working on this case? There would be no shame in leaving the rest to me or your friends," Alice said kindly.

Nick shook his head. "I'm not backing down. They need to pay. Not for deceiving me, but for all their killing and thievery."

"Then there's something I can do to make things a little easier for you. Read and sign this," Alice said, offering him a stack of papers.

The top page was an application to become a temporary Sun Knight employee. Alice and this station's commander had already signed it. The rest of the pages detailed the conditions for the contract. They said he had to obey the law, refrain from overstepping his authority, and follow the orders of superior knights while on duty. His work hours and wages were also written in detail.

Nick actually recognized this document. He had seen fellow adventurers flaunt it before. It actually wasn't uncommon for the Order of the Sun Knights to temporarily hire adventurers. Assisting the order and gaining their trust to land a job as a Sun Knight was one route to success available to adventurers. Former adventurers couldn't rise as high in the order as Sun Knights who entered on the fast track to leadership, but they could gain plenty of money and prestige.

Alice wouldn't have been able to offer Nick this contract if he hadn't gained a decent reputation among the Sun Knights. He would have been honored under other circumstances.

"I thought you'd made this a competition, Alice," Nick said, confused.

"Martha Canning," Alice responded.

"Huh?"

"She was originally laid to rest in the morgue of a public cemetery in the Garbage Heap. I heard what happened from the gravekeeper. He's a funny man. He was terrified, but he insisted that I donate because it would mean trouble for him if someone of my station didn't. I like him."

"You went there?"

Nick clearly remembered the gravekeeper's face. He was a strange man; he was timid, yet strict with anyone who didn't follow the rules, status notwithstanding.

"I'm sorry for not understanding you," Alice said quietly.

"…Okay."

"Anyway, sign this."

"Hold on," Nick protested.

"Let's just say I lost our competition. This is your victory trophy," Alice said. She was so overwhelming that Nick retreated a step. "This contract will allow you to maintain your reputation, no matter what happens. You can stay the night if you don't want to sign it. You need a shower."

Alice gave him a look that said he would be confined for much longer than one night if he didn't sign. He could be stuck here for a week or even a month. Despite her easygoing attitude, she was passionate, and that passion didn't prevent her from calmly looking ahead.

Nick found her terrifying.

"Tch… Guess I've got no choice," Nick said.

"Hmm-hmm, don't worry. I won't restrict you in any way, and you'll be paid for your work. Moving on… Garos took Eishu's stock of counterfeit tickets. He must be plotting something. Let's stay focused and resolve this case quickly," Alice said.

Nick quickly read the contract and the conditions as he listened to Alice. There was nothing that would cause any immediate problems, and the period of his employment was expressly stated.

"Come on, man. Didn't you hear me say 'quickly'? I guess you're the type to actually read contracts," Alice complained.

"I don't sign anything without reading it first," Nick said. Once he decided there was nothing problematic about the contract, he signed it and returned it to Alice.

"Excellent. Make sure you tell me anything you learn. I assume you're going to meet up with your party members?" Alice asked.

"Yep. I'm the party leader, after all. I can't just leave the whole job to them," Nick said.

"I could learn from you. I'm always shoving stuff I don't wanna deal with on to my subordinates."

"Don't send anyone to follow me. You might be able to pull it off, but I could easily lose most Sun Knight captains."

Alice smiled. She must have tailed Nick when he was tailing Eishu. There was no way she could have been there to join the fight otherwise. And given her position in the Order of the Sun Knights, it was likely she had subordinates nearby ready to follow her orders.

"You're a member of my team for now. I wasn't lying when I said I want to recruit you... You've impressed me," she said, putting a finger to her chin and laughing.

"Thanks," Nick responded flatly.

"I truly mean that. You've proven yourself capable of pursuing the truth without being flustered by your former party member's crimes or carried away by resentment. I thought you would be more hot-blooded, but you've surprised me with your maturity," Alice said.

"That's..."

Thanks to Karan, Nick thought. If not for what she said, it was entirely possible he would've acted rashly when he found Garos and gotten himself killed. He might also have failed to break Eishu's illusion. Nick felt that Karan did more to watch his back rather than the other way around.

"I'm the party leader. I can't make a fool of myself just 'cause my companions aren't around," Nick said.

"You have a good party. I think I might be jealous. All right, I'll look forward to hearing good news from you," Alice said.

With that, they parted ways. Nick intentionally passed through busy shopping districts, slipped into back alleys, and annoyed people by occasionally taking the Steppingman's road—fences and rooftops—to shake off whoever was likely following him. He continued through the city in this manner until he reached his destination—Woods Credit Check Office.

Nick had entrusted Hector with investigating Garos. Now

that he knew Garos was a demon-god worshipper, he needed to tell his detective friend to look into him more thoroughly and carefully. Also, Eishu was acquainted not just with Garos, but with every member of Combat Masters; they needed to investigate Nick's former party as well.

Nick considered the best course of action until he found himself in front of the detective office.

"Sorry I took so long, Tiana. A lot happened," he said.

"Same here. I need to fill you in. Keep in mind this is all still conjecture," Tiana replied.

She repeated what she'd told Bond during the concert. Nick was astonished by what he heard.

"So you're saying Jewelry Production is performing some kind of ritual," Nick said.

"There's no other way to account for the strength of the false paladins. What do you think?" Tiana asked.

"I think you're right. It lines up with what Garos said," Nick said with a pained expression.

"Nick..." Karan seemed worried.

Nick smiled to set her at ease. "I don't care about that. Jewelry Production has been suspicious this whole time... If they're performing rituals, though, one thing doesn't add up."

"What are you talking about?" Tiana asked.

"If they're performing ritual magic to gather mana, what are they using it for? If they're not using it on the spot, are they storing it somewhere? Is mana so easy to store and withdraw later?" Nick said.

Tiana didn't have a reply. She hadn't figured that part out yet.

"They must have an artifact that can store a colossal amount of mana," Bond said.

"If anyone would know something about that...it would be Coleman or Diamond," Nick responded.

Nick remembered Diamond's words. *I'm counting on you, my*

bodyguard. He now wondered if it was the rituals she was telling him to protect.

"But the idols take their singing so seriously. They're not acting like they've been roped into a conspiracy," Karan said.

"It is possible they are being deceived, or that information has been concealed from them," Bond replied.

Karan's expression stiffened. Anger flashed across her face; she probably wanted to make whoever was deceiving the idols pay.

"...Anyway, it's that place with the sign. I hope Hector's learned something useful," Nick said, pointing to a sign that said WOODS CREDIT CHECK OFFICE.

Tiana eyed the building suspiciously. "It looks fishy... Is the detective reliable?" she asked.

"He seems skilled. He can immediately search an entire bookshelf just by saying a word or name," Karan said.

"Why is a person with librarian skills working as a detective in Labyrinth City? That's really difficult magic," Tiana said.

"He said he was run out of the capital after he seduced someone's wife," Karan answered.

"I suddenly feel an affinity with this man. We could be friends," Zem commented, earning a weak laugh from Nick.

The party reached the door to Woods Credit Check Office. The lights were off, suggesting Hector had already closed for the day.

"Should we go in?" Tiana asked.

"I'll drag him out of bed if he's asleep. He might not be here, though," Nick answered. He reached for the doorknob just as someone opened it from the inside. "Oh, sorry, didn't know you were there, Hec— Huh?"

"What? Nick?"

"Daffodil?"

Unexpectedly, Daffodil opened the door. She was holding someone over her shoulder—Hector.

He was clearly unconscious, and she didn't appear to be going to find medical attention. Daffodil was wearing a completely black outfit that resembled dance clothes, Hector was on her right shoulder, and she was carrying a bag of books in her left hand. By all appearances, she was robbing and abducting Hector.

"Huh?! Wh-what the hell are you doing?!" Nick shouted.

Nick and Karan had asked Hector to look into Daffodil, but he didn't think for a second that she was dangerous, like Garos. He was simultaneously shocked to find someone connected to the enemy here and angry that she'd betrayed Karan's concern for her.

"I could ask you the same thing! What are *you* all doing here?!" Daffodil shouted back.

She grabbed the doorknob and pushed with tremendous force, and Nick reacted by grabbing the opposite doorknob and trying to keep her from leaving.

"Grk," Nick grunted.

Daffodil pushed as hard as she could, turning the doorknob in the opposite direction. Karan's cousin had the strength advantage, and it felt like he was taking a beating through the doorknob.

"Dammit!"

"You stubborn little...!"

Nick and Daffodil both gripped the doorknob as hard as they could, entering a stalemate in which neither could let go. Whoever did would get immediately slammed by the door.

"You're stronger...than you look! You must be...using some kind of spell!" Daffodil shouted.

"And you're way too strong...for an ordinary dancer!" Nick yelled back.

They pushed the door back and forth slightly, as if being pulled by a magnetic force, neither making much progress. Either one would be knocked back the moment they let up. The hinges groaned loudly in the midst of the battle.

"Bond! Go around the back! Break a window and jump in!" Nick ordered.

Bond immediately moved to circle around the building, and Daffodil realized her disadvantage.

"Aaaarrrrggghhh!" she screamed, using brute force that matched—or even surpassed—Karan's to rip the door off its hinges. Twisted bits of metal went flying through the air, and Daffodil charged forward, using the door like the shield of a heavy infantryman.

"Gah…!" Nick yelled.

"Sorry, but you're in my way!" Daffodil shouted.

Zem rushed over and used a healing spell on Nick, who had been knocked backward. Nick immediately jumped to his feet and chased after Daffodil.

Daffodil dashed through a back alley to avoid being seen. She seemed strangely accustomed to these kinds of escapes; she whipped garbage can lids at the Survivors as they pursued her, jumped over chain-link fences, and even ran across verandas. She quickly left Tiana and Zem in the dust, who both had to stop and pant. Karan and Bond couldn't jump over the obstacles, forcing them to leave the pursuit to Nick.

"Be careful, Nick!" Karan shouted.

"Got it!" Nick called back.

But as impressive as Daffodil's flight was, Nick was perfectly capable of keeping up. His combat experience and newfound skill with Stepping gave him agility that surpassed an ordinary human's.

"Wha…?! You're so weird!" Daffodil shouted, glancing back at Nick.

"Whaddaya mean, 'weird'?! Let Hector go!" Nick yelled back.

"This crappy detective is your friend?! I misjudged you!"

"He may be an adulterer, but his detective skills are hardly crappy!"

Nick had caught up enough to speak to Daffodil. He was well on his way to stopping her and being able to ask Hector himself what had happened.

But just when Nick was about to catch her, something strange happened. A strange tingling sensation ran through his head. He thought he was receiving a telepathic message, but no one said anything.

"Bond, did you say something?" Nick asked.

"No, I did not," Bond answered.

"It felt like someone was speaking to me...," Nick said. He didn't know what was happening, but he had a bad feeling.

"Th-that's bad, Nick! Cut off Telepathy now! It might be too late, but...!" Bond yelled telepathically.

"Huh? What're you—?"

Nick was interrupted when the assault began.

"GAAAH?!"

The tingling strengthened in intensity until it felt like an earthquake in his brain. Like lightning had split the heavens and struck him directly. Nick was so confused that he actually thought some kind of natural disaster was occurring, rather than an assault on his mind.

"OooAAAOOOAAAOOOAAA!"

The noise grew to a thunderous roar, throwing off his sense of equilibrium. He instinctively reached up to plug his ears, but that did nothing to quell the disturbance penetrating his brain.

He couldn't think. The voice he heard contained such rage that it left no room in his brain to even let his life flash before his eyes. He screamed for help, praying desperately for it to end.

"Looks like we caught a rat. They always appear when I'm busy. I wonder who they're working for?"

Nick faintly heard a familiar voice amid the roar, and it reminded him that he was holding a magic item for this. He had been told to use it if anyone directly assaulted his mind.

"Grk... **Discommunicator**...!" he gasped after weakly pulling an orb out of his pocket.

The orb activated, and silence fell immediately. It was as if the roar had never happened at all. The silence felt wonderful, but Nick quickly remembered what he was doing. He reflexively grabbed a hand as it reached toward him.

"Grk...!" Daffodil grunted as he grabbed her with a locking technique.

"What are you doing?!" Nick shouted.

"I should ask you the same thing! I thought you were on our side!" Daffodil yelled back.

Hector had been laid down on the ground beside them. Nick was both relieved to see he wasn't dead and worried that there had been a terrible misunderstanding. However, the odds of Daffodil working with Garos had definitely increased. He struggled to decide what to do until he heard a familiar voice.

"Umm... Is that you, Nick?"

A person wearing simple workout clothes and with elegant pink hair that could not have looked more out of place approached with quiet footsteps.

"Sorry, but could you please let her go? I think there's been a few misunderstandings. You stand down, too, Daffy. You can let the detective go."

It was Diamond.

"I had a feeling something was off about this," Nick said as released Daffodil. "That attack—if it can even be called that—was you, wasn't it?"

"Yep. I set traps around the concert venue. They're set to activate when a person who can use Telepathy passes through them. I told Daffy to hurry over here if she ran into trouble," Diamond explained.

"What happens when other people pass through those traps?" Nick asked.

"They don't hear Pop Song, my false Mantra. Shutting it out was the right decision. You wouldn't have suffered at all if you had done that a little sooner, though, so I can't give you a perfect score," Diamond said.

"False Mantra?" Nick repeated. That was an ominous-sounding term, and he raised his guard a little more. "It looks like you knocked out Hector the old-fashioned way, though."

"Don't blame me. That was all Daffy," Diamond said.

"Diamond!" Daffodil protested, sounding embarrassed.

"Ah-ha-ha, sorry. I told her to do it. But I can explain myself. That detective trespassed into a concert hall that's under construction," Diamond said.

"That hardly excuses hunting him down at his detective office and abducting him," Nick said.

"You think so? Should I give him to the Sun Knights, then? Alice might take him," Diamond said with a grin.

Those words actually calmed Nick down a little. "That's a pretty tame threat. I'm sure you have plenty of other ways to torment me."

"Hey, don't assume that I attack people like that all the time. I kinda did just attack you, though…," Diamond replied peevishly.

Nick was even more confused now; he had half expected Diamond to flip out and try to chop his head off.

"You have no idea how agonizing that was. I thought I was gonna die," Nick said.

"I—I said I was sorry! Please forgive me!" Diamond apologized, breaking under Nick's glare.

The danger seemed to be past, but this strange conversation had left Nick unsure what to do. His party members finally caught up shortly afterward.

"Nick! Are you okay?!" Karan shouted.

"Yeah, somehow. But…" Nick trailed off.

Karan saw Daffodil and Diamond and tensed. Tiana, Zem, and Bond also assumed combat positions to support Nick.

"Hold on, guys. Calm down. I don't know what's going on, either," Nick said.

"Really?" Karan said, confused.

"Hector's just unconscious, and all they did to me was rattle my brains. Can you heal him, Zem?" Nick asked.

Zem cast a healing spell on Hector, who woke up in a state of confusion. He glanced around frantically at first, but he breathed a sigh of relief when he realized he had been saved.

"So... What're we doing? Don't tell me we're gonna keep fighting," Nick said.

Everyone responded with awkward expressions. They didn't know what to do.

"It's late, so how about we pick this back up tomorrow? I don't wanna stay up until midnight, and I don't wanna keep my girls or you all up, either. Don't worry, I'll explain everything," Diamond assured them with a smile.

There was a quiet beauty to Diamond under the moonlight; Nick couldn't believe it belonged to a simple girl who was a head shorter than he was. But the dark shadow over her face was certainly not part of her idol personal.

All Nick could do was nod.

They split up while still in a daze over what had happened and gathered again the next day for Diamond to explain everything. Unexpectedly, Diamond didn't choose the Jewelry Production headquarters as their meeting place. Instead, she said to meet at a concert venue.

Starmine Hall was its name, and it was the largest concert venue in Labyrinth City. It was funded in a joint project between the Organization for Labyrinth City Development, Teran Event Planning, and Jewelry Production. The venue's opening concert was going to be none other than the Jewelry Production One Hundredth Anniversary Idol Appreciation Concert.

"This place is almost finished," Nick commented.

"The acoustics and the lighting aren't ready yet, but the construction is finished," Diamond replied.

The Survivors and Hector entered Starmine Hall from the back entrance. Diamond, Daffodil, and Agate were waiting for them there. Nick was surprised to see Agate, and when he opened his mouth to ask why she was there, Diamond cut him off and explained. "She wanted to come."

Agate bowed her head guiltily when Nick and the others approached.

"You look like you know something," Nick said a little sharply.

"Um, honestly—," Agate began, but Diamond stopped her.

"Hey now, be patient. I said I would explain everything," she said.

"Oh, I wasn't blaming her," Nick interjected.

"You overstepped, Nick. Let's just hear her out first," Karan said.

"S-sorry," Nick said, feeling thoroughly raked over the coals. The atmosphere relaxed a little, and there was less tension in their steps.

Diamond led the group into an equipment storage room behind the stage. Magic items for casting Amplification and other strange machinery Nick didn't know the purpose of were scattered about with no apparent rhyme or reason.

"Here we go," Diamond said, touching with practiced hands the control panel on a machine. A section of a wall opened with a loud *thunk*, revealing a hidden door. "We're going underground."

Diamond walked through the secret entrance and started going down the stairs without explanation. Nick and the others hurried after her. The staircase went surprisingly deep; five minutes of walking later, they still hadn't reached their destination.

"Don't tell me... Is this...?" Bond muttered, looking pale.

"What's wrong?" Nick asked.

"N-no... It's nothing," said Bond. "I do not sense a trap. It's okay to keep following her."

The room they eventually reached was remarkably orderly. The floor and desks were made of the strange, featureless material typical of ancient ruins. Nothing was more conspicuous, however, than the giant diamond in the center of the room that towered like a pillar. Nick and the others were mesmerized by its beautiful shine and austerity. They also glanced at a middle-aged man who was mopping the floor next to it, wondering what he was doing there.

"Ah, my apologies. I'm still cleaning, as you can see. I'll prepare the room," he said.

"What are you doing here, producer?" Diamond asked.

"I hurried over to prepare as soon as I heard you were having a meeting here. You should have told me sooner."

The man cleaning was Joseph. He hurried over to the side of the room where a long collapsible table and foldable chairs were scattered about by the wall and began to set them up. The others jumped in to help, too.

Once everyone was seated, Diamond began. "Thanks for coming, all of you. I'm sure you have loads of questions, but first... Hector."

Hector jumped with surprise when she called his name. He looked totally perplexed by the situation.

"Y-yeah?"

"I want to start by complimenting your investigative ability. You're truly impressive. How much did you figure out?" Diamond asked.

"...I had no idea this place was here. It appears to be an ancient ruin. All I learned is that you've been active nonstop for the last one hundred years and that you bought this plot of land with your own money," Hector said.

"One hundred years?" Nick said.

"I looked through the old issues of that occult magazine you gave me and found someone who looks almost exactly like the current Diamond. It said she revived ancient idol culture, and that the people of the ancient civilization fled to outer space and have now returned to rule the world…or something like that," Hector explained.

Nick guessed that article was probably written by Olivia. Recognition dawned on the Survivors' faces.

"The content of the article was nonsense, of course. But a thought occurred to me—what if all the Diamonds throughout the last century have been the same person?" Hector continued.

"All the Diamonds, huh…? There have been a lot of them. There's the original Diamond and the one at this table, and I've heard of a Pink Diamond and a Black Diamond," Nick said.

Hector nodded in confirmation. "They were all active at different times with no overlap. The name is supposedly passed down, but I don't think that's the case. I believe one person has used different variations of the name over time to avoid people realizing the length of her life span," he said, gaining confidence.

"Why do you think that?" Tiana asked curiously.

"I have a skill that allows me to say a term or name and search a collection of documents and relics at once. I used it to investigate species with long life spans, and I found something that matches Diamond. Elves who live too long and cease using the name of their tribe lose their identity and develop a memory disorder. Sentient magic items can't change their name without it having an effect on their function. I thought Diamond could be holding on to her name for a similar reason… And I believed it was most likely that she's not a person, but a magic item," Hector answered.

Everyone turned to Diamond. She began to clap.

"Good job. I'm impressed you figured that out. But you got one thing wrong," she said.

"I did?" Hector responded.

"The original Diamond, whose name was Hibiki Diamond, was

my wielder. I borrowed her name and face. I mutated to appear like her, and another mutation would put not just my function but my life in danger. I'm limited in the variety of pseudonyms I can use because my name has to remain close to Diamond," Diamond said.

"...Your wielder?" Nick repeated.

"That's right. Hibiki Diamond was an adventurer who, just like you all, wielded a holy sword," Diamond said.

The Survivors—especially Bond—were unsure what to make of this.

"What is your name?" Bond asked.

"Hibiki Diamond named me the Sword of Resonance. It's nice to meet you, Sword of Bonds," Diamond said.

The Survivors were astonished. Encountering another holy sword would have been surprising enough even if it didn't work as an idol.

"Hey, Bond... Is she an old acquaintance?" Nick asked timidly, but Bond was still too stunned to speak. He realized that Bond was surprised for a different reason than the rest of them. "Hey, what's wrong?"

"There is no Sword of Resonance. At least, not when I was forged. I did not even see it as a proposed project name," Bond finally said.

"As I said, that's the name Hibiki Diamond gave me. I originally had a different name. You've grown so much. Grown cuter anyway. Though I only ever saw your sword form," Diamond said.

She sounded as if she were speaking to a relative she hadn't seen in ages. That only made Bond more nervous.

"My original name was Hizumi. I'm the Divinity-Class Mental Fortress, the Sword of Distortion. This place is the former site of Distortion... Which means you're currently inside me."

There were two central figures in the war to subjugate Skiaprelli, the demon god. One was the hero, Setsuna the Swift. He wielded the holy sword called the Sword of Tasuki in the final stage of the war and inflicted the decisive blow to send the demon god into a deep sleep. The other was Hizumi, the Sword of Distortion and the director of Distortion, which was a facility built to distort Mantras. She rescued humanity from certain defeat at the beginning of the war.

Not much was remembered about either one—their names were only known to select sages and scholars—but the former was always spoken of with awe while the latter was spoken of with revulsion. The reverence shown to Setsuna was because he defeated the demon god. The legends—while not necessarily completely credible—painted him as a noble person who everyone recognized as a hero.

Hizumi earned her loathsome reputation from the misdeeds she performed after turning the tide of the war—namely exploiting young men and women and disposing of them when she was done with them. She gathered young people from throughout the country to offer prayer to her, and even transported beautiful young girls in lavish cages. The road she used was still called Maiden Highway today, though few remembered the origin of the name.

"I needed to do that to prevent the entirety of Teran from being turned into a labyrinth. About half of the city consisted of research facilities, military arsenals, and wealthy residential districts, while the other half resembled today's Garbage Heap," Diamond said.

"An entire city could be turned into a labyrinth...," Tiana said. "I've heard of that but wasn't sure if it was real."

Diamond nodded. "The demon god could create labyrinths and grow existing ones to expand the inhabitable land for monsters. Labyrinths also warp the minds and bodies of any people or protists who stay within them for too long. People and monsters are like pieces on a game board, constantly battling for territory, but the demon god has the ability to instantly end a game by turning a city or a village into a labyrinth. The more negative emotions and hatred a city has, the easier it is for the demon god to do it."

"So you created Distortion to combat the demon god and protect the city," Tiana said.

"Yep. I wanted to fight both socially and magically, and I made its residents worship me. I lacked the power to fix society's flaws, but I could distort people's hearts so they devoted themselves to me instead of to the demon god," Diamond explained.

"You were just as guilty of taking advantage of those flaws," Bond said. "You idled away your days making beautiful men and women serve your every need, while firing them at the first offense."

"Uh… yeah. That part was just for fun," Diamond replied, turning away with a bashful laugh.

"So you admit it!" Bond exclaimed.

"I can explain myself, though!" said Diamond. "When I started taking the ones who were about to be brainwashed by the demon god's Mantras, people assumed I was doing so out of a fondness for attractive young people. I let that misunderstanding go uncorrected because it made gathering them easier. And I only ever fired the ones who tried to convert their life into mana… I can't deny my fondness for beautiful boys and girls, though."

"Excuse me?!" Bond exclaimed, aghast.

Diamond just shrugged. "I guess anything I say now will just sound like an excuse. I was destroyed in the end anyway."

"…Yes. As huge as you were, you disappeared without a trace," Bond said.

"I thought so, too… But it turns out that my core concealed itself underground while I was unconscious and began to repair itself. I remained there until about one hundred years ago, when a traveling adventurer excavated me and became my wielder. We traveled and sang together for many years. We spent most of our time singing and dancing, actually."

"It sounds like she was an unconventional person," Nick said with a weak smile.

Diamond smiled back. "She was. She stumbled across the Sword of Distortion's core on her travels and became obsessed with songs and idols after discovering some data storage from the era of the gods. The silly girl thought minstrels were idols. She was also arrogant enough to say that the one who warped the lives of millions of people needed a cuter name than the Sword of Distortion, and she renamed me the Sword of Resonance."

Diamond began to speak of the adventurer named Hibiki Diamond. She had an unconventional personality and was tremendously influential. She devoted herself to rebuilding Teran, which had been destroyed by a large-scale Stampede, and the Maiden Highway. She also spread the word that it was possible to explore ancient ruins for artifacts and gathered adventurers to revive the defunct Adventurers Guild.

She picked up ancient culture from the items she excavated, and even found some valuable documents that long predated the ancient civilization. Her incredible discoveries and insatiable appetite for more led many to call her a hyena.

Hizumi was one of the items that Diamond the adventurer had found. She had no direct combat ability, but no matter how many times she insisted that her mana had dried up, she was still forced to take up a sword and fight monsters. Her wielder also ordered her to sing at banquets even though she knew nothing about music, to use a pickax to help maintain the highway, and even to wash dishes when she screwed something up.

Those were all first-time experiences for Hizumi.

Eventually, Diamond the adventurer had said, "The Sword of Distortion isn't a fitting name for you. It sounds ugly. How about we call you the 'Sword of Resonance' instead?" Despite the gall of the proposal, Hizumi accepted the name change.

The two of them continued to spend a lot of time together

after that. They'd had more than a few fights over the years, sometimes hating each other, sometimes loving each other.

Diamond's story reminded Nick of a song. He almost quoted it right then and there, but he thought it would be rude.

"Diamond later retired as an adventurer and claimed that she was going to become an ancient idol. I accompanied her on her new journey, since I had no real choice in the matter, and because she was a genius who excelled at anything she put her mind to, her songs became popular almost overnight. I, on the other hand, never improved, no matter how much I practiced," Diamond said.

"Can't holy swords install the talents of their user?" Nick asked.

"I wasn't really made with imitating people in mind," Diamond replied. "The most I can do is copy the form of my wielder; I can't copy their skills."

Bond nodded in agreement. "You can tell that by looking at her. She is far too large for a human to pick up and wield. Her core is a monument, not a sword. In a way, this entire concert hall is her body," he said, pointing at the shining gem in the middle of the room.

Nick nodded and remembered the sight of Diamond practicing. She must have gained that skill entirely through her own training.

"You're amazing," Nick said, eliciting a snort from Bond.

"You might hesitate to say that if you knew how much she mocked other holy swords for being primitive and having to move their bodies all the time," he said.

"Hey, do you have to keep bringing up embarrassing things from my past?!" Diamond complained.

"Anyway, we know your identity. But that's not the problem," Nick said, giving Diamond a severe look. "I want to know what you're plotting, and why you're involving us. You've roped your idols and many others into this, too."

"Yeah!" Karan agreed emphatically. "The idols are all working so hard! To them, their practice and promotional activities are just as important as their concerts! And...it's all in pursuit of their own dreams! I'm sure that's true of you, too, Agate!"

Agate just balled her fists.

"Yep. I'm using the dreams of others. I won't deny that," Diamond said.

"Why?!" Karan cried.

"I'll explain. You can leave if my reasons aren't enough to satisfy you. You're even free to destroy this place."

Diamond stood up from her chair and put a hand to the diamond pillar behind her. She continued with utter gravity.

"You sit within the newly constructed Distortion, which I have made into a holy jewel resonance facility renamed Jewelry Production. Its holy jewel will reverberate and stop the large-scale Stampede. Its final objective is to stave off the demon god resurrection that has been in the works for a millennium," she said.

"A-a large-scale Stampede?!" Bond repeated, shocked.

"There have been signs of a Stampede recently. Did you not know that?" Diamond asked.

"We've noticed the signs, but...you're saying it's going to be a large one? Not a small or medium one?" Nick asked, confused.

"Yep. It could revitalize a great many labyrinths, causing tens of thousands—potentially hundreds of thousands—of monsters to spill into the outside world. It could even revive the demon god," Diamond said.

"Hold on, I thought those only happened once every few centuries...," Nick argued, but even as he said it, he was starting to believe her. There had been an abundance of strange incidents around Labyrinth City, and they had noticed many abnormalities in the labyrinths. There was plenty of evidence for Diamond's claim.

"It's been over two centuries since the last large-scale Stampede. Do you know what the signs are? One of them is the mutation of labyrinth bosses. They're reborn into unprecedented forms that can deal with the attack patterns of adventurers. A giant, agile slime appeared last month in Gooey Waterworks and swallowed an F-rank adventurer, drowning them. A six-armed devil appeared in Thousand Sword Peak and wiped out a C-rank party. In Pot Snake Cave—"

"A new pot snake specialized for attack appeared," Nick finished for Diamond.

"Exactly. The Adventurers Guild must have noticed the signs, too. I'll bet they're panicking and having round-the-clock meetings with the Sun Knights," Diamond said.

Nick grimaced, remembering how close they came to dying in Pot Snake Cave.

"The demon-god worshippers have been working in secret for a long time to cause a large-scale Stampede and resurrect the demon god, and their efforts are finally paying off... But you gave us a chance in this crisis by defeating White Mask," Diamond continued.

"So you used the concerts to gather mana with ritual magic and moved to the execution phase of your plan. But fans started using counterfeit tickets to steal mana. Is that right?" Tiana asked.

Diamond raised her eyebrows. "You figured out how they're stealing mana? We had guessed it was the tickets, but we didn't have definitive proof."

"A false paladin showed up late to the last concert. He arrived just as the show reached its climax, and his strength far surpassed any false paladins we've encountered so far. As soon as the concert ended, though, it was like he deflated. His strength was just gone," Tiana explained.

"Interesting... Joseph, how excited were the fans?" Diamond asked.

"This was Topaz's bestselling concert ever. This was as likely a concert as any to attract false paladins," Joseph answered.

"Were there any disturbances in the mana waves?"

"Yes. They were diverted more than ever before."

Diamond asked a number of other questions before seeming to come to a conclusion.

"The counterfeit tickets serve as a marker or an identification signal. They falsify the banned fan's negative emotions as the center of the ritual and shift the location where the mana is concentrated. It's not the ticket that's important but the intensity of the owner's grudge and the fans' excitement. This is ritual magic of the cursed variety," Diamond said.

"Curse magic is prohibited in modern times. Even the spellbooks are banned... Can you do anything to stop it?" Tiana asked.

Diamond's expression was grim. "We'll do everything we can. Repelling it entirely might be difficult at this point, though..."

"Oh, yeah. I should've told you this earlier, but we figured out the identity of the counterfeit-ticket seller," Nick said.

"You did?!" Diamond exclaimed joyfully.

Nick grimaced before continuing. "He was killed, though. The seller was a blacklisted idol fan named Eishu. He was a demon-god worshipper, and a partner of his named Garos murdered him to silence him. Garos stole the rest of the counterfeit tickets and vanished. The Sun Knights are looking for him, but I don't think they have much chance of catching him."

"Eishu... Oh yeah, I remember seeing his name in the fan club report. He was a real pain who harassed our idols, but I never expected this," Diamond said. Nick was surprised to hear she read the fan-club reports.

"It seemed like he was more motivated by his obsession with idols than with his status as a demon-god worshipper. That's how I caught him, but it seems like Garos and the other demon-god worshippers were worried he would expose them," Nick said.

"I see... Thank you very much for your investigation," Joseph said. "We've been working on this project in secret for some time. We've managed to thwart all attempts by the demon-god

. worshippers to spy on us over the years, but I believe we essentially revealed ourselves to them when we began the experiments to restore Diamond in earnest. Rushing our plans forward backfired."

"Did you only start the mana-gathering rituals recently? ... Oh, are you using the new magic lighting equipment?" Nick asked, remembering something that Jonathan had told him. Jewelry Production was using new magic items for lighting and production. What if those were secretly for the ritual?

Joseph nodded. "That is correct. The new lighting equipment absorbs the heightened passions of the idols and the audience, converts it into mana, and sends it here. Much of the mana is lost on the way from other concert venues to this location, however, and we were late to realize that the false paladins were stealing it," he said.

"Makes sense," said Nick. "Man, you've got guts to perform this kind of ritual right under everyone's noses..."

"It was now or never. White Mask was defeated, the large-scale Stampede is approaching, and the Hundredth Anniversary Concert is the best chance we'll ever have to gather mana. Diamond actually obtained permission to perform the ritual, which was a major gamble that we had many meetings about beforehand," Joseph said.

"Permission? From who?" Nick asked.

"This is a top-secret project approved by the lord of Teran, the president of the Teran Department of Construction, and the president of the Teran Department of Magic Safety. I am actually the lord's nephew. I was transferred from the lord's manor to serve as an auditor," Joseph explained.

"Huh?! I didn't know that!" Agate exclaimed. She was even more surprised than the Survivors.

"My apologies. I was sworn to secrecy... I had to make a number of arrangements just to share this information with you here today. You are the first idol to learn these secrets, Agate. I will explain everything to the others by the end of the day, but please keep it to yourself until then," Joseph requested, playfully putting his index finger to his lips.

"O-okay," said Agate.

"You've been lying about your identity, too... Oh, I guess we should address you more formally," Nick said.

"Do not worry about my position. I would prefer you to treat me normally... Anyway, now that we have told you everything, let us discuss your job," Joseph said.

"Our job?" Nick repeated.

"I would like you to handle security at the Hundredth Anniversary Concert," Joseph said.

Nick tensed at those words. He had a hunch that any battle that broke out there would decide everything.

"We are going to unveil Diamond's true form—the holy jewel in this room—to the audience during the concert. We'll then concentrate mana at the highest efficiency to restore Diamond to her peak strength and activate Jewelry Production," Joseph continued.

"That's your true goal," Nick said.

"The demon-god worshippers have only sporadically obstructed our concerts so far. All they've done is give counterfeit tickets to fans... And we were unsure of their intentions," Joseph said.

"Maybe they were experimenting, too. They might not have been sure if the tickets would work," Tiana conjectured.

Joseph nodded. "Yes, I believe so. But they will have no reason to hold back at the Hundredth Anniversary Concert. Please, protect Diamond... Protect our project and the idols from the demon-god worshippers."

Nick crossed his arms, stern-faced, then turned to Diamond. "Diamond. I'll ask this question again. Why did you choose us?" he asked.

"Nick…"

"The more you tell us, the more it makes sense for us to help you. It's not just about fighting the demon-god worshippers. One of our members is a holy sword just like you. If you said you want to work together as business partners because our interests align, I'd have no complaints," Nick said.

Diamond looked guilty. "That is part of why we trust you. But it's true that we tried to use you."

"I'm not blaming you. I appreciate all you've done to help us," Nick said.

"We've done very little compared with what you all have accomplished… And your apparent willingness to remain on our side even after learning my identity and plan makes you very valuable to us," Diamond said.

"Really?" Nick asked.

"There's a chance that if I revealed myself to the Sun Knights or the Adventurers Guild and asked for help, they would treat me as property or a dangerous magic item rather than as a person. I might even lose my citizenship. I do have a team of lawyers and an ideological argument prepared for that scenario," Diamond said.

"That is a concern," Bond agreed grimly.

"And that's far from the worst thing that could happen. I also need to consider the possibility of whistleblowers or saboteurs in a public organization. You never know where someone with the authority to order around White Mask could be hiding, too," Diamond said.

"Yeah, there are a lot of shady people out there. It's probably not worth the risk," Nick responded.

"I'm not really one to talk, as someone who's using an idol company for a plot, but I don't want everything to fall apart because one person betrayed me." Diamond gave a cynical smile, resting her chin on her hands. "What do you say, Survivors? I'll pay you handsomely for your work. There are a lot of risks to taking this job, but I can offer you security in return. Bond is in a similar position to me. I can share the preparations I've made if I'm discovered as a holy sword... However!"

Diamond raised her voice suddenly. The others in the room watched her in awe.

"I don't want to just entice you into doing this job with payment and promises. I want you all to protect me. Just like the paladin who fought to save an idol. You all are worthy subjects for my songs. I have no desire to sing about someone I detest. That's why I'm leaving myself naked before you," she said.

"Can you not put it that way?" Nick quipped.

"Then let's say my organs are vulnerable. There are no walls and no mana protecting me. You could easily cut me apart with your dagger. If that's not enough to satisfy you, I'll bare this body for you as well."

Diamond took off her coat. She was stark naked underneath, leaving everyone stupefied.

"H-hey!" Nick shouted.

"I'm betting on you all. What do you want to do?" Diamond asked.

She stood there in the nude—with no hint of embarrassment or coquettishness—and waited for their decision.

Joseph ended the meeting by admitting that he and Diamond had been hiding a lot and that he would leave it to everyone's individual discretion if they wanted to continue working together, though the others thought it was a bit late for that. Then everyone except for Diamond, Joseph, and Hector left the underground storage room and returned aboveground to take a break in a waiting room. It had been three hours since they'd arrived at this venue, making it a good time to eat lunch.

They found Topaz and Amber in the waiting room with snacks; they had come to Starmine Hall to check on them out of concern. The girls handed out baskets with donuts and bread and magic bottles containing coffee and tea.

"Wait, I just realized something. Isn't this backward? As staff, shouldn't we be providing food to you?" Nick asked.

"I just realized something, too. You're very nitpicky," Agate said. Everyone else was quick to agree.

Nick muttered for them all to shut up, then relented and drank his tea.

"Oh yeah, what happened to Hector?" Karan asked casually.

"He stayed behind with Joseph and Diamond 'cause he's the only one who hasn't signed a nondisclosure agreement. He's gonna be treated as a temporary employee, too," Nick answered.

The room fell silent after their short exchange. Karan started eating, and the others followed her example, unsure what else to do with themselves. Once they were done eating, they all realized how much they needed to talk about everything. No one was sure where they should start or who they should speak to first, however, so they simply drank and refilled their tea in silence.

"Haah. Can I say something? This silence feels depressing," Daffodil said, finally breaking the ice.

"That'd be great. I wasn't sure where to start," Nick responded.

"I've been keeping this a secret, but I've been working for Diamond in pursuit of revenge. My husband—well, we were never married, so... My boyfriend, who was in the same party as me, was killed by White Mask. Oh, that makes it even more depressing in here, huh? Eh, whatever," Daffodil said nonchalantly.

The idols gulped and listened attentively; this must have been their first time hearing it, too.

"You were a D-rank adventurer...right?" Nick asked.

"Yeah. Dancing was my main job, though. I worked as an adventurer on the side to help me achieve my goal of dancing in large venues and gaining popularity... Then one day, my party found an ancient treasure in a labyrinth," Daffodil said.

"A treasure, huh?" Nick mumbled.

Daffodil smiled bitterly. "I was so excited. I thought my life was made, and that I'd be free to pursue my dreams... But then White Mask attacked us on the way home. Our leader drew White Mask's attention so we could escape, and when we got adventurer reinforcements and returned, we saw no sign of his body or the treasure. All of us who survived were heartbroken."

Nick remembered Leon telling him that many adventurers had lost companions to White Mask. It made sense for a person with a personal grudge against the demon-god worshipper to choose to cooperate with Diamond.

"And as if that wasn't enough, I learned I was pregnant when I returned to Labyrinth City... I was very conflicted over what to do. Should I forget the kid and seek revenge? Or should I live on for their sake? I even considered throwing everything away and ending my life," Daffodil continued.

"Daffy...," Karan said.

"That was when Diamond saved me. She said I didn't have to give up on having my child, getting revenge, or my dream of dancing, and she helped me build a stable foundation in my life," Daffodil said.

She explained that Diamond revealed her secret and situation to her shortly afterward. Claiming she would eventually gain the strength to oppose White Mask, she had asked for Daffodil's assistance. Daffodil agreed to help her, initially serving as a guard rather than as a choreographer or dance instructor. Eventually, however, Diamond saw the potential of Daffodil's dancing talent and had her start teaching the idols.

"Before long, I was teaching the girls and raising my boy, and I was actually enjoying my life. Diamond told me to become an independent dance instructor, and my desire for revenge faded... And then I heard that you all defeated White Mask. I thought I might be angry that my chance for revenge was stolen, but instead

I felt great relief. I've wanted to thank you all this time, Karan. I'm sorry for keeping it from you," Daffodil apologized.

A solemn mood fell over the room. Noticing this, Daffodil hurriedly stuffed donuts into Agate's, Amber's, and Topaz's mouths and urged them to eat. The idols protested, saying they weren't in the mood to eat, but Daffodil insisted and offered them more bread and donuts.

"Wait, we heard you were scammed when you opened your classroom," Karan said as she took a bite.

"I actually found out my broker was working for the demon-god worshippers, so I pretended to be deceived and—hold on, how do you know about that?!" Daffodil exclaimed.

"You were keeping too many secrets, Daffy. And you looked into us, too," Karan said.

Daffodil averted her eyes—she had no argument for that—and changed the topic. "Y-you three already knew about Diamond's true identity, right? What did you think of it?"

"Uh, well, I honestly don't understand any of the big picture stuff, and I don't really care," Agate admitted.

"I get that," Topaz responded.

"Right?" Amber agreed.

"Hey, you three could be putting your lives at risk. Are you okay with that?" Nick asked in disbelief.

Agate quickly argued back. "My job is to sing and dance! I don't know the first thing about Stampedes or holy swords or any of that stuff!"

"Sure, but Diamond's been using you! Don't you care about that?" Nick asked.

"Ah... About that. I don't know if I should say this or not, but..." Agate hesitated and glanced at her fellow idols as if asking if she should continue. They seemed just as hesitant.

"Whatever you say stays between us. You don't need to hold back," Tiana said.

Agate made up her mind, still a bit nervous. "Okay, I'll say it... Are we sure Diamond is doing all this for the just cause of saving the world and bringing about peace? 'Cause I don't think so," she said.

Nick and his party members weren't sure what Agate was saying. They might not have trusted Diamond completely, but she had won them over emotionally. They'd assumed she was mostly telling the truth.

Daffodil was initially as confused as the Survivors, but then she said, "You...might be right, actually."

"Hold on, I don't know where this is coming from. Does she have more secrets?" Nick asked.

Agate rushed to calm Nick down. "I don't think this is a big deal at all. I just don't think everything she said was from the heart. She is taking the project seriously, but I think it's a means to an end, rather than her purpose."

"A means to what end?" Nick asked with some trepidation.

"Basically, it doesn't feel like she's going through all this effort just to bring peace to Labyrinth City. I think she wants peace so that she can devote herself entirely to her idol career," Agate explained.

"There's nothing she wouldn't do to continue working in this industry," Topaz said.

"Right? I think she kept changing her name slightly and debuting over and over because she couldn't stand not performing," Amber agreed.

"She's not performing idol concerts for the plan. Gathering people, spending money, and building facilities has all been for the purpose of spreading idol culture... She's not in it for the plan at all," Daffodil said.

Nick was confused at first, but their claims were beginning to make sense.

"...Are Diamond's songs—particularly the love songs—all about her past wielder?" he asked.

"Probably. I think Diamond has made writing about her past girlfriend her thing. She's not a villain who wants to destroy the world or a hero who wants to devote herself to society. Anyway, you have to admit it takes a real pro to write lyrics about a past love affair," Daffodil said.

"Hey, don't say that out loud! I almost said it during the meeting, but I kept it to myself!" Nick shouted.

"So you realized it, too!" Agate exclaimed.

"That's not a bad idea... I occasionally write poetry and send it to women. Perhaps I should try writing an idol song," Zem said.

"Oh *now* you're interested, Zem. Do you ever stop thinking of women?" Nick said.

The group began discussing rumors about Diamond and analyzing her lyrics for hints of romance. It was a very mundane topic they were getting excited about, especially given the magnitude of the stakes at hand. With every lyric they deciphered, the unvarnished truth about the relationship between the legendary S-rank adventurer Hibiki Diamond and the most popular idol in Labyrinth City became clearer.

"Wait a second, I'm gonna look at the lyric sheet," Tiana said.

"I'll reference dictionaries for ancient words and poetic terms. There might be even more hidden in her lyrics," Bond said.

"Oh my. These lyrics are steamy," Zem commented.

"I-I'm not listening!" Karan shouted.

Bond and Tiana worked to find meaning hidden in the connections between modern and ancient words. Zem put his formidable deductive skills to use and periodically offered comments. ("The flower and the bird are a metaphor for the two of them," "This is a passionate love song disguised as a graduation song," "This song is unabashedly erotic.") The idol Diamond's love for the adventurer Diamond could not have been more obvious as they peeled back the layers of her lyrics.

The group was getting a clear picture of the dense world the two Diamonds shared together. Karan blushed furiously and covered her ears; she even looked like she could faint.

"Man, I'm dead tired... What should we say to Diamond after this?" Nick said when he ran out of steam. He leaned back in his chair and put his feet up to rest.

"Huh? I thought we were having fun," Tiana said.

"This is fun, but I wanted to talk about what we're doing next," Nick replied.

"Oh, right. I kinda forgot we need to discuss that."

"Sorry, I got too engrossed," Zem apologized.

Embarrassed, they both looked up from the lyric sheets and dictionaries they had been poring over.

"So what are you going to do?" Agate asked. "Are you going to protect us at the concert or not?"

Nick didn't answer right away. He sat up, put his fingers together, and spoke slowly. "Joseph said we can break off our contract."

"Yeah, he did," Agate responded.

"But he didn't say anything about exempting us from the penalty for not fulfilling the contract or paying us the reward we were promised, right?"

"No, he did not," Agate said.

"I didn't hear him say that," Karan added.

"Good observation. That man is crafty," Bond said.

"You've got that right. We have to talk about money before discussing quitting," Tiana agreed.

"This company is rampant with crafty people. I don't think we can trust them," Zem said.

The Survivors all chuckled together.

"There you have it," Nick said.

"Who knew our paladin was so distrustful?" Agate said, and everyone laughed.

*   *   *

There were no more concerts until the Hundredth Anniversary Concert at the end of the month. Nearly all the agency's idols were devoting themselves to preparations, and the managers and staff were very busy as well.

This was Jewelry Production's largest concert ever, and the agency was also busy with the secret plot to activate Diamond's holy jewel resonance facility, also called Jewelry Production. Furthermore, now that the Survivors had uncovered how the counterfeit tickets worked, the agency was working feverishly to counter them. They had enlisted Thunderbolt Corporation—a magic item factory that supplied the agency—to work on a jamming device that would release mana to obstruct the counterfeit tickets.

Joseph had to oversee all the company's progress, and he was so busy, he barely had time to sleep. There weren't many people who knew all the agency's secrets and could handle the paperwork. As a result, the Survivors were roped into planning the concert's security. Tiana had taken the lead in this matter and was spending her time working out how best to deploy the guards. Joseph had pulled some strings behind the scenes to recruit soldiers from the lord of Teran to help with security, but while they were capable fighters, there was no commander to lead them.

That was where Tiana distinguished herself. During her aristocratic school days, she had taken a class called Siege Defense for pure interest and had earned good grades on her military simulation exams. She put this knowledge to use to give precise feedback. Given her natural disposition as well, she quickly earned respect from both the Jewelry Production guards and the lord of Teran's soldiers.

It could also be said that the Survivors were being taken advantage of.

"Are you sure it's okay for you to be slacking off like this?"

"You're the one who summoned me here! Can't you use your authority as a Sun Knight to help me?"

Nick was meeting with Alice again. They were at a window seat at the Knocker Donuts near Jewelry Production, which was where Nick and Karan had met Daffodil. It had begun to rain outside, and peddlers were holding bags over their heads and running down the street to find cover.

"Don't say that. I know I have the ability to help you. Security is our specialty," Alice said.

"I hate that you're not lying," Nick said regretfully, and Alice laughed. "By the way, have you found Garos?"

"I was afraid you'd ask that. We've found no trace of him. I did find multiple documents that could be detailing murders Garos committed, though," Alice said, passing him a brown envelope filled with documents.

"Isn't this the statement I wrote? Do I really need to review that?" Nick asked.

"It wasn't easy getting permission for this. There are comments from other people in there, too. Look it over when you have time," Alice requested.

"Sure. I appreciate it."

"Are you sure you don't have any ideas for where Garos's hideout could be? Has anything else come to mind?" Alice asked.

Nick grimaced. "I told you all the places I could think of, and I don't have any other ideas... But something else occurred to me."

"Give it to me. I don't care how unlikely it is," Alice urged happily.

"You know how White Mask gave Nargava a phantom king orb?" Nick asked.

"Yeah."

"The demon-god worshippers should have a couple other powerful magic items that were excavated with it. They're called the Butterfly Sword and the False Root Staff. The Butterfly Sword is apparently a magic sword that can be used to perform illusionary attacks."

"What?"

"Do you...think the round thing attached to Garos's katana was a bell?" Nick asked.

Alice nodded. "Yeah, it was an antique bell from Nozomi. They call them 'suzu' over there."

"I've been told the Butterfly Sword has a bell attached to both the blade and scabbard," Nick said.

"What?! Why didn't you say that earlier, you dolt?!" Alice exclaimed, grabbing Nick by the collar with tears in her eyes. Nick shook her off, briefly worried she was actually going to cut off his air.

"I'm sorry! That's no reason to strangle me, though! That's not the important part anyway!" Nick shouted.

"What is, then?" Alice asked.

"The False Root Staff. It's a magic item that lets you manipulate magic dolls and golems at will."

"Okay."

"The Labyrinth of Bonds can't be the only ancient ruin or sealed underground labyrinth in this city. The Labyrinth of Bonds is officially managed by the Adventurers Guild, but there've gotta be other ruins the general public doesn't know about."

"The underground isn't like the rooftop routes that are only accessible to Steppingmen. The underground passages and waterways are mapped out and managed by the Order of the Sun Knights and the Organization for Labyrinth City Development."

"Really? Then any ruins that we think are inactive could just be blocked by a golem masquerading as a door or something?"

Alice didn't answer. Her expression said the chances weren't zero. "If we assume he's using a secret ancient ruin as a safe house... Is searching above ground pointless?"

"I wouldn't say pointless, but...we'd have little hope of finding him. I think we'd be better off waiting for him to come to us," Nick said.

Alice sighed deeply. "Then we should focus our efforts on the concert."

Nick nodded silently.

"But it was Eishu who was obsessed with idols, right? And Garos stole the counterfeit tickets. Isn't it possible he'll use them for a different purpose?" Alice asked.

"The counterfeit tickets require a crowd's worth of prayers to function. He'll come," Nick said.

"Can you beat him? Garos has a whole stack of counterfeit tickets, and this is the biggest concert yet. He could send dozens of false paladins at once," Alice said.

"That won't work," Nick said, shaking his head.

"What makes you say that?"

"Jewelry Production is working on a device to block counterfeit tickets from activating within the venue."

"That's great news."

"There's one problem, though... While it'll be able to block individual tickets fueled by a weak grudge, it won't be able to stop someone with a massive grudge and dozens of tickets."

"A massive grudge, huh...? I don't like the sound of that."

"I guess it's also possible one of their leaders will reveal themselves for the first time and attack the concert directly."

"That won't happen. They're saving their strength for the moment of the demon god's resurrection, so they won't spend it early. Doing so would lead to an all-out battle, which I'm sure neither side wants. That's why they're having individual mercenaries like Garos and Eishu do their bidding for them. The leaders who truly desire the demon god's resurrection won't appear until they absolutely have to."

"Then don't try to get the concert canceled. You've probably already gotten the directive from the lord, though."

Alice glared at Nick. "Ugh, who knew that girl could pull strings like that? That simple persona of hers really is all an act."

"That's why I came to apologize and share information. You should know Diamond's plan now, too," Nick said.

"I'm still upset about that... That was humiliating for the order," Alice said.

Diamond and Joseph had actually met with the Order of the Sun Knights and told them about her plan. The revelation sent a huge shock wave through the order, and there were many knights who vehemently opposed it, but Diamond had made arrangements beforehand to prevent them from doing anything about it. The presence of a certain captain and her temporary subordinate also helped to prevent the Sun Knights from trying to forcefully cancel the concert.

"We got lucky, though. Make me look good out there, my temporary Sun Knight," Alice said.

"Does that mean you approve of our plan?" Nick asked.

"If you succeed, I'll have no complaints. If you fail, Garos will probably kill you. You're no use to me dead or a coward."

Nick couldn't help but laugh at her bluntness. "You're ruthless."

"Don't die out there," Alice said.

"...I'm not a betting man, but people who bet on me always win," Nick replied.

Nick got up from his chair, took a donut from Alice's plate, and bit into it.

The sun had been shining without a cloud in the sky since early morning, making this a perfect day to spend outdoors. The beautiful weather alone wasn't enough to explain the gargantuan line that stretched outside of Starmine Hall, however. The area was loud from complaints about pushing and warnings from staff to not run.

The line wasn't exactly well organized, but the fans were unusually understanding of the staff's difficulties. This was the largest idol concert ever held, and thinking about that fact turned all feelings of irritation to joy. The rising excitement for the concert was palpable.

"Skewered eel! Who wants some skewered eel?!"

"I've got water! It's important to stay hydrated! You don't want to faint during the concert! I've got ice, too!"

"Donuts, donuts! Nothing better at a concert than donuts!"

Street vendors were forcing their way toward the line to set up stalls or peddle their wares on foot. Some had received permission from management to sell outside the venue, but many had not, assuming stubbornly that they would be able to slip into the crowd unnoticed and perform monetary calculations in their head. It wasn't only the fans who were looking forward to this day of celebration.

"Man, Nick has some horrible luck. I can't believe he has to miss the greatest concert ever staged!" Willy, an adventurer idol fan, excitedly said to Jonathan.

"Mm-hmm... Let's have enough fun for him, too," Jonathan replied, fervently repressing the desire to tell him about how that bastard had betrayed them and was currently working alongside the idols. He had to keep his word, and Nick did get him a signed card.

"Oh yeah, some weird people have been showing up at concerts lately. If you see any, leave them to the adventurers and run. At the last concert, I gallantly rushed to Lady Tiana's aid—she's one of Nick's friends—and saved her life. I can feel it. She's fallen for me," Willy said.

"R-really? I hope nothing happens, though. Everyone's been looking forward to this concert," Jonathan responded.

He looked at the concert venue, Starmine Hall. It had the majesty of a cathedral made to worship the gods, yet there was something pure about it as well. He was simultaneously awed by its beauty and a little scared of it. It was like a fortress built to protect the girls from evil.

Good luck, Nick, he thought.

There was a small room in the upper floors of Starmine Hall built for operating the lighting equipment and performing maintenance on the vents. A small window—built at an angle so that it could not be seen from the ground—in the room offered a sweeping view of the area below. The Survivors had stationed themselves in this room to watch the situation.

"This is an impressive crowd. I see many of Nick's friends. Oh, there's Jonathan," Bond said, straining his eyes curiously.

"Be careful, Bond. We don't want anyone we know to see us,"

Nick warned. Bond assured Nick—not very convincingly—that he understood. "Man, I wanted to be a part of that line."

"You can't be serious," Tiana said, rearing back.

"Of course I am! Concerts are supposed to be viewed from the stands!" Nick argued. "I'm sure you feel the same way for dragon races. There are long lines for those, too."

"Grk, I guess I can't argue with that," Tiana admitted, looking away to avoid Nick's smug grin.

"It's a little hot in here… I'm quite jealous of those in the air-conditioned waiting room," Zem complained.

"The idols are in here, so of course it's air conditioned. Do *you want to try wearing these clothes, Zem?*" Karan said indignantly through Telepathy.

"*This isn't easy for you, either. I apologize,*" Zem said.

"*You bet it isn't. As long as you understand.*" Karan harrumphed.

Karan was the only member of the Survivors not in the small room; instead, she was with the idols in the waiting room. The Jewelry Production security staff and the soldiers Joseph had procured were handling security throughout the venue, while it was Nick, Tiana, Zem, and Bond's job to wait in a location from which they could quickly deal with any demon-god worshipper threats.

Defending Diamond's main body was their top priority, however, and they needed to assure the safety of the idols as well. The barrier surrounding the stage would make it difficult to reach, and no matter how quickly the rest of the party dealt with the demon-god worshippers, they needed someone close to the performers. They selected Karan for that job.

She wouldn't be able to protect Diamond from the wings of the stage or from below it; she needed to be onstage with the idols and somehow remain inconspicuous. They decided the best way for her to do this would be to dress as an idol and join them.

Karan wouldn't sing, of course—she would essentially perform the role of a stagehand. The costume was simply a disguise so that she could blend in when the idols needed to gather onstage. There was no better way to allow her to respond immediately to trouble and fool their enemies. They didn't want anyone to realize she was a guard.

Karan was fine with being assigned to defend the idols, but she protested vehemently against the costume. It took Nick and all the other Survivors, along with Agate, Daffodil, and Diamond, to calm her down and convince her to do it.

"I don't know if you'll make the most convincing stagehand," Tiana said.

"None of them look like stagehands. Even the people who will clean the stage are wearing slightly simpler versions of the idol costumes. That's what Diamond prefers. She said I couldn't wear black for that reason," Karan explained.

"Interesting...," Tiana said.

"Anyway, is everything okay over there?" Nick asked.

"A fan got excited and tried to force his way back here, but venue security caught him. No one has gotten into the waiting room. Everything's fine," Karan answered.

"There's nothing to do but wait for the show, then. We should go out and eat once this is over," Nick suggested. He spoke casually, but there was clear resolve in his voice. He was maintaining a calm mental state—not too tense, not too relaxed—in preparation for the fight.

"...What do you want to eat, Nick?" Karan asked.

"Hmm, nothing comes to mind right away, but...oh yeah. You mentioned northern-style barbecue recently. We're gonna have more money than we'll know what to do with after this job, so we might as well go to a high-end restaurant," Nick said.

"High-end restaurants have a dress code. You should have Diamond pick out some clothes for you," Karan said.

"That's your response? And wouldn't that be more expensive than the food?" Nick said, and the others laughed.

When the laughter died down, Karan said, "...I feel like I understand now why you took me to Pot Snake Cave without explaining yourself."

"Huh?" Nick wasn't sure why she was recalling that now.

"You had probably been keeping that concern to yourself for a while. Leaders like you and Diamond have to carry so much weight all the time. I don't know if I could do it."

"That's nothing to be impressed by. I should have talked to you."

"I still think it's amazing. I've spent so much time wondering why you wouldn't talk to me, and what you were thinking about, and I finally feel like I understand."

"Don't learn from me. Don't learn from Diamond, either, for that matter. That girl's nuts," Nick said.

"I don't mind Diamond. I'm okay with you being a little nuts, too," Karan responded.

"Really?"

"I think leaders can be forgiven for turning out that way," Tiana said.

"Diamond is quite ambitious. It actually might not be so bad to emulate her," Zem offered.

"Give me a break. I don't even want to think about having to deal with more people like her," Bond said.

Karan was happy to hear this from her party members. "You should do what you want in life, Nick. That goes for the rest of you, too. Don't be afraid to act like idiots. We're adventurers, after all," she said with a caring and encouraging tone.

Her words filled the other Survivors with warmth and confidence. They all felt the desire to protect Starmine Hall on this day of great passion.

"I'm going to do my job," said Karan. "No one will lay a finger on the idols."

"That's what I wanna hear. We'll leave the stage to you," Nick said.

"Okay!" Karan replied happily.

The Starmine Hall staff opened the main gate as the telepathic conversation came to an end. Nick looked down through the window and watched the line of people flood into the venue. Some veteran concertgoers entered calmly and got in line for merchandise or food, but most people pushed and shoved their way through the crowd as their excitement got the better of them. The crowd's noise was loud enough to penetrate the soundproof walls and shake the small staff room.

The crowd eventually calmed down, but after a short silence, the venue began to vibrate much more intensely than before. The opening song had begun.

"Do you wish you were watching, Nick?" Zem asked.

"It's fine. Experiencing a concert from the staff side for a change is interesting. Just the once, though," Nick said with a shrug, leaning his back against the wall. The vibration felt good. This was a sensation reserved for those behind the scenes.

"I sense trouble," Bond said shortly afterward.

"Okay. Where is it? How many people are there?" Nick asked.

"There is an especially sinister presence at the rear gate. It is only one person. I sense no backup... They seem quite dangerous, however. They are significantly stronger than any false paladins we have encountered thus far," Bond answered.

"Zem and I will go first. We'll switch Zem for Tiana, depending on what the enemy does," Nick said.

"Be careful," Tiana urged.

Nick gave her a reassuring thumbs-up.

""""Union!"""" Nick, Zem, and Bond shouted together, summoning a torrent of light.

Far beneath the rooftop routes the Steppingman used to avoid detection, Labyrinth City also had an extensive underground network. It consisted primarily of sewers, transport tunnels for garbage, and emergency shelters that had long since been sealed.

But while the underground was complex and mysterious, it wasn't considered dangerous like the Garbage Heap was. The reason for that was because Sun Knights had permission to enter for criminal investigations. The Order of the Sun Knights and the Organization for Labyrinth City Development—which worked directly under the lord of Labyrinth City—had mapped out the tunnels and were fully aware of their layout. Or at least, that should have been the case.

Nick's guess that there might be a safe house only accessible with the False Root Staff seemed to be correct. The ominous creature crawling sluggishly out of a manhole that connected to the underground passageways was proof of that.

The creature was beyond grotesque. It was human from the neck up, but below it was made of a glutinous, slime-like material that barely formed the shape of a human body. Tags packed tightly onto its body seemed to hold the slime together.

"*Ourruurruugghh...*"

A silver knight stood in its path, tall with a carefree demeanor. Their strange sword with four blades extending in opposite directions did nothing to diminish their pure, godly aura. Their eyes were almost foxlike, and their physique appeared both strong and handsome. Their captivating form stood in stark contrast to the revolting creature before them.

"*Ruuruugh... Who...are you...? Get in my way...and I'll eat you...*"

""It looks like a monster, but it can speak... Hmm? I recognize your face from somewhere,"" Nick/Zem said.

They realized as they studied the creature that they had seen its dreadful face before. The black hair, the unshaven jaw, the bloodshot eyes—those features belonged to a man who should have been dead.

""**Are you…Eishu?! I saw you get beheaded!**"" Nick/
Zem shouted.

"*Heh-heh… I was kept alive on the brink of death… Shit! My
arms are melting… My body is melting…! So cold… So hot…!
H-help me… I'LL KILL YOU…!*" Eishu moaned.

""**C–calm down. You're not making sense,**"" Nick/
Zem said.

Eishu sounded just as insane as his body was grotesque. His
expression shifted rapidly between rage, anguish, and pleasure,
and his words contradicted each other. Nick/Zem found the non-
sensical speech just as terrifying as his vast mana and strength.

"How cruel… No one can live as just a head and retain
their sanity," Bond said pityingly.

""**What the hell happened to him?**"" Nick/Zem asked.

"His head may have been kept alive using the life-support
system of holy armor. That power can be used to supplement
missing body parts and let them live on temporarily," Bond
conjectured.

""**How could he possibly fight in that state…?**""

"With those tickets. They are absorbing mana from the
concert and using it to compensate for the unstable condition
of his body."

Nick/Zem focused on the tags and were stunned to realize
what those tags were. They were all counterfeit tickets, and each
one was feeding Eishu a sinister strength.

""**Did Garos not behead him to silence him, then?**""
Nick/Zem wondered.

"It was probably to prevent his betrayal. If Garos told him
he would use some form of magic to restore his original body,
Eishu would not be able to oppose him. Garos could also have
influenced his mind when he lost his body and mental stabil-
ity," Bond said.

""**How deplorable,**"" Nick/Zem said gravely. Anger at the abuse of this man's life and dignity rose from Zem's soul.

"You'll pay for giving me this body... I'll make you the same as me...!" Eishu moaned.

""**You're blaming the wrong person, dammit! Say that to Garos! Where is he?!**"" Nick/Zem shouted.

"Sileeeeeence!"

Eishu bellowed angrily and tore one of the counterfeit tickets off his body, causing a gross, reddish-brown mixture of blood and bodily fluids to spill out of the hole. He dipped a writing brush into the liquid and used it to write on the ticket.

A moment later, two new arms sprouted from his back. Just like the first arms, one held a counterfeit ticket while the other held a writing brush. He repeated the process ten times until twenty gooey arms protruded from his body, each pair writing on a ticket.

""**That can't be good!**""

"Take this! Ten Lightning Burrrrsts!"

Eishu glared at Nick/Zem, his grotesque body no longer even resembling a human shape, and lifted all the counterfeit tickets he had written on into the air. A dark cloud formed above Nick/Zem and immediately struck with a tremendous bolt of lightning.

""**Grk... Bond...!**"" Nick/Zem shouted.

"I know, I know! I'll form a wall!" Bond called back, floating above Nick/Zem's head and spinning rapidly.

Bond shone with brilliant light as the equally bright lightning bolts fell like rain, and he successfully deflected them all. Just as the storm finished, Eishu struck with multiple black fists, stunning Nick/Zem with a chain of heavy blows. The fists felt as heavy as morning stars or flails. But that was only a feint.

Nick/Zem realized belatedly that Eishu had stuck counterfeit tickets to their arms. When they tried to peel them off, the tickets exploded in bursts of wind magic, slicing Nick/Zem's body with razor-sharp blades of pressure.

"**"Grk... Oww...!"**"

"Be careful! He is rewriting the counterfeit tickets into talismans! The mana from the concert will allow him to cast advanced spells of all elements!" Bond warned.

"*Heh-heh-hah! Are my Wind Blade talismans painful?!*" Eishu shouted.

Nick/Zem healed themselves as they glared at Eishu. His attacks were powerful and too erratic to predict.

"**"He's tougher than Leon was... He's truly skilled, and his body's got more strength than a monster's. But he's only human,"**" Nick/Zem said.

"He cannot survive long in that state. Even with his new body, he will not last a month. You may as well consider him deceased," Bond said.

"**"We have no choice but to take him down,"**" Nick/Zem replied.

"*Heh-heh... Ouurruruggh... Out of my wayyyyy!*"

Eishu swung his upper arms as if performing some kind of bizarre dance while his lower arms tore tickets off his body to write on them. Oil-like liquid flowed from his body with each ticket he removed.

"I take that back. At this rate, his life-support system will fail, and he won't even survive the fight! He loses mana with each ticket he uses! His body will not hold!" Bond said.

"**"What?!"**" Nick/Zem exclaimed.

"All we have to do is outlast him...though that would feel like an empty victory," Bond said.

While Bond was still speaking, Eishu attacked again, this time with fire and lightning magic.

"**"Dammit, his attacks are gonna reach the venue,"**" Nick/Zem cursed. They used the four-bladed sword as a shield

again to block flames and lightning from another set of talismans.
""Grk... Should we switch to Tiana?""

Nick/Zem's strength was hand-to-hand combat. Their healing magic awarded them impossible toughness, and their agility further accelerated Nick's martial arts skill, allowing them to toy with their opponents. Protecting a wide range from a barrage of spells was not their specialty, however.

"That would be ideal, but...only if we get the chance," Bond responded.

Their odds of defeating Eishu while protecting the venue were slim. Their opponent was insane; if he got past them, many people would die.

"You talk a big game for someone so messy."

Nick/Zem heard a cool voice as they wondered what to do. They didn't have the leeway to turn around and see who it was.

"*Ouruuruughaah!*" Eishu growled.

"Wow, someone got up on the wrong side of the bed... You may have gotten stronger, but your fighting style is the same as before. Don't think it will work on me... Consume his violent mana, Wind Whale!"

The voice's owner drew a sword, and Nick/Zem felt a strange current. It wasn't wind—the flow of mana in the air was being manipulated. The flames and lightning released from Eishu's talismans were diverted toward the sword, disappearing into fog just before they made contact.

""Alice!""

"You've changed your look since the last time I saw you. Did you cut your hair?"

""Looks good, doesn't it?""

The newcomer was Alice of the Sun Knights. Nick/Zem weren't thrilled that she recognized them as Nick—that could have dangerous consequences—but they were relieved all the same. She might have saved their lives.

"That is a magic sword that can dismantle magic spells... Those are quite difficult to master, but they are incredibly powerful under the right circumstances! They can cancel buff spells and healing that's been directed at you," Bond said.

"Well, I won't ask questions right now. Anyway...this is cruel," Alice said, grimacing at the sight of Eishu. She seemed to understand his tragic state right away. "Hold him in place. I'll finish him off."

Nick/Zem shook their head. ""**He's just a lowly criminal who's here to crash the concert. You should arrest him.**""

Alice gave Nick/Zem a stern look, as if debating whether she should say outright that that was impossible. "It's obvious he's trying to end his life. Killing him would be a mercy."

""**We should still do whatever we can. We're not assassins or soldiers,**"" Nick/Zem replied.

"This isn't a street fight. We have to do what's necessary," Alice argued. Her voice carried the weight and sharpness of one who had been through many battles.

But Nick/Zem laughed that off. ""**Of course this is a street fight. No festival would be complete without one.**""

Alice was dumbfounded, but then her eyes softened a bit. "Haah... I can see I won't persuade you. Do what you want. I'll take you both in for questioning later. Magic Absorption Barrier," Alice said with a shrug, turning her back on the fight and slicing her magic sword through the air.

A large, glass-like wall spread out before her; it was probably a magic barrier to prevent Eishu's attacks from reaching Starmine Hall.

"I made a barrier to obstruct mana. It won't hold for long. Finish this quickly," she urged.

""**Got it!**"" Nick/Zem called back.

"*Grourruuugh!*" Eishu growled.

With that, Nick/Zem sprang into action.

""Cognition Corridor!""

Particles of light shot forth from Bond and scattered around Eishu, while Nick/Zem jumped after them. Nick/Zem could scatter and pull the particles together at will, and when they stepped on them, the particles consolidated and produced a strong repellent force—essentially forming steps in midair.

"Wha...?!" Eishu shouted.

Nick/Zem jumped around Eishu with angular and irregular movements, tearing the counterfeit tickets off his body like strips of peel from an apple. With each ticket removed, more of his dark, slimy body was exposed.

"Graaaugh... Stop... I'm gonna die... I want to die..."

""Not on my watch! Recovery! Restoration!""

"Gah?!"

Nick/Zem struck Eishu under each counterfeit ticket and cast healing spells when their blows landed. Meanwhile, something resembling a tree root began to grow between Eishu's neck and his black transparent body.

""Take that! Recovery! Restoration! Hematopoiesis!""

Nick/Zem repeated the process with each ticket, punching and kicking and casting healing magic with each blow. They took a page out of Olivia's book, concentrating mana and impact into Eishu's body without knocking him away from them.

A fat white protrusion grew around the long, root-shaped thing below Eishu's neck. It steadily grew into the shape of a human body, forming shoulders, ribs to protect his organs, and arms and legs. The process sped up from there—white and pink meat you would find at a butcher's shop formed around the bones, skin grew above it, and the black substitute body melted away as it was replaced.

"H-huh? M-my body..."

The monster made of black slime was gone, replaced by a naked and relatively muscular man.

"N-no way... You restored my body from that state? H-how?" Eishu gasped.

He sounded shocked, but there was no fear in his eyes or voice, and his eerie behavior was gone. He fell to his knees, patted his body, and reacted with joy when he confirmed it was his.

Then he jumped to his feet and tried to run.

""Sorry, but I didn't restore you so you could get away. I don't want you getting silenced, so I'm gonna put you on ice for now.""

"Huh? Wh-who are you? Where'd the man go?" Eishu asked.

The handsome, black-haired man had disappeared. Instead, a beautiful woman with long blond hair stood before him.

""Ice Coffin.""

Nick/Zem had deactivated Union after they healed Eishu; while he was dazed, Nick had quickly joined with Tiana. It was obvious that Eishu would run if given the chance, and the demon-god worshippers would silence him if he got away. That would prevent them from learning the full picture and leave them unprepared for any attacks the enemy had planned.

"Grr... R-right after I got my body back, too...," Eishu complained feebly.

Nick/Tiana was trapping his newly formed body in ice. It climbed upward from his feet and was nearly at his head.

""This won't kill you. I'll release you later, and you'll tell us everything then.""

"I-it's hopeless... No matter how strong you are... You can't defeat..."

""We're not gonna lose to Garos.""

"No... Your enemy is—"

Eishu's mutterings were interrupted when the ice finished enveloping his body.

"All right, everybody! The final act is next! Let's stay focused!" Diamond chirped.

The idols in the waiting room were taking a break before the final songs of the day, and they looked so exhausted, they could die.

Some idols had already performed their songs and were spent, some looked so excited they could run back onstage right now, some were waiting as if their turn was an execution, some concentrated silently, and some looked ready to collapse from stress. Diamond spoke to each of the girls, encouraging some, scolding others, and lighting a fire under them all. Some idols pointed out that she had the most songs of all, wondering between exasperation and praise how she could possibly have so much energy left, but Diamond just laughed.

Her smile seemed to communicate one thing—that this was the most fun moment of the whole event.

Idols were a special kind of beast. Diamond had told them all her secret, but while some were angry about being used and others were moved by her noble goal of sealing the demon god, those feelings were dominated by their dogged desire to not be bested by her. They didn't abandon their respect and trust for Diamond; instead, they redirected those feelings into anger and a sense of duty. Each one of them was burning with the ambition of toppling this scheming, dishonest girl from her perch.

The idols also learned that she had slightly changed her name and makeup over the years to pretend that she was a different person and take the position of top idol in each generation. The idea of a semi-immortal girl retiring while at the peak of her prosperity was a disgrace to all idols. They each swore to themselves that, even if they didn't yet have the skill, they would someday replace her at the top.

"Karan, let's eat lunch together!" Diamond said cheerily.

"Okay."

Karan followed Diamond as she walked among the stunning idols and entered her unoccupied personal waiting room. Diamond plopped down into a chair, sighing with exhaustion.

"The show's been a success so far. Thanks for your help," she said.

"Don't thank me yet," Karan responded frankly. Diamond nodded.

A magic barrier had been erected around the stage to repel any wrongdoers who tried to rush the stage or throw things at the idols, but intentional holes had to be left to allow entry into the staff rooms and waiting rooms. If anyone got through, it would be here. That was why Karan was sticking by Diamond's side to protect her.

"I sense Nick and the others are fighting something dangerous. That might mean we're safe," Diamond said. She reclined in her chair while taking some deep breaths.

"I'm sure it's a decoy. The main attack will be here," Karan replied confidently.

Diamond shrugged. "We gave out Garos's Wanted posters at reception. Groups of fans are also circulating documents detailing him as a dangerous person who has attacked idols and is behind the counterfeit tickets."

"Then can I take off this costume?" Karan asked.

"Absolutely not," Diamond said.

Diamond and Joseph had done everything they could to prepare for this concert. But they couldn't afford to take this threat lightly.

"Would you come if you were Garos?" the idol asked.

The Karan of old probably would've rejected that question, unwilling to think from the criminal's perspective. The new Karan answered without hesitation. She had already run this through her head multiple times.

"He'll try to come when everyone lets down their guard. Probably when the idols are done performing. The guards and soldiers will relax as a matter of course," she said.

"Exactly. That's why you're here," Diamond said.

When they decided that one of them needed to be onstage to protect Diamond's main body, Karan was chosen through the process of elimination. She also ended up having to wear an idol costume so she wouldn't stand out onstage, which she normally never would have gone along with.

"But why did you lie your way into defending me?" Diamond asked.

Karan had been deceiving her party members—she had already made plans with Diamond before the Survivors discussed deployment. She told the idol that someone needed to remain by her side at all times and that she wanted her party to be influenced into choosing her.

Diamond wanted Karan to dress like an idol partially for fun, but also because she wanted to be able to continue the concert without suspending it in the event of a security problem. She hoped that if any fights broke out onstage, the fans would assume it was part of the performance so that the excitement of the show wasn't diminished. Karan used that to pretend that she didn't want the job. By complaining that she didn't want to wear the costume and having Nick persuade her into doing it, she was able to hide the truth that she'd volunteered.

She also had read the crime scene report Nick had borrowed from the Sun Knights so many times, she could recite it from memory. It detailed the positions of Nick, Alice, Eishu, and Garos at the time of the murder, described Eishu's headless neck, and conjectured about what kind of attack Garos performed. There was information Nick didn't know in the report as well, including details about other murders that were similar or could also have been committed by Garos.

Nick had been so swamped with helping to devise the security plan and guarding the idols as they practiced that—unusually for him—he only skimmed the documents. He arrogantly dismissed them, saying that it was all based on what he wrote anyway and that he knew how Garos operated. As such, Karan was the only one who read them carefully. She had predicted what Garos would do, but she didn't share her idea with Nick.

No one suspected Karan at all.

"You're like a different person from when we first met. Did something happen?" Diamond asked.

"I realized that I love Nick," Karan said.

Diamond was startled by the sudden declaration, but her eyes quickly turned gentle. "It's a good thing to love someone. But what does that have to do with this?"

"Agate, you, and your songs taught me what you should do for the person you love, and how to avoid having regrets. You need to be willing to do anything for them without getting too focused on the little things," Karan said.

Karan had been half pretending when she blushed and covered her ears as Agate and the others excitedly analyzed Diamond's lyrics. The more she thought she shouldn't listen, the less she could resist doing so. The true meaning of each lyric, the love they contained, and Diamond's commitment to her love had left a deep impression on her.

The wounds Callios had inflicted. The example Fifs had provided. The guidance Nick had given her, as well as his kind lies. The affection Tiana and Zem had shown her. Leon's harsh advice, Agate's encouragement, and the love Diamond sang of. It had all come together to birth something beautiful in Karan's heart.

"Is that why you're here?" Diamond asked.

Karan nodded without hesitation. "Nick's not the kind of person who can kill someone he likes. There's no going back from that. I'll do it instead."

"You're not invincible, Karan. Nick will blame himself if you die," Diamond replied.

"Do you expect that to happen?" Karan asked with a smile. It wasn't a vicious, beastlike smile, nor was it a show of courage. It was the smile of an adult who had been hurt, bounced back, tempered herself, ceased being a lost child, and found love.

"You've become a true adventurer. You have the strength to protect people. I think you have what it takes to beat an S-rank one day," Diamond said.

"Hmm-hmm, you bet I do," Karan replied.

"But lying and conspiring to protect the one you love is a thorny path, whether you're a person or a holy sword... Strength does nothing to ease the pain in your heart."

"Yes... I actually think being strong makes it harder," Karan said. She was sure Diamond experienced that pain as well.

Diamond accepted her kindness without comment. "You have my support. As long as you retain the intention of protecting the person you love, that won't change."

Diamond hugged Karan softly and affectionately.

Garos's fighting style was to find and take advantage of blind spots. When fighting monsters, he danced around them, hid, used his allies as decoys, and then landed the killing blow when the monster lost track of him. He couldn't rely on strength, and even if he could, he wouldn't.

He was bad at math and wasn't one to save money, but he was very calculating in combat. He was crafty, able to read one or two steps ahead and adjust based on what his opponent thought he would do. Garos used his typical careful thought process to choose the end of the concert as his time to strike.

His job this time wasn't an assassination. It was sabotage. His directive was to destroy the jewel-like pillar shining at the back of the stage. Garos didn't have much interest in what it was or why it needed to be destroyed. He knew the gist, but he didn't understand the details of how it worked. He also didn't care about the feelings of his client who thought the stone was a threat or of the idol who was trying to protect it.

He was, however, scared of his client. He used ancient relics and stopped at nothing to accomplish his goals, and he treated allies as expendable. Garos had already gotten the holy armor destroyed and lost all the information stored within it; if he failed again, he would suffer a fate worse than death. What happened to Eishu would look like a mercy by comparison.

But at this moment, he had forgotten his fear. He wouldn't be able to work as an assassin if he couldn't put aside those kinds of feelings.

Garos's mother had been a prostitute, and he didn't know who his father was. He didn't think his mother was entirely sane. She had claimed she was a member of the royal family of Nozomi and made Garos hone his swordplay so he could help revive the country, and he had obeyed her while knowing that her story was a delusion.

He wielded his sword recklessly, with no idea of what he was doing. Eventually, one of his mother's customers, a mercenary, decided he couldn't stand to watch Garos any longer and taught him how to fight properly. The man gradually paid his mother enough money to get out of prostitution, and the three of them started to live together as a family. Before long, Garos came to call the mercenary his father.

His new father was a reliable teacher, but one day he was heavily injured on a job and forced to retire. Garos's mother took care of him, but he fell into alcoholism and grew violent with his family. Garos was eventually able to overpower him and chase him out of their home.

After that, his mother began taking customers again to provide for him. Garos picked up the katana his father had left behind and used it to protect her from stingy customers and debt collectors. Outlaws and juvenile delinquents came to fear him as a monster, which changed how people in the area treated them.

Even Garos's mother grew to fear him. The debt collectors changed their tune and praised him for his skill, and eventually, a mercenary group recruited him. Garos left home and never returned.

His sharp skill and taciturn nature led the mercenary group to entrust him with secret jobs to kill traitors and people who had violated military regulations. Eventually, however, he was roped into a conflict between factions in the army, with multiple superiors giving him conflicting orders to kill or not kill certain targets. Garos grew tired of thinking and decided to just kill them all, which put him in a dicey position with the army.

However, the skill with which he operated and the business-like approach he took to killing caught the attention of his current employer. He was suddenly ruled innocent of the crimes he was being investigated for, and his new employer gave him holy armor and made him one of his personal assassins.

The holy armor housed a personality. He was belligerent with little interest in anything other than fighting, which made him compatible with Garos. His name was White Mask, and the two forged a partnership that ended dozens of lives.

One day, his employer told him there wouldn't be any work for a while and ordered him to lie low as an adventurer. He and other people he had never seen before who worked for the same employer were put together to form an adventurers' party. They had all ended up in this trade due to special circumstances. The leader's name was Argus, and the others became his pupils and fellow Combat Masters party members.

Garos was surprised to find that these fellow assassins were people who had made a name for themselves in the war, but it wasn't a problem. He was happy to learn from Argus's skill set, and he was allowed to live as he wished.

A couple of unexpected factors ended up complicating matters.

First, Garos started to enjoy himself. He had always been a stoic person when not on a battlefield or performing an assassination job, and the pleasures of Labyrinth City proved far more stimulating than he could have imagined. It was also then that he realized just how crudely he had been living.

Next, Argus adopted a boy. He was the son of a couple assassination targets.

Garos thought that the work must have finally driven Argus insane; what else would drive him to do such a thing? He also thought their employer would kill the man if he found out what he did…but unexpectedly, the choice went unpunished. Their employer actually seemed delighted to have placed Argus in his debt.

Garos and his new party members continued working as adventurers for a number of years. He spent his time delving into labyrinths, killing monsters, making money, drinking booze, having fun, training, and teaching the boy.

He wasn't sure how it happened, but over time, he shed his quiet persona for a much more talkative one. Argus taught the kid how to fight properly, so Garos taught him other things. *Use your surroundings when fighting on the street. Don't use joint locks when fighting multiple opponents. Joint locks are effective on people used to fighting on the battlefield or as guards. Always look ahead before rounding a corner or going through a door.*

The kid listened to Garos, but he spent just as much time talking back. He berated Garos for not saving money, for giving gifts to women he wasn't close to, and for drinking too much booze. Garos ignored his complaints and continued to live his indulgent, slovenly lifestyle, still teaching the kid almost on a whim. Those weren't bad days at all. He realized twenty years too late that he probably should have berated his father in a similar way.

When the kid eventually grew up, rebelled, and was kicked out of the party, Garos felt a sense of accomplishment, like he had completed a big job. The kid didn't belong in a party like theirs. After the kid was cut loose, he began to distinguish himself. He even came to wield some kind of strange ancient relic and destroyed Garos's holy armor—utterly defeating White Mask and, by extension, Garos himself.

Garos felt no regret over the incident. Far from it, actually—he found it exhilarating. White Mask took their work seriously, but he was growing tired of his second life, and he occasionally voiced a desire to face a worthy opponent with all he had. He said if he died on such an occasion, it would be long overdue. Garos smiled afterward, proud that his own pupil had delivered his pain-in-the-ass partner such a fitting end.

It was also true that the defeat placed his life in peril, however. His employer responded by giving him what was essentially a suicide mission. His orders were to obstruct the plan of an idol agency that—for reasons he didn't understand—was working with the lord of Labyrinth City to strengthen the demon god's seal.

It was obvious he would die if he failed, and even if he succeeded, the hope of survival was slim. But Garos didn't really care. His partner had ceased to function and left this world without regret. Garos had even felt the satisfaction of raising a pupil, and he had sensed for some time that he didn't have long left to live.

Once this job was over, he was going to be either killed by his pupil or silenced by his employer. That was his last thought before he woke up.

Garos had actually snuck into the venue a week ago. He had slipped past Diamond's surveillance network, the eyes of Nick and his companions, and the magic items that had been installed for detection, doing so with a special spell of his that allowed him to weaken his body significantly.

The spell, called *Dormancy*, was an advanced version of Light

Body. It did more than just reduce one's weight; it also repressed one's breathing, pulse, body temperature, mana waves, and all other life signs down to their lowest extremes, placing the target into a state of apparent death. This made Garos less detectable than a sewer rat as he snuck into the venue unnoticed, dislocated his joints, and crammed himself into a piece of audio equipment no one should have been able to fit inside. He had been hiding there ever since.

Using that spell was a gamble. Even a child could kill him in his current state, and he needed close to an hour to deactivate Dormancy and fully reawaken. But if everything went according to plan, nothing would get in the way of him destroying his target. Garos had completed many infiltration and assassination missions with such gambles. He also performed many jobs by relying on the strength of his holy armor, but this was his true style.

Garos woke up at the intended time before the concert, left the storehouse, and climbed onto the lighting equipment above the stage to wait for the right moment. He could see how idols could captivate so many people as he watched their radiant singing and dancing from above. He also found it amusing that Nick—who always used to have a bit of a stick up his ass—had become obsessed with them.

Garos had decided it was time to settle things with Nick. He spread morsels of information for him to find, half as an apology for deceiving him all these years and half to lure him here. If Nick was fixated on Garos, if he bore a grudge toward him, he would finish off Eishu quickly and show up here. It was possible he had already figured out Garos's plan and was lying in wait.

Garos listened to the concert as he waited. He noticed guards around the stage as the idols sang and danced amid all the flashy stage production. There were people stationed on the wings of the stage and below it, and one of Nick's companions had even dressed as an idol so she could walk among them on the stage. He laughed to himself, amazed they had gone that far.

The final song—called *Undying Love Song*—came to an end. In a rare moment for Garos, he thought it was a good song. The wistful lyrics lamented the end of the speaker's youth and the discovery that it really wouldn't last forever. He could relate.

The curtain lowered as the crowd roared. Nick's companion who had dressed like an idol was nowhere in sight. The guards around the stage had lost focus. Diamond was exhausted and taking a short rest in the middle of the stage.

This was his best chance.

Garos leaped down toward the holy jewel and swung his blade with all his might.

But something blocked his sword. "What?!" he gasped. He heard the unpleasant sound of metal scraping against metal. "Wha...? Where are you?!"

Garos was stunned. It felt like he was pushing his blade against a greatsword, but there shouldn't have been anyone on the stage with such a weapon. He had checked multiple times to see if there were any guards onstage, and the one with a greatsword had left during the show.

It was as if his very senses were being deceived. That was when he realized the trick.

"Karan of the Survivors! It's you, isn't it?!" he shouted.

Karan appeared before Garos.

Karan had spent the beginning of the concert on the wings of the stage, watching for trouble or helping to move around the set as a stagehand, but after a certain point in the show, she had never left the stage. She stood in a position where fans couldn't see her, picked up her sword, and waited silently. Neither Garos nor the idols noticed her there.

She'd pulled this off by using a magic item that prevented others from perceiving her. It was a phantom king orb fragment, and as long as she held it, she was as good as invisible. The fragment was one of the things Nargava had left behind in the Garbage Heap when he died. Zem had found one of them when sorting through Nargava's room and secretly taken it.

Karan put the small fragment to use.

"Dream Sword! Shine your light!" Garos yelled, and his blade released a flash of light.

He expected the idols helping to dismantle the stage after the curtain was lowered to scream, but they didn't. Most of them had already backed away and were watching anxiously. As Garos wondered what was going on, Karan sprinted toward him, ignoring the light completely.

"Heh, you're a brave girl…!" he said.

"Shut up."

She raised her sword overhead to swing it down at Garos. That was the perfect chance for him to perform his most deadly attack.

The Butterfly Sword's Dream Sword function used light and sound to dazzle opponents. Technically, however, that was the ability of the Butterfly Sword's scabbard. The true ability of the blade was that of the Reality Sword, which allowed the user to spawn a slash attack wherever they wanted within a short distance. Garos had successfully killed many assassination targets by using this ability to slice them in the back or behead them.

He created the slash behind Karan's neck, as he had done countless times before.

"What?!"

But Karan wasn't beheaded; instead, she punched Garos so hard he went flying backward across the stage. When she had lifted her Dragonbone Sword, she had let go. The sword stuck into the wooden planks and protected her back like a shield, which blocked the slash and allowed her to punch him.

"H-how...?" Garos stammered.

"Intuition," Karan said. Her opponent had no idea how to respond to that.

The truth wasn't quite so simple. Karan had used what Nick told her and the reports about Eishu's death and the other similar murders to form a concrete image of Garos in her mind. She mentally fought this image many times, getting killed over and over again until she finally found a way to win.

"You're lying," Garos said.

Karan's superior imagination had helped her win.

Garos had been knocked out of the Reality Sword's range, so he couldn't perform another attack. He was also injured too badly to stand.

Karan was far stronger than the average soldier, and she had grown since joining the Survivors by studying Nick and incorporating a number of his moves. She imitated the technique he used to knock Leon off his feet despite his smaller build, and the defensive techniques he used to best Nargava.

"Good job, Karan," Diamond said.

"Don't let your guard down. Put the jewel away now. You're naked with it up here, right?" Karan urged.

"I wish I could, but moving it will be difficult because of all the mana it absorbed during the concert. We have to handle it carefully. So..." Diamond glanced at Garos. "You're going to tell us everything, Garos. Let's start with your employer."

Garos had lost consciousness and begun to mutter to himself as they spoke, but hearing his name snapped him back awake. He took a deep breath. "Heh... You overestimate me."

"What?" Diamond said.

"I'm not nearly important enough...to know anything about

him... I couldn't care less anyway... I just thought I might die with less regret if I killed Nick or he killed me... But I didn't get that chance...," Garos muttered.

Diamond clicked her tongue, openly displeased. "He's telling the truth," she said.

"Man, you're terrifying... Bet you could just hear it in my voice..."

"You're going to give me the information I want whether you answer or not. Your reaction will answer yes or no for you. You can't hide anything in that state."

"Like I care... You're 'bout to find out anyway."

Garos smiled, bearing the pain. Diamond went pale when she realized what he was going to do.

"No! Don't use Telepathy here!" she shouted.

"*Grah...! Hey... I found the location and the enemy... The rest...is up to you!*" Garos conveyed.

"Pop Song is inhibiting telepathic communication on this stage! You'll die!"

Garos suddenly began writhing in pain. His face turned black and blue, and blood trickled from his ears.

"*Your enemy...is the idol, Diamond... She's prolly a holy sword...just like you...*"

Garos didn't make a sound, but Karan heard his crackling voice in her head. She started to worry, but for a different reason than Diamond.

"He can use Telepathy without a telepathy orb?" she said.

That meant Garos was doing the same thing as the Survivors. Just who was he speaking to?

As if in answer, a small door opened in Garos's body.

"Wh-wha—?! Th-the hell're you doing?! Ngh!" Garos cried.

This door was not a gateway to Garos's insides; instead, it connected to a different place entirely.

"You sacrificed one of your wielders to breach our barrier. To think you'd stoop this low...," Diamond said.

"I could say the same to you... I didn't want to believe it, but that radiance is unmistakable... You look nothing like your old cruel and beautiful self. I never wanted to see you take the form of a flesh-and-blood human."

The voice filtering through the door filled Karan with spine-chilling fear and a strange sense of nostalgia.

"Get lost. This place isn't meant for your eyes," Diamond demanded.

"I'll leave once my business is done. I see you're not my only old acquaintance here," the voice said.

The eye in the darkness rested on Karan. That eye—that voice—touched the deep scars in her heart.

"No... Are you...?!"

"I let you live on purpose, but it looks like you've grown a little since then. I can't say I ever expected our final farewell to be anything like this."

"Callios!"

"Curse Stake."

An arm reached through the hole in Garos's body. It looked like the ordinary arm of a fair-skinned man, but it was so rich with wicked mana that it frightened even Karan, who couldn't use magic at all.

The mana condensed and formed a kind of stake in his hand. It was made of pure, smooth iron, but the holder's mana quickly contaminated it with rust. To Karan, the rust resembled insects that were colored to warn predators of their poison.

"Dodge it, Karan! You can't fight him!" Diamond yelled.

It was only when Diamond spoke that Karan realized she was holding her sword in a defensive position. It was also then that she realized she had no intention of backing down.

Disaster struck with a thunderous boom.

After handing Eishu to the Sun Knights, Nick and the others started toward the venue to find Diamond in her waiting room. A massive explosion from the direction of the stage rocked the ground on their way back.

The fans leaving the venue were spooked by the sound. They hounded nearby staff members for an explanation, but they knew just as little as anyone else.

Agate's voice sounded throughout the venue to answer everyone's questions.

"An equipment malfunction caused a small explosion. A security guard was injured, but their life is not in danger. No idols or fans were hurt. I ask that all fans please leave the venue as quickly as possible so a damage investigation can be performed. All shops in the venue are closed as of right now. I apologize for any inconvenience."

Her calm voice rippled through the uneasy crowd. Some fans complained about the stores being closed, but there was no panic. Nick and his fellow Survivors, however, felt a sense of dread. They knew what the announcement meant.

"Let's hurry!" Nick urged.

They ran toward the stage, doing their best to fight through their exhaustion. They barely had any energy left. Zem and Bond—who had performed two Unions—appeared ready to collapse.

"These two can't keep up! Go ahead, Nick!" Tiana shouted.

"Thanks!" Nick called back.

Nick was the most worn out of them all, but he was in the best physical shape, so his body held on. The scene he found on the stage immediately pushed his fatigue from his mind.

"Wh-what...happened here?" he asked, studying his surroundings.

"I'm sorry. I failed," Diamond responded without looking up.

She was sitting next to a person who appeared to be unconscious. A ring of idols stood around them, chanting something. Their shadows hid the person on the ground, but it was obvious who it was.

The Dragonbone Sword was on the stage in two pieces. A rusty stake had pierced the holy jewel, sending cracks out from the center. Garos was dead, with a giant hole bored into his body.

Nick couldn't possibly understand what had happened at a glance. But he did know one thing—they had failed to defend their target.

"Karan! Hey, Karan! What happened!" Nick shouted.

"I don't think she'll wake up for a while. Her wound isn't that deep...but it's cursed. The assailant sacrificed Garos's life to permanently injure my main body and Karan," Diamond answered.

Nick didn't understand a word of what she said, but he swallowed his anger and kept his voice calm. "Will Karan...survive?"

"Yes. There's no need to worry. Our emergency treatment worked."

"Garos is dead, right?"

"Yeah. His employer sacrificed him."

Nick gritted his teeth in response. He held back the fury that threatened to explode from within him, schooled his face into a neutral expression, and faced Diamond.

"Are you gonna be okay? Your main body was cracked," he asked.

"My plan is ruined," she answered.

"I'm asking if your life is in danger."

Diamond smiled sadly. "You're a nice person. Karan minimized the damage by standing in the way of the attack. I call that my main body, but my consciousness—or soul, or whatever you want to call it—has been transferred into this body."

"You said Karan's emergency treatment worked. Will she be okay after that?" Nick asked.

Diamond's expression darkened. "She'll be able to live her days in relative comfort. But the curse is dense. You should assume she won't be able to continue living her current life."

"Tell me what the effects will be."

"Her stamina and mana will greatly decline. She may suffer from impaired coordination as well."

"What does that mean for her?"

Nick stepped so close to Diamond, he could feel her breath. The others watched anxiously, unable to stop him.

"She will no longer be able to work as an adventurer," Diamond said, clenching her fists tightly.

"How do we cure her?" Nick asked. He was fighting to stay calm now. While his speech sounded dispassionate, his rage slipped into his expression.

"Curses are difficult... The most reliable cure is to get the person who inflicted it to dispel it," Diamond said.

"THEN WHO DID THIS TO HER, AND WHERE ARE THEY?!" Nick suddenly roared as the dam was broken. The surrounding idols shrank away from him. "Tell me, Diamond. Why'd this have to happen to her?"

"Well..."

"I'd have no complaints if this had happened to me. I'm sure Garos was prepared for his fate, too. But Karan has a whole future ahead of her. Her road can't end here. She deserves to be happy. Why wasn't I able to protect her?"

"That's enough!" Diamond yelled, grabbing Nick's collar with a strength he couldn't believe came from her slender body. "Don't get the wrong idea, child. Karan chose to fight of her own free will. She's a true adventurer. I won't let you insult her any further."

"Shut up! Do you have any idea how much Karan has suffered?!"

"You noticed that and still chose to believe in her. You saw her potential. You knew that she was the real thing."

"Then what can I do? How do I heal her?!"

"Persuading him to dispel the curse will be impossible... The only choice will be to defeat him and weaken the curse."

"You know who cursed her."

"It was the Sword of Tasuki," Diamond muttered.

Nick etched the name into his mind with rage. "Is he…a holy sword?"

"He's a holy sword created in ancient times with a focus on recreating the abilities of holy armor. Outstanding people with the potential to be heroes are always being born throughout the world. The holy sword's purpose was to grow by incorporating not just their skills but their spirits, too. The idea was for him to eventually develop a soul stronger than the demon god's… But he's known by a human name now. He's likely been mutated," Diamond explained.

"What's his name?"

"Callios."

The idea of Callios targeting Karan again sounded like a delusional conspiracy. Or a paranoid theory grounded on pieces of shaky evidence. It was terrifying to think this was reality, but Nick pushed aside the fear with anger.

"Where is he?" he asked.

"I don't know. But…Garos wasn't the Sword of Tasuki's wielder. He was just under his control. There has to be someone else. His true wielder won't be controlled," Diamond said.

Those words made Nick realize who they should be looking for. Though it was more like he had been choosing not to look the entire time. He hadn't wanted to consider who among Garos's companions could be stationed above him.

He could only think of one person.

"Take care of Karan," Nick said.

He gently patted his friend on the head, then walked over to Garos and closed the corpse's eyes. Then he left the stage in pursuit of his new target.

The doors of the Adventurers Guild branch called Manhunt slammed open, causing everyone inside to look toward them suspiciously.

Only adventurers visited Manhunt. Doctors and traders frequented other branches to request certain materials, but those people had no business here. The only non-adventurers who ever came here were resentful victims who wanted to put a bounty on someone's head or citizens who wanted to complain about a violent adventurer.

As such, the adventurers here were used to kicking out guests who came bringing trouble. One of the regulars started to stand up, feeling excited at the opportunity for a fight.

"Oh, it's a Survivor. This is unexpected," the deerian receptionist said, surprised.

"It's just Nick. How hard is it to go through a door quietly?"

"Aw man, it's one of the dudes. Where's Lady Tiana?"

The adventurers muttered complaints, but Nick ignored them and spoke to the receptionist.

"I wanna put up a bounty," he said.

"Huh? You?" the deerian asked.

"Argus from Combat Masters. I learned he's working for the demon-god worshippers."

Everyone who had been drinking, playing cards, or perusing Wanted posters fell silent. Argus from Combat Masters was well known at the Manhunt guild. That wasn't just because his party could conquer labyrinths without relying on magic. Argus had a reputation for being potentially the strongest adventurer alive due to his barehanded fighting skill.

And Nick—his pupil who had defeated the demon-god worshipper White Mask—was going so far as to put a bounty on his head. Not a single one of the grizzled adventurers in the guild thought he was joking. Instead, his declaration struck an ominous sense of fear in their hearts.

"I wanna explain, but it's complicated. Is the back room free?" Nick asked.

"Y-yeah. Wait here as I open the conference room... Huh?"

the deerian said, pausing right before she turned around to go to the conference room used to ask clients for details.

"What?" Nick responded.

The deerian stared at Nick. Actually, she was staring behind him. A woman's image was reflected in her pupils.

Nick immediately spun and threw an elbow, but the woman easily blocked it. Nick kicked at her shins next, but she blocked that, too. He didn't feel like his movement was hindered by his fatigue at all, but he couldn't hit her.

"That's enough passion for one night, Nick. There are things you should hear and do, but for now you need to sleep. There's no way you're not exhausted after using a powerful ancient spell twice."

"...Alice!"

Alice's muscular arms wrapped around Nick's neck, and she held him until he fell unconscious into her arms.

"Good night, Nick. Rest up for the real fight."

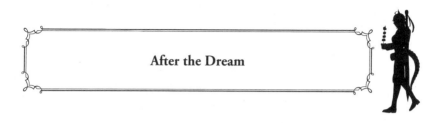

After the Dream

The holy jewel was once again stored underneath Starmine Hall. The cursed stake had been removed, but the spider web of cracks was still there. The time in which the jewel's beauty was unblemished now felt like a dream.

Diamond and Joseph stood looking at it together. They seemed disinterested in its destruction and felt no joy at having survived the day. This was a kind of ritual to help them accept the outcome they had feared would come.

"I'm not looking forward to what's ahead of us. We'll need to explain this to the lord. We wasted a lot of money," Diamond said.

"You don't need to worry about that. We didn't spend much more than the amount you've been paying in taxes for the last century to store yourself here," Joseph replied.

"I hope that's true."

"Besides, this was not a total failure. The facility functioned flawlessly as a fortress. The fact that the enemy couldn't destroy the venue and had to perform that indirect attack is proof of our defensive capabilities."

"That's because someone softened the blow for me. Even though there was no reason for her to risk her life like that."

Diamond gently stroked the holy jewel's cracks.

"I guess holy swords can't stray too far from their purpose. The Jewelry Production facility has been set back, but what about the project to remake me as the Sword of Resonance? Will it work?" she asked.

"Do you really want to do it?" Joseph responded.

Diamond's original name was the Sword of Distortion. The Sword of Resonance was only a temporary name the adventurer Diamond had given her after rudely saying her original name sounded ugly.

She used the name to deceive herself and forget that she hadn't been destroyed, lost her mana, and mutated into a form that was little different from an ordinary human's. Outside of singing, dancing, and becoming the core of her holy jewel resonance facility, she had no power. Not enough to stop the destruction that would be wrought by the massive Stampede that was approaching anyway.

"Yes, I do."

Diamond touched the broken holy jewel and prayed silently. The jewel began to vibrate, and the cracked portion fell to the ground in fragments. A few seconds later, the entire jewel shattered like a glass plate that had dropped on the floor.

"Good. The core is unharmed," Diamond said.

There was a crystal inside the jewel that changed colors as it shone. The larger jewel wasn't actually her core—just an outer shell made to store mana. They couldn't perform the original Jewelry Production plan now that it was broken, but they weren't completely out of options.

"We're going to design a new holy sword made to suit my mutated form. This is the start of a new project," she said with determination in her voice.

Joseph looked confused. "But...who are you going to choose for your new wielder?" he asked.

"Her, of course. I've trained many girls over the last century, but…I've made up my mind. I'm not gonna let her adventure end here," Diamond said.

"Is her style compatible with yours? There is no guarantee she will choose you, either," Joseph pointed out.

"That won't be a problem. Are the technical aspects ready?" Diamond asked.

"No," Joseph said, shaking his head.

Diamond almost stumbled in response. She had expected him to say they could get started right away.

"Why not?! Can't we use the mana from concerts that we've stored in the fake holy jewel?!"

"We do not have a sword from which to start. You have rejected all the blades we have shown you, saying you don't want to transfer your body into something so blunt."

"Oh yeah… I have been saying that, haven't I?"

Joseph was not subtle about his sigh.

Diamond glanced around uneasily, wondering what to do, and something caught her eye.

"Hey, Joseph. Wouldn't that work?" she asked.

"That is…that girl's sword, is it not? It's also broken," Joseph said.

"The sword can be repaired, just like I was. Nothing dies as long as the heart remains unbroken."

Diamond was pointing at the sword that had been brought underground along with the destroyed holy jewel. It was a famous greatsword passed down by the dragonians, forged from an alloy of iron and mineral found in dragon claws and bones.

The Dragonbone Sword.